MW00718024

HAVANA
PASSAGE

For Alden, who helped make it possible to include this book as part of the WASHINGTON TRILOGY

HAVANA PASSAGE

A NOVEL

JAY LILLIE

www.ivyhousebooks.com

PUBLISHED BY IVY HOUSE PUBLISHING GROUP
5122 Bur Oak Circle, Raleigh, NC 27612
United States of America
919-782-0281
www.ivyhousebooks.com

ISBN: 1-57197-452-0
Library of Congress Control Number: 2005902877

© 2005 Jay Lillie

Printed in the United States of America

Dedicated to

INGER

The love of my life.

ACKNOWLEDGMENTS

The author acknowledges the advice, assistance, and lifetime of friendship from two of the finest lawyers of this or any other generation: Robert P. Oberly of Philadelphia, Pennsylvania and Edward Reilly of New York, New York, both of whom might tell you if they were alive today that I've been writing legal fiction for years.

Thanks to author and editor Ms. Laura Taylor for helping me tell less and show more.

Thanks to Ms. Elana Gronert of New York for years of painstaking work on her own time.

I acknowledge the People to People Program and its directors and participants in the visit to Cuba in December 2003, and those fellow citizens who have learned the hard way that Americans do not have the freedom to visit Cuba.

I've said for a long time that women have everything else, they might as well have the Presidency.

Harry S. Truman
President, 1945 to 1952

AUTHOR'S NOTE

Havana Passage is intended to entertain. The story is fictional and takes place in the near future. The characters that dance across the book's pages are wholly from my imagination. However, the Havana in which much of our intrigue takes place is the city we see today. The concepts and policies that live within the corridors of power in Washington, Havana and Miami form the background for the novel's two protagonists as they tackle an important Presidential assignment.

Not all of us are familiar with Cuba or our relationship with its people. There are a few historical points and events to consider before beginning the story.

Fidel Castro is not immortal. There are those who believe that after he's gone the Cuban people will be emancipated from the tyranny under which they live, but that didn't happen in the Soviet Union when Stalin died. It happened throughout what was the Soviet empire when the ideas and dreams of the rest of the world could no longer be kept out. Who knows, freedom might have come to the Cuban people already were it not for the isolation imposed by the United States' trade embargo that has kept U.S. citizens out of Cuba for the last forty years. Let the sun shine in, and good things usually happen.

This is not to say American actions have always been good for the people of Cuba. What followed Teddy Roosevelt's charge up San Juan Hill, in the war and subsequent military occupation that gave us Guantanamo Bay naval base in 1903, was not always pretty. Ernest

Hemingway, and more recently Tom Miller, gave us a look on the bright side of Cuba. But Havana, which had always been revered as one of the more romantic and cosmopolitan cities of the New World, had degenerated by the 1950s into a frontier of prostitution and crime, often more base than that presented in *Godfather III*. Not all Cubans were unhappy when the Americans were sent packing in 1958.

Then came the Cuban Missile Crisis and Russia's cohabitation of Cuba, ninety miles from our shores. When the Russians went home as their world began to collapse, Castro was left to his own devices, and the United States, perhaps missing an opportunity, kept in place the embargo brought in to punish Russian/Cuban aggression. Despite periodic notions in Washington over the last twenty-five years to ease these restrictions, the embargo is still in place, and Americans are still not allowed to travel to Cuba.

It's hard to find anyone in international trade or politics who is neutral on the subject, but one thing seems fairly clear: the announced and stated purpose of this restriction on American freedoms (which ironically was implemented in order to bring liberty to the Cuban people) has not been achieved. Cubans have never been less free. Washington may be the only place in the world where this failure of foreign policy is not obvious.

Surprisingly, and no thanks to the Castros or our own government in Washington, Americans are not unpopular among the people of Cuba. Most Cubans would like to see more of us than the few who are licensed to visit by the U.S. Treasury Department. Those who have been given permission to travel there cannot mistake Havana for other major cities in this hemisphere. Havana is required to put its best foot forward. Even so, the city sports an old world charm that comes alive from noon into the wee hours with music, good food, and interesting people. If you don't look too closely at the man sitting at the next table, to whom the waiters are giving a deference approaching abject fear, you might even believe you're in a free society.

This is Havana today. *Tomorrow* is not history yet, but it's coming.

HAVANA PASSAGE

ONE

John Carver counted out seven one-hundred dollar bills and placed them into the man's outstretched hand. Carver watched, squinting into the high sun as his ex-crewman stuffed the bills into his pocket, threw his duffle bag over a shoulder, and headed off the dock in the direction of the nearest bar.

"Sorry sonofabitch," Carver mumbled, and began the long process of cleaning up the boat from ten days' fishing in the Gulf Stream. He was about to cast off and return his fishing boat to its permanent mooring on the backside of Key West when a long shadow fell across the deck beneath his feet. He turned to face a large man standing over him on the pier.

"Captain Carver?" the man asked in what sounded like a Cuban accent.

Carver nodded. "I'm John Carver."

"They call me Lefty," the man said. "I was told you might need a hand."

Indeed he did. "Throw off those lines and come aboard," Carver said, "if you don't mind going out to the mooring with me. It's getting dark, and we can talk on the way."

That night, the captain spoke with his wife.

"Yes, and some dark night you'll get thrown overboard so he can run drugs or people from Cuba," she said.

"I don't think so, Maisy. My gut tells me he really wants the job. I'm too old to go out there alone anymore. Look at the last three bums I've had on board." Carver took a deep breath and reached for his pipe on the table. "I'd like to take a chance with him," he said, tilting his head and looking back to his wife. "I liked the way this man looked straight at me when I spoke with him."

"You take too many risks, John. You know he's an illegal."

"I didn't ask that question. Fact is, if he's a good man on a boat, I don't care if he's Fidel Castro himself."

"Alright, John," she said, taking her husband's hand and squeezing hard. "I guess the good Lord will protect you. He always has."

Like most who go to sea in small craft to earn their keep, John Carver was God fearing and prone to superstition. He fished from a forty-eight-foot wooden boat that had been built in Nova Scotia before he was born, sixty years earlier. The new hand became a good fisherman after a half dozen trips into the Florida Straits. They were bringing home more fish, and the combination of Carver's knowledge and his Cuban mate's improving seamanship made them a formidable crew.

John Carver knew the driving forces of the Gulf Stream's swift current were the prevailing wind and the vertical movement of temperature gradients through the ocean depths. He'd learned that the big fish preferred the cooler water outside the walls of the Stream, but ventured into the warm eddies to feed on smaller forms. That's where Carver liked to fish, along the northern and southern boundaries of the Stream, moving in and out of the swirling temperature gradients.

One thing the usually thorough Carver didn't seriously consider was the consequence of being forced to seek refuge someday within Cuban territorial waters. Some of the best fishing was off Cuba's north coast. To access those international waters, it was necessary to cross the strongest currents running between Florida and the Cuban coastline. More than once John Carver had delayed crossing back over to Key West, waiting off Cuba for the elephant herds of square waves in the Gulf Stream to subside.

"I've never been in Cuba," he said to his mate in the bright sunshine one day while fishing the south wall of the Gulf Stream.

His mate shrugged and went on working.

"I guess it's the last place you'd want to be," Carver said, looking to draw a response, but not getting any.

That was as close as the two men came that day to discussing what might happen if they were ever forced to seek a harbor of refuge in Cuba.

★

Kate Stevens was painfully aware that the end of her second year at Georgetown Law School was fast approaching. A break from the pressures of meeting *Law Journal* deadlines and preparing for finals would be welcome, but she wasn't looking forward to two months at another summer tennis camp.

Teaching the game bored her, and moving back into the college scene as an adult was like being the only sober person at a cocktail party. She felt out of place and uncomfortable, being hustled by the other coaches. The environment at law school was more study oriented. Something about tennis players . . . maybe she'd figure it out someday. Meanwhile, she had to put the finishing touches on the film she'd talked the Law School into letting her produce.

The opening sequence of the film still bothered her. "We need to put our issues in a setting that will draw the viewers in," she said to the student director from the coast who was assisting.

"Okay, we've prettied-up the entrance to the Supreme Court Building. What's missing?"

"What makes this whole thing so stupid is that Cuba is practically next door to Florida. I mean, Key West is closer to Havana than it is to Miami. Do you think the average American realizes that?"

"He does if he took geography in school."

"That's my point, Jeff. Haven't you seen all those articles that show most high school kids can't place Chicago on the map, let alone Havana?"

"So let's show them Disneyland."

"Very funny. Anyway, that's in California. Disney World is the one in Florida."

"How about one of those shots from the NASA satellite?"

Kate slapped her hands together. "That's brilliant, Jeffrey. Yes, get a shot covering the area from Canaveral to the west end of Cuba. Make sure it's a clear day. I want to see the ocean."

From space, the blue-green of the Gulf Stream ocean river carved a languid serpentine shape, moving north and bending around the western tip of Cuba. It gathered itself in swirls and headed east to bisect the Florida Straits between Havana and Key West, before returning to a northerly direction near Key Largo and sweeping up the east coast of Florida. The resulting optical effect joined the north coast of Cuba and the Florida Keys at the hip.

"That's it," Kate said in triumph to the young man from Berkeley. "Jeff, you're a genius."

★

Emily Harris was eighteen when she came into the District thirteen years earlier to work for Gordon Cox.

"We're a good team," she liked to tell her one close friend.

Emily still lived at home in suburban Maryland, taking care of a widowed mother who suffered from poor health worsened by advancing age. The office, and working for the firm's senior partner, was the enjoyable part of Emily's life. She watched her coworkers count the minutes left in the working day before going home to family or meeting friends. Emily dreaded the end of the day, the bus ride home, and the demands her mother carefully crafted to make accomplishment impossible.

Emily's outlook and attitude changed for the better each day as she boarded the bus at seven-thirty in the morning bound for 17th Street NW, Washington, D.C. In the hour it took to reach the office, she read the Washington Post for events that might shape her day. By the time she arrived, she was in good spirits, anticipating vicarious involvement in one or more of the city's or the nation's happenings.

Emily loved calling the White House for her boss. Many on the staff knew her by name, even though the new President had been in office only a few months. She enjoyed the year Gordon Cox worked on the President's campaign. She knew how much winning the election had meant to him, but she was pleased when he decided to remain in private practice.

Sometimes, Gordon asked her to work on Saturdays, and other times she came in on the weekend just to get out of the house.

"Mother, I'm sorry, but it's my job. I have to go in today." . . . "I know it's Sunday, but there are a few things I need to prepare for tomorrow." . . . "Yes, I'll be back in time to give you an early bath and supper." Lying to her mother made her feel guilty, but sometimes it just seemed necessary.

In her wildest fantasies, before drifting off to sleep at night, Emily saw Gordon Cox and herself as the perfect pair. Neither was beautiful outside, but they both knew how to get things done with a minimum of fuss and fanfare. She loved the sparkle that came to his eyes when he shared with her an amusing incident or another person's silliness. They seemed to know in advance what the other was thinking. Gordon had dubbed Emily "The Implementer."

"Go see The Implementer," he would tell one of the firm's young associates. That would always bring a smile to complement Emily's deep brown eyes.

When she arrived at the office one day in early May, she found a note from Gordon on her desk.

"Emily, good morning. As you've already figured out, I'm not here. In fact, I'm over at Pennsylvania Avenue," their code for the White House. "I probably won't be long. Tell Brad Howe I'm going to need his report on the Jackson case. Thanks, Gordon."

Brad Howe hadn't come in yet, so she walked down to his office and left him a message. She'd follow up later to make sure he was informed. Meanwhile, she opened Cox's mail and looked around on the chance that Howe's report had already been put in her inbox.

★

The two men stood together in stark contrast, Gordon Cox in his double breasted, pin-striped suit, towering over Charles Black, and the White House Chief of Staff holding his ground with his clipboard in one hand and adjusting his reading glasses with the other. Long hours spent battling for the President's election, sharing the belief that their candidate was the right leader for the times, had opened and maintained an easy line of communication between the two. Their dealings were clear of excessive ego and many other hurdles to men of action dealing effectively with one another. There was no need to pull punches or walk on eggshells when Charles Black and Gordon Cox were harnessed together. The President knew this, and enjoyed watching them move toward solutions that might escape others hung up on the importance of their own agendas.

The President had been unable to convince Gordon Cox to join her administration.

"I'd be a liability to you, Rebecca. You need people like Charles Black, who don't have so many enemies. I'm not going anywhere. I'll be around if you need me."

Cox gave advice when asked, and was available for assignment to projects too sensitive for those encumbered by bureaucratic agendas.

Charles Black was no salesman, as both the President and Gordon Cox could be when the situation demanded. But it was Black who steered the President's ship through the conflicting interests that appeared every day on the White House steps. His appointment as Chief of Staff was a brilliant move on the President's part, and he wasted no time on this occasion getting into the subject she'd summoned Cox there to discuss.

"Gordon, you know how critical she's been of this country's policy towards Cuba."

Cox cocked his head and looked down at an angle at the Chief of Staff. He paused for a moment, and then nodded.

"She's got some ideas, and we'd like to try them out on you."

"What's it like in Havana these days?"

"It depends on how you slice it," Black said. "On the surface, not much has changed over the last twenty or thirty years. It's still a repressive, authoritarian government, accompanied most of the time by a hypocritical smile flashed in the direction of European tourists. Small pockets of individual expression are allowed from time to time in areas where foreigners can travel and trade. The military is not as potent as it used to be. They can't afford it and, despite the rumors, no one else has been willing so far to give them weapons. It's a good show the Cubans put on for the Europeans; but make no mistake, scratch the surface and you'll find a regimented and penal society. The country remains vulnerable to manipulation by outside forces. The President thinks it's as much our fault as anyone's."

Cox recalled earlier discussions with the President. For more than four decades, the United States had tried unsuccessfully to isolate and squeeze Fidel Castro from power. By those very measures, they had helped to keep him there. Not an altogether enlightened policy, they'd decided, but doing something about it was for another time. Black seemed to be telling him that the time might be now.

"There's always the swing vote in Florida," Black said, hitching up his trousers to meet a slightly protruding stomach.

Cox nodded. "Is she prepared to put that at risk?"

"Do you remember the idea you threw on the table during the Florida campaign?"

Cox squinted one eye, and shook his head.

"It was the night we came back from the session in Coral Gables. I remember it, because I never had any idea what the World Bank actually did."

"You mean to have the Bank finance Cuban restitution payments to Cuban-Americans."

"Yes, that's the notion."

"It was just an idea, Charlie. I don't know if we can make it work. There are a few things, like Cuba becoming a member of the Bank, which would need to happen first."

"It's just a thought," Black said.

"So who will be the next Cuban strongman? Are you getting reliable intelligence?"

"Not enough . . . that makes sense anyway. They think he's had a mild stroke. He's been out of the public eye for sometime."

The lawyer's eyebrows rose, which Charles Black knew was Gordon's way of expressing polite cynicism.

Black got down to the business at hand. "We need to generate support in Congress for dealing with Havana. Now, here's the thing," the White House Chief said, switching his clipboard from one hand to the other and hitching up his trousers again, like he was embarrassed by his subject. "One of the students out at Georgetown Law School produced a film this winter which questions the constitutionality of some of the actions taken by the Executive Branch over the past fifty years or so. It focuses on our placing Cuba off-limits for U.S. citizens. We want your advice on its merits. The history professor in her is coming out. She thinks we can make something good come of it."

Cox's slow half-smile showed Black he'd been right in expecting the lawyer to be skeptical.

"My two cents might be worth exactly that," Cox said, opening his briefcase, balancing it on his knee, and taking out a pair of reading glasses he'd previously neglected to put in his pocket.

"Who else can she ask, Gordon? Certainly not the Attorney General. He has too many connections in South Florida. Sometimes I think those people would like nothing better than to see a Cuban civil war, or a coup sponsored by Venezuela to put a new strongman on the throne. Then they'd pressure us to use force and make the way clear for them to take over."

Cox's silence told Black nothing. He'd taken it as far as he was able. It was the President's damn fool idea. She'd have to deal with Gordon Cox. "Come on," he said, giving Cox a gentle poke on the arm, "we'd better get in there. She has a busy morning."

The two men surfaced again in the West Hall. They were in light conversation as they walked through to the Oval Office. The figure of the President emerged behind them from the alcove occupied by her secretary. Willowy, tall, and impeccably dressed in a white silk blouse and navy skirt that swished as she moved, she quickly greeted the two men. The President's striking features and steel blue eyes always caught Gordon off guard. Today was no exception as she strode toward him with her hand extended in greeting to an old friend. A few inches shorter than he in low heels, her eyes looked straight into his as she cocked her head to the side and smiled, like she was flirting with him.

"Hello, Gordon. Where've you been hiding? I thought maybe you were angry with us or something."

They both knew the distance maintained between Cox and the White House wasn't all the lawyer's doing.

"Madam President, you're in my thoughts day and night," Cox said, their eyes in uninterrupted contact. "It's good to see you."

The President moved around him, and glided across the room. She placed a folder on her desk, and without ever losing eye contact, came back to where he stood. She took his hands in hers and accepted his kiss on each cheek.

"Well, if you weren't so good at keeping some of the members of my Cabinet on their toes, we might see more of you. I wish you were still on our team, Gordon, but I guess you already know that," she said.

Cox nodded as the President sat down in front of her coffee table, crossed her legs, and got down to the business at hand.

"Did Charlie tell you what's on our minds?" she said, glancing first at her wristwatch and then at her Chief of Staff.

"I think I've got it," Gordon said, hoping to make a response from Black unnecessary.

"Good," she said, motioning Cox into a place opposite her. Gordon took his seat and placed his case on the rug near his feet.

Charles Black remained standing. The President smiled and addressed her Chief of Staff.

"Is the film set up, Charlie?"

Black took her question as his cue to leave them alone. "I'll double check," he said.

Charles Black departed, closing the door to the Oval Office behind him.

It was the President's initiative, and Cox waited as she eyed him, gathering her thoughts.

"Thanks for coming over on such short notice, Gordon. We really have missed you around here," she said, gesturing with her hand. "We haven't seen much of you on the Washington scene either. All work and no play, is it? When are you going to find a good woman to share your life, Gordon? It gets very lonely out there. Take it from someone who knows."

Cox hunched his shoulders, his thoughts for the moment on the death of the President's husband several years before.

The President continued. "I don't think you enjoyed the politics much, did you? God, you were good at it, though. I wouldn't be sitting here in this office if it weren't for you."

"Not true, Rebecca. This was your destiny. But you're right; I prefer the courtroom to the kinds of hypocrisy you have to deal with every day."

"I don't blame you." The President paused, changing the subject. "Speaking of what we deal with around here every day, I've been sitting on my hands, waiting for our intelligence experts to tell me when the next real crunch is going to come in Cuba. The French, Germans, Chinese, and countless others continue to move in down there. There are four new hotels under construction along the north shore alone, to add to the dozen or so already flourishing there. I hate to see all of this going on under our noses. Cuba is a natural market for U.S. business, but at the rate things are going, the Europeans and the Chinese will own the place and we'll still be enforcing that damn trade embargo and using the naval base at Guantanamo Bay as a prison."

"I don't know, Rebecca, those businesses are taking a real gamble that the Cuban government won't take it all back some day."

"You sound like our esteemed Attorney General."

Cox laughed. "So you think maybe the time has come to do something?"

The President hunched her shoulders. "Castro's legacy is not going to last forever. Vacuums are dangerous. I don't want another strongman coming in there, making his case by trashing the USA."

Gordon nodded, and the President continued.

"I can't tolerate an armed camp sitting on our doorstep under the influence of others. And I don't want another fifty years of diplomatic pouting that accomplishes nothing and makes us look like chumps. Have you heard about this film on the Constitution?"

Cox shook his head.

"You're excused," she said with a sly grin. "It's a film about how some of our laws, well intended originally but long past their relevance, can be used to step on the toes of our freedoms. The part that interests me is a satirical piece on our fifty-year-old trade policy with Cuba. I saw the film several weeks ago. If you tell me it holds up professionally, we're going to show it at dinner to a crowd that includes most of the political movers and shakers with a stake in Cuba's future."

"Who funded it?"

"Aha, that's my Gordon. Good question, but it's not what you might think. First of all, one of Georgetown's students, or her parents, funded it. She's no zealot, except maybe on the tennis court. She was on the winning NCAA Women's Tennis team at Stanford a couple of years ago. They chose the Cuban Embargo as one example of ill-fated and unconstitutional foreign policy that violates the Fifth Amendment. She got the idea for making a film to expand on a note she helped write for the *Law Journal*. The work is very creative. I've seen the film and was impressed. I want to be sure it's not too academic. You're the only person I can trust to give it to me straight. So come on, let's go next door. If you give the film the green light, I'm going to show it to the group at dinner here in the East Room."

TWO

The pastor of John Carver's church asked him to take on as temporary crew a young man who came to South Florida looking for fun in the sun, but found instead a dependence on cocaine and destitution.

"You needn't pay him much," the priest at St. Michaels said. "The best place for him right now is out there with you."

Carver said he wouldn't do it unless the Cuban he called Lefty agreed. It was both their lives on the line, and an inexperienced hand on board increased everyone's risk. "At sea," he explained, "trouble breeds trouble, and bad things can happen very quickly."

"He'll be secure in your hands," the priest said, totally missing the point.

"We will take care of him," the Cuban said later when Carver asked for his consent.

"It's not the boy I'm worried about."

"We'll take care of her too," the mate said, meaning the boat.

Late in the spring, a storm fitting the captain's definition of trouble surprised even the weather experts. The strongest winds hit Carver's boat and crew from the east, when they were northwest of

Havana around one o'clock in the morning. The seas built quickly to the height of small buildings.

Carver turned to his Cuban mate. "We've got some fish in the hold. I'm going to head for home. If it's too bad in the main current of the Stream we can head back south and motor off the Cuban coast until this thing blows through."

The mate nodded. He had seen his captain's seamanship at work and had confidence in his judgment.

Carver eased the boat onto a northeasterly course, feeling his way into the lines of waves that galloped from the east in the darkness. Once inside the south wall of the Stream, the small wooden vessel began to labor in steep, breaking seas, undercut by the driving force of the Gulf Stream current. Finding the best course to parry the largest waves was difficult in the darkness. Carver was about to turn back when the boat motored through the breaking crest of a steep wave with a concave backside and fell fifteen feet onto her side.

"What was that crash?" the youngest crewman shouted vainly from his bunk through the noise of wind and crashing waves.

The captain knew his old boat had been hurt falling off that big wave. "Go check it out," he ordered the mate, and quickly turned the vessel back toward the Cuban coastline, throttling back and climbing over another big sea that suddenly rose up before them.

The mate crawled through the boat's forepeak into three inches of water. The boat's sharp pitch made him weightless over the top of each wave and crushed his chest into the bilge as she buried her bow into the trough below. The Cuban knew immediately there was little they could do at sea to stem the flow. The sea forced water through two cracks in the planking each time the bow dove into an oncoming sea. He braced a mattress against the cracked planks with a long oar, which he hoped would slow the sea's intrusion. The pumps were fighting a valiant but losing battle against the sea.

Climbing back on deck, the Cuban told Carver, "You'll have to go in. We'll not last the night out here. Havana Harbor is your only choice. The entrance at Hemingway is narrow and not well lighted. None of the others will have any lights."

The captain didn't argue. He knew the last thing his mate wanted was to enter Cuba, from whence he might never return. "Here, take the wheel," he said. "I'll get us a course back out of the Stream and into Havana. If the boy comes topside, start him bailing."

★

The film was Kate Steven's idea. She wanted the important issues they were raising to be generally presented and not limited to volumes on the shelves of the nation's law libraries. A film, freely available and linked to the university law center's web site, was the idea she pushed.

Drama, she argued, was needed. "The play's the thing," Kate joked, quoting from Hamlet as she spoke to the professor who would approve her idea, "wherein to catch the conscience of the king," or in this case, Congress and the White House. Her professor acquiesced, but the law school expected her to cover the costs.

Kate's father came across with the funds, which assured her final editing rights. Robert Stevens knew his daughter would resist working with anyone she might have to fend off. He found her a brilliant young student film director who wasn't particularly interested in women.

Kate housed, fed, and teased him for five weeks while they worked around the clock. They produced three hours of film, which Kate then cut to thirty minutes. The two of them added special effects at her father's advertising studio in Los Angeles. The actors, playing the parts of indicted defendants, lawyers, and questioning Supreme Court Justices, were all students, except for two children who belonged to the family of one of her favorite professors. The reviews at the law school were good, but she was shocked when she picked up the *Law Journal* office telephone and found the President of the United States on the other end of the line.

"Ms. Stevens, Professor Smith tells me this film on Cuba was your idea."

"Yes, Madam President, but it's not really about Cuba. We only used the Embargo as one example of abuse of executive power."

"I understand. I'd like to see it. I asked your mentor if you and the others who helped you would like to come to the White House one evening and show it to us."

Kate thought, *Are you kidding me?* and she answered too quickly. "We could do that. Yes, ma'am," she said, struggling to get the right words to come out. "I mean, we'd be pleased to do that, Madam President. We have it on DVD. Is that alright?"

The President paused before answering. "I'll tell you what, Katherine. That's your name . . . Do I have that right?"

"Yes, ma'am. Katherine Stevens."

"Someone from the White House Staff will contact you and make the arrangements. Nice to chat with you, Katherine."

And that was that. What followed was an evening in the Diplomats' Room of the White House with a dozen people, half of whom Kate knew by name, and the President. The film was shown, and immediately thereafter, the President left without commenting "to take an urgent call."

Convenient, Kate thought at the time, and expected to hear nothing more from the White House. She received a personal call almost immediately from one of the men who attended the showing. She declined the invitation to join him for a drink.

"Can't make it, sorry."

Then a few weeks later, she received the call from the staff person with whom she'd first dealt, inviting her group to repeat the showing at an official White House dinner.

The last White House call gathered Kate up in a swirl of attention around the law school. Those who thought they were seeing her for the first time were in fact doing exactly that. Kate's instinct was to live like she played tennis, hitting for the baseline. Off the tennis court, and especially at law school, she felt uncomfortable letting herself go. The result was that people thought she was withdrawn or snobbish. Now, she was liberated to an extent that made a difference. Everyday life became more fun, and her true personality began to emerge.

With her first exam over, she treated herself to a bottle of white wine, slapped a wedge of Brie and a hotdog onto a baguette, like she and her father used to do, and walked the short distance to the small park below the Capitol Building. Relaxing was not something she ever did knowingly, but competitive tennis had taught her to pace herself, and that was engrained. She ate her lunch on a bench that gave her a long view down the length of the lagoons to the Washington Monument. She thought about where she was, what she was going to do the following year to get ready to practice law, and how she could make the best of her job at the summer tennis camp.

She finished off the last of the Brie, pulled the cell phone out of her waist wallet, and placed a call to her father in Los Angeles. Their usual subjects exhausted, Kate told her father about the most recent call from the White House. She loved ambushing him with dramatic news amidst the more mundane subjects.

"Yes," she answered when he asked her to repeat what she'd just said, "at dinner in the East Room."

She could sense his mind getting into gear. "My reunion is on Saturday night," Bob Stevens said, thinking out loud as he continued. "Your White House dinner is on Friday. I'm taking the red-eye Thursday night. Who will be at that dinner? Did they send you a guest list?"

It reminded Kate of the time she'd called to tell her father she'd won the Pacific Coast No.3 singles title. He'd missed the match, and swore it would never happen again. She knew he wanted to be there when the film was shown.

"All I know is some Cabinet members and Senators, the Attorney General—God help me in that case—and a dozen or so corporate types like you."

"Like me, then why not me?" her father said. "Who've you been dealing with at the White House? Do you know who's in charge of invitations?"

"The person who's been in touch with me works on the White House Staff. That's all I know. Can you really manage to get yourself invited, or do you want me to try?"

"No, you'd better not. Give me your contact's name. I'll let you know how I make out. Either way, we're on for that Saturday affair. You promised you'd attend the reunion with me."

"Sure, Father. Are you going to stay through Sunday?"

"Yes."

"Good, we'll make it a weekend."

★

The President placed the Mexican Ambassador on one side and the Canadian on the other. The Secretaries of State and Agriculture joined them at the head table, and Senators and Representatives from Florida, New York, Kansas, and Minnesota were sprinkled around the room. In the center, farthest from the head table, sat Kate Stevens, other students, and several law professors from Georgetown.

The President began her remarks when the meal was finished and the dishes were cleared. Cox's suggestion had been to save dessert, champagne, and coffee as the bribe for mingling afterwards so as to give Charles Black the opportunity to gauge reactions.

"We have with us tonight representatives from our friends in the hemisphere and right here at home. I hope you've enjoyed your meal and the wine, which was provided by our neighbors in Chile. Thank you all for joining us. Now we have a special treat for you. Professor Smith, will you please stand?"

Kate watched her law school advisor stand as the President continued speaking.

"Professor Smith will introduce some of the members of the *Law Journal* at Georgetown University Law Center, one of whom will give us a synopsis of the film we're going to see. Professor . . ."

Kate introduced the film. The deep breath she took before beginning what she had to say matched that of some of the men sitting nearer the dais as they turned to look.

"Thank you, Professor Smith, and thank you, Madam President and distinguished guests," she began, after blowing an imaginary strand of blond hair from her right eye, like she did when she really needed her first serve to be in.

"When we started this project, it was to give some publicity to our research. We wished to highlight legal opinions several of us reached concerning federal laws and regulations that infringe on our constitutional freedoms. Not all of these have been tested before the Supreme Court. We chose laws passed decades ago by Congress, enforced on and off by Presidential Order and Regulations of the Treasury and other agencies. One of these laws prohibits U.S. citizens from dealing with or visiting the peoples of another nation with whom we are not at war. What could possibly be the justification for such an extraordinary measure, and why has it gone unchallenged in the courts for such a long time?"

At this point, she leaned over her table and took a swallow of water from her glass. All eyes were riveted on her as she moved. She gave her audience a shy smile and continued.

"What you are going to see are fictional case histories acted out by members of the *Journal* staff and our friends. This is a legal treatise. We don't intend to make a political statement, though we are not so naïve as to think one will not be inferred. We attempt nothing more than to dramatize what can happen to unsuspecting individuals when Congress and the Executive Branch of our government step over the line and there is no one there with the means or the will to call them on the transgression. There are adequate legal remedies. We do not need to parade in the streets to have our case heard. We dramatize because we know how easy it is to take such loss of liberty for granted when it doesn't hit home in the course of most of our daily lives. We intend to point out that no matter how well intended originally, these laws became insidious to our freedom the moment the circumstances giving rise to them ceased to be extraordinary. If you can recognize some of the ironies presented, then we'll consider our efforts successful."

[19]

Kate took her seat, but it was not until the lights dimmed that many stopped watching her.

The film concluded with the student playing the part of the government attorney making a point, with suitable thespian gestures: "These regulations do not say you can't go to Cuba, Your Honor. They say merely that you can't spend any money or conduct any trade while you are there." At this point, the East Room of the White House filled with ironic laughter. The noise rumbled as the lights came on. Kate glanced at her father and saw his thumbs-up from across the room.

The President stood tall for a long moment, her patrician features enlivened by the impact of the film on the audience. She raised a glass in silent toast to Kate, and invited her guests to stay for dessert, champagne, and coffee. She said she hoped they'd address their questions to the students who created the film. Following Gordon Cox's advice, she refrained from substantive comment.

After the film, the President mentioned to a small gathering of the corporate executives in attendance that she liked this creative approach to explaining legal points of view. To the group she also said, "That young woman, Katherine Stevens, is quite impressive, isn't she?"

"She's my daughter," Robert Stevens said.

"You should be very proud, Mr. Stevens," she said, giving him a closer look and winking at him. "I understand she's quite a good tennis player as well."

Kate's father smiled and nodded as the President moved on.

No one other than Charles Black took special notice of the Attorney General and Congressional Representatives from the Miami area leaving together before champagne was served. The Chief of Staff drifted through the crowd, putting together a consensus from four factions. Business wanted to get into Cuba before the Europeans and Chinese sewed up everything for themselves. State and Commerce wanted to get the monkey off their backs and resented a foreign policy designed to placate a few hard-line ex-Cubans in Miami. The Canadians and the Mexicans were tired of being bullied by the U.S. to comply with the trade embargo. The group that left early did not want anyone free to trade with Cuba until they were allowed to go back and reclaim what was taken from their families a half-century earlier. Black was right. It was a lively evening, and he informed the President that the consensus favored the course she had in mind.

"Call the Attorney General first thing tomorrow, Charlie," she said as the last guest left. "We need to get his nose back in joint."

It was after eleven-thirty when Kate and her father got into his rented limo and made the trip back to her apartment near the law school, and almost two in the morning when fatigue overtook Kate. She pushed her father out the door and into a cab back to his hotel.

Father and daughter were accustomed to celebrating Kate's successes and analyzing her failures. The subject on this night was their President, and the champagne Bob Stevens had brought with him for the occasion fueled Kate's impish sense of humor.

"She's single, Father. Why don't you call her for a date?"

"Very funny."

"You're right, she's too old for you. But don't you think she's sexy?"

"Power is sexy," Bob Stevens said.

"No, I mean physically sexy."

Kate's father smirked and shook his head. "She's very charming," he said, in a tone that ended the matter.

"Do you ever wish you were back here on the Hill in your old job?"

"Goodness no, child, that was kindergarten. Besides, I don't think it's as much fun as it used to be. So, how's law school?" he said, changing the subject. "Still like it?"

"I love it, and I'm very glad I came here rather than continuing at Stanford."

"Why? Stanford's a great school."

"So is Georgetown. Anyway, I needed a change of scene."

"How's your mother?"

Kate had been waiting for this. Her mother had ended the marriage. Daughter handled father's question delicately.

"She's the same. They seem happy enough."

"Get to Princeton much?"

"Not very often. I said I'd visit them after exams, before I leave for California and that damn tennis camp."

Stevens finished the wine in his glass, and moved to open another bottle. Kate stopped him.

"It's late, Father. You've got a big day tomorrow. I'll call you a taxi."

★

John Carver knew the immigration authorities and the Cuban police would demand to interview all crewmembers listed in the landing documents. The Cuban would be recognized for what he was, and subject to immediate arrest.

"I'm going to list only two in the crew," he said quietly to the mate as they rounded Morro Castle and entered the relatively calm waters of Havana Harbor. "You stay out of sight until we plug some of this leak and get out of here. I'll list the boy and we'll just pretend you're not here."

The mate understood the captain was risking confiscation of his boat if the Cuban authorities discovered he'd left a crewman off the official documents that had to be filed when entering a foreign port. He also knew that if they found out who was really on board, John Carver and the boy would be thrown in jail and the keys to their cells thrown away.

"Maybe we trade some of this fresh fish for a bottle of rum?" the Cuban said.

Carver nodded, and with a wide smile frozen on his face, turned the wheel to steer the listing boat for the lights he could see near the innermost section of Havana Harbor. The boat settled heavily onto its new course.

The Cuban came up to Carver's shoulder and spoke to him in quiet tones. "You know, John, we're going to need assistance putting a temporary patch on those sprung planks and cracked ribs. There's no way anyone coming on board to help is not going to see me. I don't think the fishermen will sound the alarm. We'll just have to take the chance with them."

"Are you sure?"

"Yes. I'll hide back aft under your bunk until the immigration officers and harbor police leave. They'll be concentrating on the sprung planks up forward to confirm your reason for coming here. Give them each a good fish to take back to their family. I'll come out when they're gone, and arrange a work party of local fishermen in the morning. I know how to blend in. You don't want to make the crossing back to Key West until she's seaworthy."

Carver looked hard at his mate, but nodded his assent. The captain was risking his boat, but the Cuban his life.

The mate continued. "These fishermen are pretty good at fixing old engines like yours. They can't get replacement parts in Cuba, so they keep them running with paper clips and rubber bands. I bet they'd fix those sticky valves of yours for a few pounds of fish."

"Okay," Carver said. "You take her while I explain things to the boy. He needs to know what's going on."

THREE

The reunion party of Congressional staffers of Bob Stevens' vintage was in full swing on Saturday when Kate and her father arrived. Kate stayed in one place while her father prowled the room looking for an old friend here and there. She was sustained by the high she was on from the film showing at the White House, and looked radiant in spite of a night of adrenaline induced insomnia. She enjoyed seeing her father in his element, watching as he circulated among unfamiliar faces, revisiting the issues of his days on the Hill. Still privately distracted by several issues that surfaced during the Q&A session following the White House dinner, she managed to keep up an endless stream of small talk for her father's benefit.

Kate heard a voice call her father's name from across the room and over the din. Its resonance belonged on the stage, and drew the attention of everyone in the room. She turned to see if her father would respond, but her glance was intercepted by the man who'd spoken. As their eyes met, she drew in a sharp breath of instant recognition. She flushed. They both looked away in the same moment.

Kate focused on her father, watching as he moved quickly toward the other man. The two met each other midway across the room and embraced. She studied them, trying to imagine the content of their conversation, when her father's companion intercepted her gaze again. The eye contact unsettled her, but this time she made him look away first. Her father was motioning for her to come and join them.

She excused herself from the small group around her and made her way across the crowded room. She stopped in front of her father. Only then did she allow herself to look up at the man standing next to him. Several years her father's junior, taller, and more battle-scarred, he was her father's opposite in the color of his hair and eyes. His face was so homely, it was almost beautiful. His sparkling eyes and brilliant smile muted the acne-scarred cheeks and over-sized features. He possessed a style and presence and broadcast a level of self-confidence that fit well with his actor's voice. He was dressed like he'd come to commune with royalty.

"Katie, I'd like you to meet Gordon Cox, the man your mother and I used to spend most of our fun time with here in Washington. He thought when he first saw you that you were Elizabeth."

"Guilty as charged, Katherine. Your mother was a very beautiful woman."

Kate felt the flush of embarrassment return to her cheeks. "She still is," she said, glancing at her father.

The edge in her voice did not escape either man. "Please forgive me," Cox said. "I didn't mean to put your mother in the past tense."

Her father was less compassionate. "Katie!"

"That didn't come out quite right, Mr. Cox. I apologize."

Gordon Cox's eyes spoke kindness. He waved a huge hand, as if to say no apology was needed. Then he asked, "How is your mother?"

"Well, very well in fact. She's living in Princeton, New Jersey now."

He smiled. "I've heard of it."

"Katie, Gordon is one of those Washington lawyers we read about in the newspaper every day."

"Don't over do it, Bobby."

"With the President one day, and keeping some politician out of jail the next."

"I know who Mr. Cox is, Father. He's a legend at Georgetown."

"You're here at the Law School?"

"Yes."

"What year?"

"Second. I went to the seminar you gave in October."

"Then you're on the *Law Journal*. Well, I'm in trouble now, Bobby. Before this gets any worse, why don't you and Katherine join me for dinner? At least we can have a decent drink that my Irish father would have approved."

Bob Stevens deferred to his daughter. "Katie?"

"That would be lovely," she said. The look on her father's face rewarded her for making the right decision.

The lawyer paused as the three of them exited the assembly. He studied Kate for a moment, as if trying to recall some thought from the back of his mind.

"Of course, your name was on the film credits. Were you at the White House last night?"

"We both were," she said.

"How did your audience respond?" he asked.

Before Kate could answer, Cox raised a forefinger to his lips, and said, "On second thought, not here. We'll talk about it over dinner."

Caught in the moment, Kate could only nod.

★

Gordon Cox arrived at his office late Sunday morning, the day after his unexpected meeting with Bob Stevens and his daughter. There were several young lawyers already hard at work at their computers, researching in the library, and marking up documents at their desk. Gordon saw the message light blinking on his phone as he cut through Emily Harris' side office to take one of the empty mugs she kept at the ready. The caller, whoever it was, could wait.

He poured the coffee, picked up on the way in from his place in the Watergate complex, into the more drinkable mug and unwrapped the bagel he'd brought with it. He avoided his desk, arranging breakfast and the Sunday Post on a small round conference table in the center of the room. He sat with his back to the blinking red light on his phone.

His head hurt and the tips of his fingers tingled from too much cognac the night before. What twist of fate had brought the Stevens woman across his path? He'd become aware of her mother's divorce from Kate's father only when he'd read the announcement of her new marriage. Since then, he'd entertained no more fantasies of what might've been. What a cruel trick to play on him now. Or . . .

"Or what?" he mumbled to himself. "For chrissake, Gordon, stop this nonsense and get to work."

He finished the last of the now cold coffee, and moved to his desk. His nose crinkled as he snorted lightly and punched the message play button on his phone. Cox recognized the recorded voice of his favorite cousin, a Jesuit priest working with a refugee organization in Boston.

★

Kate thought it unlike her father to prefer what she considered the stodgiest hotel in Washington. The ex-beach boy from California, she fancied, should be staying at one of the more contemporary places. She guessed his choice went back to some earlier view of where you were supposed to stay when you'd made it in life. Like a merit badge.

The breakfast room was carpeted on the floor and on some of the walls. Father, of course, was nowhere in evidence. She used the house phone and caught him in the shower.

"I'll be down in a couple of minutes, Katie. Have them rustle up some scrambled eggs and get me half a grapefruit."

She eyed the headwaiter, who stood by his churchlike pedestal drenched in somberness. He escorted Kate to a small table close to the swinging doors into the kitchen.

"I'm not going to sit at a table next to the kitchen, sir. My father is a guest here. Since he'll make you move us to one of those other empty tables when he comes down, we might as well do it now."

She was down two cups of tea and halfway through the front section of the Sunday Post by the time her father appeared, clean shaven and looking like he was ready for whatever the day might bring.

"Sorry it took so long, kitten. You know it's only 6:00 A.M. my time."

"I noticed that phenomenon last night," she said with a laugh, "when you and Mr. Cox were on your third cognac."

Bob Stevens chuckled. "So what did you think of my friend Gordon?" he asked, joining Kate at the table just as the eggs she had ordered for him arrived.

Kate's smile filled the room. Father's timing, as usual, was perfect. "I enjoyed meeting him, but it seems he was as much a friend of Mother's as yours, Father," she said, sipping some tea and looking over the edge of the cup to see what kind of a reaction her remark would yield.

"He was in love with your mother, Katie. You got that right," her father answered, pushing the grapefruit aside and starting in on his eggs. "I came along later."

"And you're still friends?"

"It was all a long time ago. To tell you the truth, I don't think he ever got over their romance. I think your mother walking out was what sent him back home to Boston and to law school. Be sure to tell her that you ran into him," he said, with a fiendish grin that Kate recognized came with the joke.

"I'll think about it," she said. She wondered if Gordon Cox went to the reunion in hopes of seeing her mother. Instead, he met father and daughter.

"Are you going to accept the offer he made to work with his firm this summer?"

"Maybe. I had no idea he and you . . . and Mother . . . were such good friends. It would be far more interesting than teaching tennis again. Trouble is I've already said yes to the darn tennis camp."

"So help them find a replacement. Why not one of your old college teammates?"

"I'll get on it. Good idea, Father dear."

Kate and her father spent the next thirty minutes at the breakfast table trying to outdo each other at pointing out some of the more ridiculous events considered newsworthy by the Post. It was a game they started playing years before when her father accompanied her around the country on junior tennis trips.

She waited until the moment seemed right. "Father, why don't we go for a walk? It's a nice morning. This place is suffocating."

They emerged from the hotel into bright sunshine and walked along 16th Street. Kate took her father's arm as they crossed into Lafayette Park, moving in silence toward the north side of the White House, which now held a special meaning for Kate. They strolled together through the security of the cement barricades and around the South Lawn. Then, putting the Washington Monument behind them, they continued along the Mall toward the Capitol.

They talked lightly about the past two days, revisiting Friday night's dinner at the White House.

"She has amazing presence," Kate said, referring to her impressions of the President. She's not overpowering, not intimidating, just strong with depth. The impression I have is similar to what I've read about Abraham Lincoln's effect on people, except," she said, giggling, "the President is better looking than Old Abe was. You'd met her before the other night. Did she remember you?"

"I'm afraid not," Bob Stevens said, "but I know what you mean. It's as if she can see right through you, yet when she gives you that look, you're left with a warm feeling."

"Hmmm," Kate muttered, still picturing the President's appearance in her mind.

Bob Stevens continued. "Has this encounter given you any ideas about government service, or maybe running for office some day?" he said, and reminded of a related question he intended to ask his daughter. "Have you figured out what you're going to do yet, after you graduate next year?"

"Not really," Kate said. "I've so little exposure to anything real in the law, I don't know what I want to do."

"So take Gordon Cox up on his offer. That could make for an interesting summer."

★

"Hello, this is Gordon Cox."

"Oh, Mr. Cox, it's Kate Stevens. I didn't think you'd be in the office. I was going to leave you a voicemail message."

"Hello, Katherine. I was just about to call it a day. Nice to hear from you. I hope you're going to tell me you'll be with us this summer."

"Yes, well, I have to find a replacement for my job at the Stanford tennis camp. Subject to that, I can do it. I really appreciate your giving me this opportunity."

"Wonderful. I'll leave a note right now for my secretary. Her name is Emily Harris. Call her in the next couple of days. She'll get you started. I'll see you when this damn trial up in Wilmington is over. Is your dad still in town?"

"Yes, he's right here. Hold on."

"Gordon?"

"Hey, Bobby. Thanks for dinner last night. I didn't intend for you to pay."

"You're welcome, Gordon. It was a great evening, but I've learned never to let your lawyer pick up the tab. You get charged for the time too."

Gordon laughed. "You've got that right, Bobby, but this time I owe you for introducing me to that talented daughter of yours. The film she made is the talk of this town, and it's already causing quite a stir over on the Hill." Cox paused for a moment, and then continued. "Now that I think about it she might need to be prepared for what could be coming. Can you put her back on for a moment?"

Bob Stevens handed the phone to his daughter.

"Hello?"

"Katherine, I just wanted to mention . . . just so you know where to come if things start to get rough. Your film has become a politi-cal football. There will be criticism, and some of it will be focused on the law school for letting you make what will be characterized as a political statement. The White House has already received a call from the Dean. Some of this is going to come home to roost. Your best course is to avoid getting involved. Accept no interviews and don't let yourself get roped into making any kind of statement."

"I'm not really surprised. I guess that's what we were doing. Making a controversial point, I mean."

"You know the list of people invited to that dinner Friday was not by chance. It was a phalanx of various sides on the Cuba issue. The film served as the President's catalyst to initiate the debate and to make the contrary argument look foolish. Your film accomplished part of that task for her."

"Law and politics do mix."

"Exactly. Let's hope the tempest is short lived. We'll get together when this case of mine is finished and I'm back in town. In the meantime, if it gets too rough, call my secretary and tell her you need to speak with me. She'll know who you are and what to do."

★

"Bless you, Cousin Gordon."

Paul Hennessy's call to his cousin Gordon on Saturday night concerned a small Florida fishing boat intercepted and boarded by the United States Coast Guard returning to Key West from Havana, Cuba, where it was forced to dock during a severe storm in the Gulf Stream.

"Apparently," Hennessey began, "the captain, a man by the name of Carver, was anxious to tell his wife they were on their way home. He used the boat's VHF radio coming out of Havana to make the call. The Coast Guard picked it up, got a bearing on the transmitter, and made the intercept."

"Is that all?" Cox said.

"No. Unfortunately, they had a Cuban crew member. He was taken off the boat at sea and into custody. This got the Coast Guard skipper's attention, and he ordered a thorough search of the fishing boat. They found a box of Cuban cigars and a half consumed bottle of Havana Club Rum on board. The captain insisted the Cuban had been a member of his crew for over a year, but his name wasn't on the landing documents filed in Havana. The boat was then turned over to the drug enforcement division of the Justice Department in Key West to search for drugs."

"Things went downhill from there. Poor communication between the Coast Guard and the DEA on the circumstances of the intercept resulted in the drug enforcement agents assuming they were dealing with a typical group of foreign drug traffickers. They thought the boat was confiscate, so it made no difference if they trashed it. The easiest way to find illegal substances on board was to tear the vessel apart. That's what they did, and with it went this man's means of making a living."

"Carver was charged with a violation of the Trading with the Enemy Act, arrested, and incarcerated in Miami. We were solicited by a church in Key West to aid the man's family," Hennessey said, "but he needs a good lawyer and his boat back in one piece. What do you say *Cuz*, can you help us out?"

Cox agreed to do what he could. The following morning he called in Brad Howe, one of the firm's litigation associates. Howe had shown Gordon he had the ability to manage others while preparing for trial. Not all of them could do that. Litigators, the good ones, tended to work alone, trusting no one to frame their answers or pose their interrogatories. Howe had a knack for delegation and was good at following up, and one was no good without the other.

"Brad," Gordon continued, "enter an appearance on behalf of that old fisherman and the American crew member. We're not going to defend the illegal. We'll let the 'usuals' in Miami handle that. We're doing this *pro bono*. Use Kate Stevens on it. She's the new summer associate. Let her take it as far as she can."

"I've heard about her. She was the one who did that film on the Embargo."

"That's right. Let her work in the constitutional angle if she wants."

"Okay. Uhh . . . mind telling me what our interest is in this case?"

Gordon looked for a measured amount of aggressiveness in the firm's young litigators. The price he paid for engendering this spirit was putting up with questions from them that often bordered on insubordinate. He loved the give and take.

"Well, does it sound right to you, Brad, that this old man's livelihood was taken away by our friends over at Justice, because he traded a few fish for some ice and a bunch of lousy cigars?"

"They had an illegal on board," Brad pointed out. "Transporting people from Cuba into Florida is a felony, Gordon."

"True, but that's no excuse for tearing the man's boat apart, is it?"

"There is a lot of drug trade coming out of Cuba, and there probably was reason to do a search."

"I'll grant you that, but they had no right to confiscate the man's boat. They found nothing. They also destroyed his catch, which I understand was a month's good wages."

"So that's our interest, justice for the downtrodden? Or is it the Justice Department we don't like these days?"

"Brad, we've been asked by the Catholic Church to give this man and his family a little help. If, in the process, we make a monkey out our esteemed Attorney General, I for one will be very happy. Does that answer your question?"

Howe knew when to get in line. "Yes, sir. Do you want to see the papers before I file them?"

"This is your case, Brad, until Kate Stevens is ready to take it over. Come back if you want my input. Otherwise, you two handle it. There's something else you should know. The team handling our project financings is doing some research for me on the possibility of using the World Bank to make reparations in Cuba. Have one of them give you a copy of all information generated. There might be data in there you or Kate Stevens can use in support of any motions you might consider worthwhile."

So, the young lawyer thought, walking back to his desk with a grin on his face, *the senior partner is after the Attorney General again.*

The *cognoscenti* inside the Beltway had assumed Gordon Cox would be named to the top legal position in the government when the person he effectively supported won the Presidency. There were too many vanquished enemies of the Irishman lying in ambush on Capitol Hill and inside the federal bureaucracy. The President's appointment of Conner Omega to head the Justice Department sailed through the Senate confirmation proceedings. He was a virtual unknown outside the precincts of Dade County, where he made his name conducting an all out assault on the illegal drug trade in south Florida by coordinating efforts with the DEA and U.S. Coast Guard coming out of Cuba and Central America. Many thought this was the background needed at the Department of Justice, especially when the position also included supervising the FBI and the drug enforcement staffs. Omega's connections within the community of Cuban hard-liners in Miami went unnoticed, or were quietly swept under the political rug.

★

"It's the perfect case for you," Gordon told his new summer associate during her brief orientation to the firm. "We've taken it *pro bono,* so you don't need to worry about time spent, fees, and the like. You'll be working with Brad Howe, one of our promising young trial lawyers. When it's over you can add it to your film collection," Gordon said with an alluring twinkle in his eye.

"I can't wait to get started on a real live case, involving the Trading with the Enemy Act no less. And thanks for the summer job, Mr. Cox. Oh, by the way, I spoke with Father last night. He sends his regards."

Cox smiled and shifted in his chair. "Kate, one thing you will soon notice around here is that just about everybody calls me Gordon. And please give your father my best."

"I also spoke with my mother." Kate embellished what she said with a devilish look that made the corners of her mouth tilt upward.

"Did you tell your mother you're working with us this summer?"

Kate laughed softly. "If you remember anything about my mother, you know she has a low tolerance for surprise."

In the silence that followed, Gordon's eyes stopped dancing. He looked vulnerable. Kate deflected the awkward moment with the first thought that came into her head.

"How long have you and the President known each other . . . Gordon?"

Cox's features came back to life. "Since I was in law school," he said. "Your mother and I left our respective staff jobs on the Hill about the same time. The Boston congressman I worked for helped me get accepted to the Harvard Law School, and I got a job teaching political science to Harvard undergraduates. Rebecca was head of the history department at that time. Later, when she was elected Governor of her home state, I took a summer off and worked in her office. When she ran for the Big Job, I did what I could to help out. How'd she do the other night?"

"I was overwhelmed, but to be the first woman President . . . well, that's pretty impressive in itself."

"Maybe you'll get the chance to meet her again."

"I'd like that."

FOUR

It was a long drive home from the Federal District courthouse in Miami. John Carver's bail was posted by a lawyer in Washington he'd never heard of, and his local parish church provided the ride back to Key West. His fishing boat was up on the hard, dry land, where the DEA people had finished with it. There wasn't much left. "Not enough to float, anyhow," the captain's wife had told him over the phone. She was right.

His Cuban crewman, taken off the boat at sea, was presumed to be on his way to Guantanamo Bay. It had been a mistake to use the VHF to call home so close to Havana Harbor. This was a red alert to the U.S. Coast Guard, and it was easy for them to intercept his course home. He should have known better, and it cost him his boat and the Cuban his freedom. Carver wondered what they'd do to him back in Cuba.

What in hell had this world come to that a man couldn't go into a foreign port to save his own vessel? He didn't "trade" with anyone, and he didn't know Cuban fishermen were the enemy. They wouldn't believe him that the Cuban had been on board in Key West. Carver's trial was set for the following January. Until then he was free to fish in U.S. waters. All he needed was a boat.

★

"I'm Kate Stevens," she said, peeking around the door into Brad Howe's office.

"Hello. Yes, Kate, come on in. If you can find an open space somewhere, you can even sit down," Howe said, picking up a stack of books from the only other chair in his small office. "There, have a seat," he said, unable to disguise his appreciation for Kate's blond hair and remarkable blue eyes.

"Thanks," she said, taking in the room at a glance. Clutter, stacks of documents on the floor, picture on the credenza with wife or lady friend skiing in Colorado, diploma from the Penn Law School, desktop computer and a view of bricks and glass across 17th Street, N.W.

"I guess you'd like to have the file on the Key West fishermen," he said.

Kate nodded, still taking in the clutter.

"Did Gordon fill you in?"

He had, but Kate's instincts told her it smacked of favoritism. "Not really," she answered.

"Well, I have to admit it's an interesting case, though I don't for the life of me think it's one the firm should be handling."

"Why not?"

"It's all downside, and make no mistake it will be damn difficult to win."

"Is that because we're taking it on *pro bono*?"

"No, it's because having any dealings with the enemy warrants tough measures these days. No judge will let this case go to the jury."

Kate wanted to argue that Cuba technically was not our enemy, but she held back. She also doubted Brad was right about getting to the jury, but she needed to get up to speed on the facts and applicable law. "I'll be back for help when I reach that dead end. Will you help me?"

"You bet. Do you have anything on for lunch today, Kate? I'll introduce you around. We'll go across the street to the greasy spoon."

"That's very nice of you Brad, but I've got to get over to the law school and get my desk cleaned out for the summer. May I have a rain check on lunch?"

Slowly at first, then with unleashed energy, Kate immersed herself in the assignment Cox and Brad Howe had given her. She worked well into the night, a habit from her time with the *Law Journal*. She left a pile of notes and a few suggestions for her teammate to consider the next morning. A light in Gordon's office was still on when she walked by on her way out. She was tempted to poke her head in and say hello, but decided against it.

On the late-night, firm-subsidized cab ride back to her apartment, Kate thought about her mother and Gordon Cox. They would have made an interesting couple, though her mother was two or three years older than Gordon. She decided the relationship could not have lasted. Kate knew her mother too well. Gordon Cox was not beautiful. What looked like an athletic body under his pinstripes was offset by a four-cornered face with remarkable eyes that looked out of place on either side of an unseemly large nose. He possessed none of the sculptured good looks that were reflected in her mother's taste in men. He'd been a poor boy in those days, with less of a future than her mother would have demanded. But the magic was there for a time. That much was clear.

Kate couldn't sleep. Tired, and still on the adrenaline rush from her first day in a real law office, she spent most of the night sliding in and out of sleep, wrestling with her own relationships with men and the never ending battle to establish independence from the beautiful, strong-willed mother who still wanted to control her life. Tennis had been her ticket to escape from both. It had earned her a scholarship to one of the best universities in the country. She could have attended an Ivy League school, but chose one just as good in Palo Alto, as far away from her mother as she could get.

Success had followed in almost everything she did, except in relations with the opposite sex. She liked men, but men liked her too much. She didn't function well on the defensive, and that's where she found herself on dates and in short order after meeting an interesting man. In college she tried changing her hair color from natural blonde to brunette. When that didn't ice down the male testosterone, she got rid of her frustrations by hitting tennis balls where her opponents weren't.

The heavy doses of competitive tennis that Kate Stevens experienced throughout most of her young life required concentration amid multiple distractions. She learned how to focus on controlling what she could, and to disregard the rest. The more she studied the facts of the John Carver case within the confines of the Trading with the Enemy Act, the more she became convinced that an unconstitutional seizure of personal property and a deprivation of liberty had taken place.

She went through all relevant cases involving the Cuban Democracy Act and Treasury Rulings and penalties assessed for trading with the enemy in Cuba. This was all part of the work she'd already done for the film. She began to concentrate on federal law enforcement in south Florida, particularly in the area of persons dealing with Cuba. She began to experience firsthand the highly charged political emotions that ran amongst the Cuban communities in Miami when anyone tried to return to Cuba or was caught visiting or trading with Fidel's old crowd. These politics were the driving force behind the Embargo, and she thought were also the immediate cause of her government's excessive actions in this case. Clearing the fishermen and restoring the old man's livelihood became Kate's crusade.

★

The first call came in from the Attorney General, himself a product of the politics of south Florida. "Your people are stirring up a lot of hard feelings back in my old neighborhood, Gordon. Is it all really necessary?"

Cox possessed little respect for this Attorney General. He thought him to be overly political and often arrogant. But he was also the Attorney General, so his calls were answered. "Like what, Conner?"

"Well, for starters, why get the Catholic Church involved in civil matters?"

Cox couldn't resist the gambit. "I'm sure I don't know, but didn't the Pope's visits to Cuba set everything in motion? Maybe you'd better check with the State Department. They encouraged it."

Conner Omega dismissed the comment. "And some associate in your office has been trying to drag up all the old sins in Dade County, I suppose trying to show the arrest of those two fishermen was part of a pattern of harassment. Well, it's dangerous country, that."

"Do you have his name?" Gordon asked, fully aware that he meant Kate.

"No, but it's a she, not a he."

"I'll look into it, Conner, but tell me . . . is it?"

"What?"

"A pattern of harassment?"

"Of course not. Those guys had contraband on board."

"Oh, come on . . . a few cigars and a half empty bottle of Cuban rum."

"It's the principle that's important here, Gordon. You know that."

"No, I don't know that. Your people took his boat apart and threw the man in federal prison. For what—a few smokes?"

"The captain of that boat was transporting an illegal into the U.S. For all we know, he intended to bomb the White House," said Conner.

"An illegal to whom your department will now offer asylum."

"Okay, okay, we may have overreacted a little bit. Have the man plead to a lesser. We can work this out."

"Does he get his boat back . . . in good shape?"

"You know I can't do that."

"Then no deal."

"I'll get back to you."

"You do that."

"But you call off Joan of Arc. I've told my friends in Miami I'd throw some cold water on all this fuss. If you want my cooperation, you'll need to rein her in. The President is worried about any adverse publicity right now, with Congress rethinking the relationship and all."

If he only knew what the President was worried about, Cox thought. "Get back to me," he said. "In the meantime, no deal."

Cox asked Emily Harris to order two sandwiches and have Kate Stevens come to his office.

She arrived looking vibrant, with an armful of documents. Emily gave her a thumbs-up, and helped her pick up two papers that fell off the pile. "He got you a sandwich," she said.

Kate strode into Gordon's room and sat down in the chair in front of his desk with the papers still balanced in her arms. Gordon smiled as he watched her lower the stack to her lap, blow a curl of blond hair from her right eye, and give him a big hello. How did he manage before meeting this creature? She brightened up his day.

"I don't know what you've been doing on that case you're working on, but whatever it is, keep it up. I received a call from the Attorney General himself. He wants to deal."

"What does that mean?" she said, using her best law school class demeanor, and placing the stack of documents on the floor next to her chair.

"We don't know yet, but you've managed to put some pressure on somebody. He wouldn't have called me otherwise. What have you been up to?"

Kate took a quick breath and exhaled it. "I don't understand why our government made such a big deal out of an old fisherman limping in and out of Havana. I began checking the Internet and Nexus. When I found something similar to the treatment these fishermen received, I called around to see how it all ended. I've spoken with several Miami lawyers who have handled similar cases. I also found a very helpful source in the Dade County Clerk's Office. Our case is unique, but there is very definitely a pattern of going after anyone who tries to deal with Cuba, especially if that person isn't one of the Cuban expatriate inner circle."

"What about the younger generation, Kate? Or are these strong feelings limited to the fathers and their sons who remember what happened at the Bay of Pigs?"

"That's a great question. Two of the lawyers I spoke with were of Cuban parentage and in their twenties. They certainly didn't go along with the type of excesses they talked to me about. I'm not sure, but I think it's limited to the men who were there, plus a small number of politicians who won't let the people forget. There are certainly those who hate the Castros for what they did and will not rest until Cuba is returned to them, but the vast majority seems more interested in getting on with their lives."

"So what's your legal theory for getting Captain Carver off the hook? Shouldn't we make a deal with Justice?"

"I guess it depends what the deal is. The only person totally free is the illegal who was on board. Ironically, he's the one the Cuban community is concerned about. That's because the government was going to send him back to Cuba. The other two are out on bail, but that's thanks to you. So, maybe if Justice returns the boat to the captain—repaired, of course—and if they drop all charges, then I'd say we should take the deal. Otherwise, nothing doing. My theory is no due process."

"When will you finish your research?"

"I'm almost done. Another couple of days."

"Alright then, let's have a session on Friday evening. I'll hold off the AG until then."

Kate flushed. "I was going up to spend the weekend with Mother. Can we do it on Thursday? I don't mind working late."

"Good. Thursday it is then . . . around seven?"

"I'll be here," she said with a smile, picked up the papers, and headed back to her office.

Gordon Cox swiveled his chair around so that he was gazing out the window onto 18th Street. Kate Stevens was going to be a very good lawyer. She had her mother's style plus a refreshing attitude toward life and a no-nonsense approach to her work. He found himself attracted to her. He was almost twenty-five years her senior, and his own mother was right when she told him he wasn't pretty. Yet, women seemed to be attracted to him. He had his share of relation-ships, so why not the real thing? He thought he'd had this with Kate's mother, for a while anyway, until that weekend he took her home to Southie. Was it wrong to be attracted to the woman's daughter? An irrelevant question, he decided, "And thank God for that," he mumbled, suddenly realizing Emily Harris was standing by his desk with a quizzical expression on her face. He was happy the rest of his thoughts had not been voiced.

★

The second call was a death threat.

"Brad's outside, Gordon," Emily said, uncertain what was going on with her boss. "He needs to speak to you."

Howe looked ashen. He had trouble holding some papers in his right hand, it shook so much.

"Did the call specifically come in to you, Brad, or did the switch-board just send it up to you?"

"No, no, the caller asked for me by name," the lawyer answered as Kate joined them in a rush. She'd passed Brad in the hall and had seen how upset he was. She'd followed him back to Gordon's office, walked right past Emily Harris, and joined the two in desperate discussion.

"He knew where I lived, as well as my wife's name, where she worked, and what bus she took to the office," Brad said, his voice raised to a higher frequency than normal.

"What happened?" Kate asked.

"Brad has just received his first threatening phone call. It was from Miami."

"Oh no, I've touched too many nerves down there."

"Sit down, you two. Let's talk this out," Cox said. "I assure you, working in this town, doing what we do, this may not be the last time you receive a threatening phone call."

Emily was standing by the open door. "Please close the door, Emily," Gordon said.

Cox spent the better part of an hour with Kate and Brad Howe, talking through Howe's fears for his wife's safety. He told the younger lawyer to replace his name on the court documents with his own. Then, he suggested Kate should ease off on her politicizing activity in Dade County. He said he thought the AG would be back in touch in a few days, and he'd take up the matter then. There was no reason, he told them, to expect the worst.

Kate seemed satisfied, but Howe was still clearly shaken. To get his mind on other things, Cox took the young lawyer with him to a scheduled meeting with the Secretary of State. Howe could talk to his wife about the meeting when he went home that night, instead of what some idiot in Miami had said to him over the telephone.

FIVE

Carlos "The Orphan" Diego laughed aloud in his Coral Gables office, a sight his confederates seldom witnessed.

"You told him in Spanish he was a dead man? What happened then?"

"He said nothing. I think he was frightened."

"Enriques, you're a fool, but I love you. Do you have five dollars in your pocket?"

The man fumbled through the greenbacks in his hand and picked out a five-dollar note.

"Place it on the table," Diego said. He reached into his own pocket, pulled out five dollars, and put it next to his man's. "Now, we're going to have a bet, amigo. If my friend Conner Omega doesn't call within two hours to find out what we're up to, the ten dollars is yours. If he calls, you lose. Okay, now find out where the deserter we rescued from Guantanamo Bay has gone. Probably back to Key West."

Carlos Diego was made an orphan by Fidel Castro. Diego's father was one of the few industrialists in Cuba who was favored by the revolutionaries immediately following Castro's overthrow of the

Batista regime in 1958. That warm and fuzzy relationship didn't survive Castro's embrace of communism, and if you weren't the revolution's friend, you were its enemy.

At seven years old, Carlos came home from school one afternoon to find his mother and teenage sisters lying naked in pools of their own blood in various rooms of the house. Upon learning of his wife and daughters' rape and murder, Carlos' father went gunning for Castro. The dictator's guards easily cut him down.

Since that day, every waking hour in Carlos Diego's life was spent working to even the score. Diego was determined to make Fidel Castro and his supporters pay for what they did to his family. Carlos would return to Havana on that day and reclaim what was rightfully his. He staged daily combat to gain power in Havana, but retained fewer and fewer allies as time passed. Compatriots in Miami looked elsewhere for help in establishing a sympathetic government in Cuba. His following in Havana was bought with Yankee dollars and the promise of even greater rewards when Fidel Castro was gone. Diego was hard put to keep his hard-liner group together. He needed something to happen, and soon.

★

Kate went to Princeton on Friday after work. Being there reminded her how much her mother had wanted her to attend Princeton University instead of Stanford. One factor loomed large in each of their minds . . . her mother would have been right next-door. Kate knew that wouldn't have worked. It was still a nice place to visit. She arrived in time for a late dinner.

The subject of Gordon Cox did not come up until Kate and her mother sat alone over coffee on the screened porch.

"You've gone to work for him?" Kate's mother asked, genuinely surprised, if not disapproving.

Kate became defensive. "Yes, Mother. He's a lawyer. I'm in law school. He offered me a summer job, and I took it. There's not a student at Georgetown who wouldn't kill for this opportunity."

"Extraordinary," Elizabeth mumbled to herself.

Kate didn't catch her mother's remark.

"What?"

"I was just thinking what a small world."

"Yes, well anyway I'm really looking forward to seeing what an honest-to-God law firm is like."

"Hmmm," Elizabeth said. "Maybe we can see more of you this summer."

By the time her mother and stepfather drove Kate to the train on Sunday for the trip back to Washington, Kate had learned more about Gordon Cox. He came up in conversations whenever mother and daughter were alone and during a shopping trip on Saturday when her mother was being girlishly candid.

"We were very young then, Katherine. Times were good, and we had fun being around the halls of Congress. We all thought we were something special, maybe with the exception of Gordon Cox. To him, it was just a job."

"I think he was really in love with you, Mother."

"It was fast and furious for a while. He was fun to be with, and a very good kisser."

Kate laughed hard at her mother's choice of words. She knew she meant "lover."

"What are you laughing at?"

"You, Mother dear, you. I suspect it was more than fast. My bet is it was totally torrid!"

"Don't be silly. He was interesting and fun to be with. I was a little uncomfortable that he was younger than I was. The woman should always be younger than the man."

"I think he's very sexy. So do the women in the office. He pays no attention to any of it. I don't think he even has a girlfriend."

"You wouldn't know, would you? He wouldn't play around the office or even in D.C. He's too well known."

"Well, it doesn't seem to stop anyone else in Washington. No, I think he's still carrying the torch for you."

"Well, think what you wish, Katherine. I guess he's good to work for."

★

Most of the outline of John Carver's fishing boat was intact, but the inside bulkheads and under the cabin sole had been ripped apart. There was no insurance to cover what DEA agents had done. If he'd driven the boat onto a reef or had a fire on board, his insurance would cover most of the loss, but this was his alone to bear. He prayed for the lawyers in Washington to tell him the government would fork over the money for a new fishing boat.

"Thanks again, Father Kelly," Carver said, leaving St. Michaels with the money sent to him from the church in Boston. "I'm sorry about the boy's job."

"That's alright John," the priest said. "He's gone back to his family in Illinois. The time with your crew did him a lot of good. I understand your other mate is back living on the wreck of your boat."

"Yes and why not? At least it's good for something."

"Will you be at the service tonight?"

"Yes, but Maisy can't make it. She's working in the kitchen over at Bud's."

"This'll all be over soon, John. Don't you worry."

"Please thank those fathers in Boston. We couldn't make it without this money."

"You've helped the Church out a good deal, John. It's the least we can do. See you tonight."

Carver took the call on the phone he'd moved from the boat to his den.

"Captain?"

"This is John Carver."

"Captain Carver, we got a fishing boat you might be interested in having a look at."

Carver gave his stock reply to all those who called when they heard he'd lost his boat. "The insurance hasn't come through yet. No point in my getting excited about any boat."

"The owner of this one can wait. He ain't in no hurry, and this'n has all the gear you want. It's been fished all this year up in St. Mary's. They brung it down here to sell."

"Where is it now?"

"Do you know where the old bridge was taken out over by Boca Chico airfield?"

"Yes, but I don't know any docks over there."

"No, it's up on a big trailer behind the buildings. She'll be moved tomorrow onto a mushroom buoy in the old harbor. I could show her to you around seven, just before it gets dark. This one ain't gonna last long."

Carver thought for a moment. He couldn't place the spot that this caller was telling him about, but maybe it would get him back in business sooner than he'd thought. His prayers were being answered. "Okay, I'll be there after church, if I can find the place."

Three men were standing by a large pickup truck parked in front of the first building as Carver pulled off the main road into the old helicopter base. He couldn't see any boat, but the first man waved a greeting, and Carver stopped alongside the truck.

"Captain Carver?" the first asked.

John Carver nodded, and stepped out of his car.

★

The Attorney General reached Gordon Cox in his office late on Monday. He commented that Cox's associates seemed to have complied with his wishes. Cox told him it was because one of them received a threat to his family.

"I was afraid something like that might happen," the AG said.

"I want it looked into, Conner. I'm sure with your connections in Miami, you can convince the right people that threats of violence will harden, not soften, positions."

"I'll do what I can. I don't condone this sort of thing."

"I should hope not," Cox said sharply. "You're the Attorney General, for chrissake."

"So I am. We're dropping the case with prejudice."

"What about the old man's boat?"

"No boat is going to do him any good. He's dead."

★

The next step, following notice of John Carver's death, was to send Brad Howe to Key West to inspect the remains of the old boat, meet with the fisherman's widow, and fill in the missing pieces about the old man's estate. Howe's wife thought about the threats he'd received. She wouldn't agree to his going back to Florida on this case.

"That's a job for the marshals, Brad," she said. "You don't get paid to risk your neck running after criminals."

When Kate arrived at the office Tuesday morning and learned of the plan, she was furious. She found Cox in his office, standing in front of his antique podium desk.

"It's my case, Gordon. You've got to let me do this."

He shook his head. "It's too risky, Kate."

"For me, but not for Brad Howe? Come on, Gordon."

"It really should be a lawyer."

"Why? It's just fact finding. I can handle it."

Gordon smiled and raised both hands in mock surrender. "All right, Katherine," and he called for Emily to come into the room. "As long as you are going, Kate, do it right. Don't cut any corners. I want to know how we get the government to pony up some real dough for that man's family, or my cousin Paul will disown me. And be back here in two days. I have another assignment for you that won't wait."

Kate squealed, "Yes!" and taking a long step forward, rose to her tip-toes and planted a kiss on Gordon's cheek just as Emily Harris entered the room. It happened quickly, and Cox was momentarily stunned. Kate blushed profusely, and gave Gordon a friendly poke on the arm. Then she turned and walked past Emily, acknowledging her presence with a half smile.

Gordon and Emily Harris stood for a moment looking at each other, not sure what to say. Cox broke the ice.

"Emily, please arrange for Katherine's flight to Key West. She'll give you the details. I don't think she's ever been down there, so you'll have to pick an appropriate place for her to stay over."

Emily nodded, but remained speechless. Gordon spoke as she turned to leave his office. "Emily, that wasn't what it might have appeared," he said.

She looked back at him, but try as she would, she couldn't muster the smile she knew he wanted.

★

Kate saw the darkly tanned shoulders of a man standing chest-deep in the shallow Gulf waters along the north shore of Key West. His back was turned to the afternoon sun as he fished with light tackle. Kate waited in the deserted boatyard until the man, naked and carrying two small fish on a string, emerged from the water. He pretended to ignore Kate as he strolled past her and climbed up and into the wreck of an old wooden fishing boat.

It was this boat and this man she had come to see. She waited a few minutes before pounding on the hull of the old wooden vessel. The man reappeared, looking down at her. This time, he wore a pair of faded khaki shorts.

Kate climbed up the ladder under his amused gaze, mumbling "Now what?" to herself as she reached the deck of the boat where he was standing. He motioned her to sit down on the combing around what was left of the boat's fishing platform.

She spoke slowly in Spanish, asking questions, listening to his one-syllable responses, and seeking clarification when she didn't understand his replies. She stayed on the offensive.

"My name is Katherine Stevens. I understand you're known as Lefty. Is that right?"

He nodded in the affirmative.

"I've just come from the widow of your late captain. She told me that's what you're called."

This engendered no additional response.

"I've come here at the request of a charitable organization that is helping the captain's family. We were trying to get the government in Washington to agree to give the captain a new boat, because they destroyed this one." Kate paused for some sign that she was being understood. Getting none, she plowed ahead anyway with a rhetorical question that was not very lawyer-like. "Since the captain died in a car accident, what good is the boat?" she said.

Her question seemed to spark interest in the man.

Encouraged that her Spanish was getting by, she moved on. "So what will you do now? What's your job, now that the boat no longer goes out fishing?"

"Want a beer?" he asked in clearly spoken English.

Taken aback, Kate sputtered, "Uh, sure. Thank you."

The man disappeared into the dry deep bottom of his wooden home, returning by some miracle, she thought, with two cold Coronas.

"No lime," he said.

"That's fine. Thank you very much," she said, adding her best smile.

He smiled back, lifted his beer under her watchful gaze, and took a long, slow swig. He wiped his mouth on his wrist, and sat back as if to say, "Okay, now I'll answer your questions."

Kate took such a quick sip of her beer it made him laugh. She continued carefully in English, "What will you do now that the boat no longer goes out fishing?"

"I have work."

"It must be tough though not having a work permit."

"I get by."

"Did you like fishing? The captain thought you were a very good fisherman."

"I like fishing."

"Well . . ." Noticing the man had almost finished his beer, Kate took as big a sip as she could manage before continuing. She swallowed wrong, choked, and coughed her way through the next question, all to his quiet amusement. "I was thinking. If we can get the widow a new boat, would you be willing to work it for her? You and the captain's family could split the catch. Is that a good idea?"

"The feds aren't going to let me run a boat."

"Maybe my boss can get you a work permit which would allow you to operate the family's boat."

He shot her a skeptical look. "How's that? You work for Jesus Christ?"

"No," Kate said, unable to repress a twinkle in her eye. "But he's negotiating right now with the feds, as you call them, on behalf of the captain's widow."

"Well, I might do that, señorita. The old man was good to me. Another beer?"

Kate was ready this time. She didn't want to drink the man's beer. She wanted to relocate to neutral ground. "My turn," she said, "and my treat. Is there a bar nearby?"

They walked down the road to a small outdoor cantina that stood in contrast to the side of town where Kate's hotel was located. Barrels topped by planks served as the bar. A cook in a stained apron worked at an old stove under a corrugated tin roof, making conch fritters. Kate ordered another beer for the Cuban. They sat down at the edge of the water at a weather beaten picnic table.

"So, any chance they'll try to send you back to Cuba?" Kate asked as they sat down.

The question stopped him for a moment. He looked harder at her, as if trying to see if he'd missed something. Maybe it was the beer or her good looks, but his moment of doubt seemed to pass.

"No, the Orphan is the only one who could do that," he said.

"Who?" Kate asked.

"Never mind. You don't want to know. But the Cubans in Miami have contacts in Washington, too. I guess you know that." He held up his empty bottle as he fell silent.

Kate got them both some conch fritters and Lefty two more

bottles of beer. The man grew more talkative as the beers went down.

"What did you do while the boat was in Havana? Weren't you searched?"

"The captain filed his entry papers with only two in the crew. He took a big chance. They take the boat if they discover that he's filed false papers. I just stayed down below. We were there for two days. If any Havana fishermen saw me, they didn't report it."

"What happened when the Coast Guard caught up with you?" Kate asked.

"When they saw I had no papers, they took me off the boat in shackles and locked me down below in their cutter."

"Were you treated all right?"

"Sure," he said, "but I knew I was headed for Guantanamo."

"The Navy base?" she asked.

"Yes, the U.S. Naval base in Cuba, where they took the ones from Afghanistan. It's been used for years to hold Cuban migrants who don't make it to Florida."

"That's convenient. It's in Cuba," she said.

"Right, but that's the way it is."

"Why did you think you were going to be taken to Guantanamo?"

"If a Cuban makes it ashore here, he either fades into the crowd or is given asylum. If the Coast Guard intercepts him at sea, he is taken to the Bahamas and then back to Guantanamo Bay."

"Why didn't they do that?"

"I don't know. I guess they thought we were running drugs and I would be a good piece of evidence. That's what the Orphan's lawyer told me."

"So, they let you go and kept the other two—both American citizens—in jail."

"I never saw the captain again."

Kate wasn't sure she believed what he said. "My boss got your captain out on bail, but you were free to go?"

"As I said, the Orphan has connections. His lawyer said I

was lucky that Washington didn't want any more publicity on Cuba right now."

"So how did the captain die?"

The Cuban frowned, as if suddenly struck with a bad migraine.

"The police got a call that a car was in the water off the causeway by the old Naval Air Station. They hauled it out the next morning. The captain was in the driver's seat. His seat belt was still fastened."

"Was there an investigation?" Kate asked.

"They said he was drunk, but . . ."

"But what?"

"I never saw him take a drink."

"So what do you think happened?"

"I don't know, lady. He's gone."

Kate changed the subject. "Is the fishing good out in the Gulf Stream between here and Cuba?"

"Yes, it's very good, but this is a dangerous place to be sometimes. The sea can get very rough when the Northers go against the current in the Stream."

"What, pray tell, is a Norther?"

"You know those storm fronts that come across up where you live?"

Kate nodded.

"Well, their tail ends come whipping through here, bringing strong winds and bad seas. We got in one that night. She fell off a wave and two planks were opened up. That's why we went into Havana."

"And you want to go back out there?"

"Sure," he told her. "Most of the time, it's beautiful. It's better than sitting around here. And a whole lot better for me than in Cuba." He lifted another empty beer bottle.

Kate got him a fresh one, and then asked, "Would you ever want to return?"

"To Cuba? What in hell for?"

"I don't know, maybe to get a friend out?" she suggested.

He didn't have any friends.

Kate knew her scheme to provide for the captain's family depended on being able to trust this man to fish and act responsibly. She was testing, looking for some indication that they could depend on him.

"So, what would you do if you saw a raft of Cubans adrift out there? Would you pick them up?"

"Of course. It's the law of the sea."

"Would you bring them back here?"

"Of course."

"Would you report them?"

"I would tell the Orphan."

"And let him handle it?"

The Cuban nodded, lifting the beer to his lips.

"Would you go to Cuba to get someone out?"

"It's very hard to get people out of Cuba if you are working from here," he told her. "It's better if they make their own arrangements."

"Suppose you were offered money to go in there and get someone. Would you do it?"

"It would need to be a lot of money," he said, but the direction their conversation was taking seemed to change the Cuban's demeanor. "Who are you, lady?" he said suddenly.

"I told you," she said too quickly.

"So tell me again."

Kate was suddenly on the defensive. This shy man, with whom she had become comfortable enough to let down her guard, had suddenly turned on her.

"I told you that I work for the Church. I came here to help your old captain's family."

The Cuban glanced over Kate's shoulder at a man taking a seat at one end of the wooden plank that served as the cantina's bar. She thought he didn't understand what she said.

"I'm here to help the widow."

He looked back at her. His jaw was set hard and his eyes

narrowed. His sudden change of attitude alarmed her. Beer is not sudden.

He bellowed, "So, are you going back to your little hotel, lady, or do you want to come back to the boat and fuck me?" he challenged, leering at her.

Kate froze.

"Because if you don't, old Lefty here has had enough of your damn questions. I'm going home for a nap."

"Excellent idea," she said, her tone sharp enough to draw blood.

"Let me know when you get the money to fix up that boat," he half shouted on his unstable rise from the weathered bench. "Like I said, I sure do like to fish." He turned and stumbled away. Catching his balance, he looked back at Kate. "I like to fuck too, lady, so if you change your mind about that, you be sure to let me know."

Kate felt the eyes of a half dozen men on her as she walked across the cement slab of the cantina, and back onto a rutted dirt road still full of puddles from the previous night's rain shower. She kept a fast pace into the setting sun until she came to an area she recognized from earlier that day. She hailed a taxi at the first opportunity. Safely inside the vehicle, she thought about the Cuban fisherman, and what had transpired over the course of the previous few hours.

He drank a half case of beer, but didn't seem drunk until it suited him. Was he playing with her all along? The more she thought about it, no obvious explanation made any sense. She felt foolish, and frustrated that her ingenious plan for helping the widow depended on this Cuban doing the fishing.

The view from Kate's hotel room looked south over a white sandy beach to the clear, blue-green waters of the Gulf. She indulged in an early morning swim before contemplating defeat and heading back to D.C. empty-handed. She thought she'd found a solution to Gordon's charge to help the family of the dead fisherman. Her solution had suffered from a sudden rush of testosterone, the story of her life.

The man she ran into as she came off the beach in back of the hotel wasn't a ghost, but he startled her. Dressed like a normal person, he no longer resembled the derelict from the sea she'd first encountered. He was clean-shaven and his hair was slicked back. He looked like an amalgam of Rudolph Valentino and Bumpy the Seal.

"Oh, hello," Kate barely managed.

"The waters are good here," he said. "It's very nice in the morning. The front desk told me you were swimming. I came to apologize."

Kate wanted another shot at making her scheme work. "Can you wait a few minutes? I'll go upstairs and change. We can have a cup of coffee in the breakfast room."

"There's better coffee down the street," he said.

She hesitated, and then nodded. "Give me a few minutes."

The coffee he had in mind was Cuban. It had a consistency that reminded Kate of the coffee grounds she usually threw out, but it tasted good. The café was mostly on the sidewalk and a busy place. They were seated inside at a small table in the corner. Patrons came to the take-out counter and went away with small containers of the heavy, dark brew. The girls, and an occasional man, gave the Cuban a flirtatious look, and some of the men tried hard to get Kate to look in their direction. Kate thought it was unnecessary to drink the coffee; the aroma was so strong you could breathe it in. She drank three small cups. The first two were social. The third motivated her to finish what she'd begun the day before.

"Lefty . . ."

"My name is Santiago. That's my real name."

Kate blinked. "Alright, Santiago, I accept your apology. Are you still interested in doing a deal with the captain's family, if I can pull off a boat for them and a visa for you?"

"I will do it."

"Good. Now, tell me what happened yesterday?"

"I took too much beer, señorita. That's all."

"Who was that man?"

"The one who followed you?"

"What? He wasn't following me!"

"He told me he was."

"I think you better explain, Lefty . . . ah, Santiago."

"I told you about The Orphan."

"Yes."

"Well, that man works for him in Miami. He was under orders to follow you from the airport."

"Why?"

"That I don't know, señorita. He didn't tell me, and I didn't ask."

"Did you see him before?"

"No, but his name was on my list when I was in Cuba. I know who he is and what he does. He only knows that I was a fisherman, which I wasn't always."

"What list when you were in Cuba?" she asked, confused.

"I had a list of names with pictures of all the Castro brothers' enemies in the United States. I memorized the list, and this man was on it."

"You were in Castro's secret service? Oh great, so you're a spy, for God's sake," Kate said, eyebrows raised to her hairline. She paused for a furtive glance at the ceiling, and then continued. "So, if you had to make a guess, why do you think he was following me?"

"The Orphan wants to know what you are doing in Key West. What would you like me to tell him?"

Kate spoke her thoughts now as they came to her. "Are you a spy?

"I am not a spy, señorita. I was such a person in Cuba, but I only spied on my own people. I got tired of that. That's why I'm here now."

"How did The Orphan know I was here?"

"As I told you yesterday, señorita, Diego has many contacts in Washington. His man told me who you are and where you work. You're a lawyer, and you represent the captain against the Orphan's friends."

"Against his friends? Who the hell are his friends?"

"He is dealing with people in Washington. They all do what suits them."

"What people in Washington?"

"The people you're fighting. I don't know."

"We are 'fighting,' as you so correctly put it, with our country's Department of Justice, the Attorney General of the United States."

"Then that's who Diego is working with."

"Are you kidding me, Santiago? Do you expect—"

"Is he not the one who let me go? Instead of sending me back to Guantanamo Bay?"

"I doubt he personally—"

"He has a name that is Latin or Greek."

"Conner Omega?"

"That's the man."

"So you're telling me you heard his name. Do you know him?"

"I don't know him, señorita, but Carlos Diego does."

"Is that man still around here in Key West?"

"Yes, he's sitting outside this café, waiting for you to come out so he can follow you some more, and get my report. That's why we're sitting inside."

Kate glanced out the window of the café. "Your report?"

"Yes, Diego expects me to give him a report on what you are doing here."

"You spoke to him?"

"He called me last night to remind me he could have me sent back to Cuba."

"Does he know you and I are meeting?"

"Yes."

"Does he know about the deal we made?"

"No."

"Will he?"

"Not from me."

"Thanks for small favors," Kate said.

"You're welcome," the Cuban said, not recognizing the idiom.

"Santiago, I'll be in touch as soon as I have news on what your friend Conner Omega will do. Will you check in with the captain's widow once in a while?"

He nodded. "I have a phone, señorita. Everyone has such a phone."

"Give me your cell phone number, Santiago." Kate absently blew a strand of hair away from her right cheek. "Now, I'm going home."

SIX

It was after three the following afternoon when Kate finally managed to see Gordon Cox.

"How did it go, Kate? Come on in and sit down. How was Key West?"

Kate gave him a big smile before answering.

"I had two meetings with the captain's widow. She's surviving, but just barely, on what the Church is sending her."

"That can't go on forever. What's your idea?"

Kate took a deep breath. "It's unlikely we're going to get cash money out of Justice to settle, but the DEA has dozens of boats suitable for commercial fishing that have been confiscated. The government auctions them off. My idea is to have them replace the boat they wrecked with one of those."

As was his habit, Cox probed for softness in an idea that appeared very clever. "What good is that going to do with the captain dead?"

Kate smiled in anticipation. "I asked the widow about the Cuban who worked on her husband's boat. She said he was a very good fisherman, and that she trusted him to run the boat for her."

"The fellow they took off the boat at sea? Where is he?"

"That's a long story. I met with him twice. The bottom line is that he'll do it if we can get him a visa. They'll split the catch."

"Can we trust him?"

"I'm not sure, Gordon. I have a gut feeling that we can, although there is nothing in his background to suggest he is anything but untrustworthy."

"Gut reactions are usually pretty good. What's he done that's so bad?"

"Well, for starters, he was Fidel Castro's *numero uno* bodyguard. Now, he seems to be cozy with the man they call The Orphan in Miami. That man is a notorious anti–Castro hard-liner. He's been linked to just about every crime in Florida that has involved Cuban disaffection and, if you can believe it, he seems to be in close collaboration with our Attorney General. I was followed the whole time I was down there. Santiago, that's his name, told me that the AG informed the Orphan I was coming and when. How did any of them know I was going down there?"

Cox hunched his shoulders. "That's worth thinking about," he said. "Since the captain's death, those with something to hide would be waiting for us to start nosing around."

Kate hummed a bar, and continued. "Santiago said the Orphan was in tight with our 'enemies.' When I asked him what he meant by enemies, he said the people you are fighting with over what they did to the old man's boat. He recognized the name Conner Omega."

Gordon showed no immediate reaction, but Kate was flushed with indignation.

"How could the President appoint a person like that, Gordon? Brad says you were supposed to be the Attorney General. What happened?"

Cox's actor features lighted up in an ironic smile that came close to being a laugh. It was contagious. Kate's frown melted and a smile came across her face as Gordon spoke.

"I'm not the one to answer that question, Kate, but the drug war was a hot issue in the Presidential campaign. This firm successfully defended a couple of poorly documented but highly visible drug enforcement cases brought by the government. Omega made a name in Miami as a ruthless, no-holds-barred prosecutor of dealers and importers. He seemed the answer to keeping Rebecca's promise to get tough on the drug trade, especially since they made an alliance with others who were clearly not friendly to America. Omega's a bit heavy-handed and often more interested in what he reads about himself in the papers than upholding our laws. I can see him being used by people with strong convictions to shortcut the rules in order to get what they want—but actively conspiring with them? I have a hard time with that."

★

"Charles Black called while you were at lunch, Gordon," Emily Harris said. "He'll be here in ten minutes. I hope I did the right thing."

"That's fine, Emily. Thanks."

"The Attorney General is raising hell about your handling the case of a Key West fisherman picked up coming out of Havana with a Cuban national on board." Charles Black smiled as if to draw Gordon into a conspiracy. "What's going on?"

"Another case of Justice Department overkill, Charlie. This guy went into Havana in a bad storm. The boat was taking on water, and I guess he had no choice. It was either that or drown. Coming back out a couple of days later, the Coast Guard picked them up and arrested a man on board believed to be Cuban. They also found some rum and a few cigars. When they got back to Key West, the Guard turned the boat over to the DEA. The captain and a crewman were taken into custody by the FBI, and the suspected Cuban national was contained by Immigration. The fishing boat was taken apart at one of the local yards and left there. A hold full of fish on ice was confiscated. We've been asked to defend the captain and recover his fishing boat."

"What about the Cuban?"

"I understand that he's been given asylum even though they

picked him up offshore. The captain told the Coast Guard he's been his first mate for over a year, and denied picking him up in Cuba. The trouble is his name was not on the landing documents. The captain told the FBI that he'd hidden him below so the Cubans wouldn't find and arrest him."

Black had a hard time keeping a straight face. "The AG says your people are stirring up a lot of trouble in Miami. Conner has made sure the case is receiving a good bit of attention on the Hill."

Gordon buzzed Emily Harris on the intercom.

"Yes, sir."

"Emily, ask Kate Stevens and Brad Howe to come up here, please."

"Brad's in court today."

"Okay, tell Kate we need her help."

Charles Black watched Kate stride into the room and put on the brakes as she spotted him.

"I think you two had dinner together at the White House," Cox said, his eyes dancing with delight.

"Hello, sir," Kate said, extending her hand.

"Ms. Stevens, it's a pleasure to see you again," Black said, rising to his feet. "Gordon tells me you've moved on from filmmaking to working on active cases."

"Yes, sir," she said, smiling as Gordon motioned her to a chair.

"Kate, why don't you tell Charles what you've been uncovering down in Miami?"

Kate took a moment to organize her thoughts, and then related to the White House Chief what she'd previously told Cox. Black listened carefully at first, but as she wrapped up, he began to fidget, like he had something else on his mind, and glanced several times at his watch. If Kate noticed, she wasn't distracted.

When she finished, Black was very quick to ask Gordon, "Don't you need to visit Havana on this case?"

Taken aback by the question, Gordon awaited further explanation.

Charles Black's expression shone with anticipation. "Won't it help your case to have evidence that the old boat was half sunk when it came in, or that all Carver did was trade a few fish for help fixing the hole in the bow?"

Kate saw something important pass between the two men, but waited in vain for enlightenment.

"Kate," Gordon said, realizing he and the White House Chief needed to speak privately, "why don't you and Brad look into this? I suspect we'd need a license from Treasury to go to Cuba, and a visa from Havana."

Kate got to her feet quickly, and shook hands with Charles Black. "I'll get right on it, Gordon. Brad should be back by four-thirty. I can go over it with him them."

"Sharp young lady," Charles Black said after Kate had left.

Gordon nodded. "So you want me to go to Cuba?"

"Look, here's the idea. You make your living going into situations where you know very little about the people involved or the issues that will arise. You are very good at this or you wouldn't be as successful as you are. Your clients depend on the advice you give them following meetings and your analysis of the persons and subjects that develop. So she's your client. The situation is the government of Cuba. Just tell us what you need to go down there and come back with an assessment of who's who."

"Isn't that what the State Department and Global Security are supposed to do for you?"

Charles Black nodded his head with a knowing smile across his face. "Of course, but we're not ready to do that. We need more backing in Congress before doing anything officially with Cuba." Black leaned back in his chair. "Let's what-if for a moment. What if, there are situations or people down there we've overlooked? Before putting the wheels of government into motion, she wants to get a feel for the place. You're the next best thing to her going herself."

Cox's eyebrows rose. "They'll have a fit over at State."

"That's where your case for the fisherman comes in. We need

you to have a cover, not for the Cubans, but for all the bureaucrats here who would have their nose out of joint if they knew what you were really doing. This case is perfect, and all the smoke the AG is making will make it work even better."

Cox thought for a moment. "What's the timing you see on this, Charlie?"

"I don't know. I'm sure you've already figured out the whole idea is the President's. The AG was driving us crazy complaining about your firm and this case of the Key West fisherman. She called me with the idea after Conner left the Office last night. The timing depends on you."

"When we apply for the Treasury license, it will let the cat out of the bag."

"Leave that license to me. Can I tell her you'll do it?"

"Absolutely."

Gordon called Kate as Emily Harris, following Gordon's protocol with important clients, escorted Black to the firm's elevator bank.

"Kate, can you come back up here for a few minutes?"

When she arrived, Gordon came quickly to the point. "Tell me more about this man who was Castro's bodyguard."

"He's living in Carver's old boat. He worked for the captain for over a year, and was trusted by Mrs. Carver as well. He's intelligent, and speaks English. I have the impression from the way he says things about Cuba and the government there that he was well up in the hierarchy."

"How long has he been in Florida?"

"Three years," Kate said.

Cox leaned back in his chair, wrestling with an idea. Kate waited patiently for his thoughts to become vocal.

"Does this man . . ." Cox started, and then stopped to switch gears. "Can you get him to come up here and speak with me?"

The request took Kate by surprise. She thought carefully before answering.

"I don't know. He's the suspicious type, probably for good reason. If this Orphan character knew that I was coming to Florida, he'd probably figure out that Santiago—that's his name—was coming here to see you. The Orphan seems to have a good bit of control over refugees in Florida, and a pipeline into Washington."

"So, we'll go to Key West. Tell him it's to help the captain's widow and to get him a visa."

"Is that the truth? He'll know if I'm lying."

"We'll make it the truth. If he can help us in the manner I have in mind, the White House will get him his visa."

Kate was reticent to probe, but looked at Gordon for an explanation. Cox decided to bring her into his confidence.

"Kate, the President has asked me to go to Havana to test a couple of ideas she has about reaching some level of understanding with the government there. Neither the State Department nor the AG knows this yet, so you must keep it to yourself. This man Santiago might be my ace in the hole."

Kate nodded. "I can call Santiago," she said, and her voice trailed off as she saw Cox was deep in thought.

"No, let's you and I sneak out of here tomorrow night. We'll fly into Key West and you can call him from there in the morning. I'll be the surprise."

Emily Harris made flight and hotel reservations for her boss and Kate Stevens to and from Key West. She handed the electronic ticket information to Gordon with a twinge of jealousy that made her right hand shake ever so slightly. It had been clear to her from the first time she'd heard Kate's name that a special relationship existed between the boss and Kate's family. Emily was quick to pick up the ways in which Gordon treated the new summer associate differently from her peers. No one other than Emily might have noticed. She doubted that Gordon Cox himself was aware of the subtle deference he showed to Kate Stevens. Now they were traveling together to Key West, Florida.

"Emily, please call me as soon as we hear from counsel to the

World Bank; and when Baker calls on the Firestone matter. I'll keep my cell phone fired up."

"I will, Gordon," she said, and handed him a small suitcase in which she'd placed one new dress shirt and tie, along with a pair of slacks and sports shirt she'd bought down the street at Brooks Brothers. "I put a bathing suit in there for you. The hotel has a nice pool," she said with an ironic lift of her chin.

Cox laughed. "You're going to make some lucky man a great companion one day, Emily. Thanks."

She thought to herself, *I'm that now*. But she knew what he meant, and the comment didn't bring a smile to her face. The new summer associate arrived at that moment, suitcase in hand.

★

Kate made the call to Santiago's cell phone the next morning from the pay phone near the hotel pool. Gordon was doing laps in his new bathing suit.

"Santiago?"

"Señorita? Is that you?"

"Yes, Santiago. I'm in Key West. I need to speak with you."

"Will you come here? Where are you?"

"I'm at the same hotel. Tell me which place would be the most private. What I have to say is very important."

"There is no one here in this yard."

"I will be there within the hour."

Kate stood at the bottom of the boat's ladder and knocked on the old wooden hull. When Santiago appeared, she smiled and greeted him warmly. Then she opened the door for Gordon.

"Santiago, I have Mr. Cox here with me. He's the man I told you about. He will get your visa and make the deal with the government in Washington."

Kate waited while the Cuban glanced around the open space of the yard for Gordon's location.

"It's alright, Santiago. You can trust us," and as she spoke, Gordon

[69]

came out from under the hull of the boat to where the Cuban could see him.

"Hello, Santiago. I'm Gordon Cox. May we come up and talk with you?"

It was mid-afternoon when Gordon and Kate returned to the hotel.

"Santiago was very happy with that envelope you gave him. Did you see his face light up?"

Gordon nodded.

"I guess you got your money's worth?"

"Kate, I've got to call the office. Why don't you go for a swim? Our flight back is not until late."

"I thought I'd make some notes about what he told us while it's all still fresh in my mind. I'll work out by the pool and get some sun."

"Good idea. I'll join you if I finish in time."

Kate put everything down on paper that the Cuban had told Gordon. Then she went back through it, added her own comments, and condensed everything to a summary of its relevance to the issues she thought Gordon was going to meet in Havana. The people they'd talked about stuck in her mind.

Gordon asked about several of the names that he'd been given by Charles Black, who in turn had received the names from the Department of State.

"The man Hernandez," Santiago said, "I don't know him. I don't think he was around when I was there. I do know the man who almost certainly drives his bus. His name would be Eduardo Santos, and he's a force to reckon with."

This was one of the other names given to Cox. "How do you know Santos?" the lawyer had asked.

"He and I both reported to Raul Castro. We were competitors, and in that environment, we soon became enemies."

"Is that why you left?" Gordon asked.

The Cuban looked sharply at Cox, and took a sip of the Corona Kate had remembered to bring along to lubricate their discussions.

"Raul did not appreciate the way I did business. Santos was able to exploit that. They are professional criminals. I was an amateur. Besides, I like to fish."

Gordon suppressed a smile. "So why would this man Santos become involved in matters involving the United States?"

"He's the Deputy Minister of Defense. They are convinced an invasion by the United States is coming some day. This is always on their minds. Hernandez is in the Foreign Office from what you've told me, but Santos likes to deal from the back room. He always has someone out in front to take the heat when things go wrong. Maybe that fits Hernandez."

"Will Santos be head of the Cuban State someday?"

"Who knows," Santiago said. "He has a good many enemies and few friends. People are afraid of him. Unless he's gotten religion, the man is ruthless to the extreme. I imagine he's very busy watching his back. If not, he'd have long ago sent those that do such things over here to take care of me."

"How are you a threat to him?"

"I know too much about his personal habits."

"Do they know where you are?"

The Cuban laughed, and took a swig of beer. "I do not hide," he said, still laughing at Cox's naïveté.

"How does this man Carlos Diego fit into the picture?" Gordon asked.

"The Orphan? He's nothing but hot air. He thinks he's a player, but he's irrelevant in Havana. In Miami, he talks big, and knows important people in your city; but he is used by others more than he is able to be the user."

"You gave Kate the impression he's powerful in Florida."

The Cuban looked at Kate and smiled. "I didn't want her to get hurt. Women and children . . . and defenseless old men . . . are The Orphan's favorite targets."

"I see," Gordon said. "Did he have Captain Carver killed?"

"That was the stupid sort of thing that Diego would think about doing."

"What would he stand to gain from Carver's death?"

"The captain's case was going to be an embarrassment for Diego. Your lawyers would defend him by making a mockery of the Embargo being used against a poor fisherman who was only trying to save his boat and its crew. It would be in all the papers and Diego would lose a few more supporters. Also, it would have made me important, because I was there. I don't think Diego would care for that. If he kills him, it's over."

"I see," Cox said. "So he could do the same to you."

"He knows I can handle myself. I'm not an old man who trusts people. I would see them coming, and after I finished with them, Diego knows I'd come after him."

Cox waited while Kate handed another beer to Santiago. "Who in your opinion will succeed Fidel?"

"Raul Castro, assuming he is in good health, and for a while anyway, until he becomes ineffectual."

"When might that be? I mean, how could that happen?"

"You need to understand that Fidel has been in place for the entire life of everyone in Cuba under the age of fifty. They don't know anything else. Some people think it would be easier for a completely new person to come in after Fidel is gone—not his brother, who is not generally well liked. Certainly not the way Fidel is. You've also got to understand that outsiders are going to move in as soon as he's gone."

"Why is that? What do you mean by outsiders?"

"There are people Fidel has flirted with, like the Venezuelan strongman, and the Chinese. But it was just flirting, to keep Washington and Cuba's creditors guessing. Fidel likes things just the way they are, but others—and I don't know who they are—would see those contacts as opportunities to get rich and build their own empires."

Gordon asked the question he'd held back until he'd decided the Cuban might be of help to him when he was in Havana.

"Can you think of some way I can communicate with you from Havana?"

"To do what?"

"As I meet people, to call and see if you can give me any insight."

"When are you going?"

"Soon."

"That would be very difficult without compromising me and your mission. I don't think Santos would be pleased if he discovered you were in communication with me."

Gordon had been thinking about this possibility for the previous several minutes. "What about using the Catholic Church?" and he looked at Kate as he said it.

Santiago drank some of his beer. "How would that work?" he said.

"The Church has us involved in helping the captain's wife, and now his widow, in her case against the government. I will be taking evidence in Cuba to help us in that matter. The Cuban Ministry of Justice will grant me the opportunity to speak to Cubans who might have seen you in Havana and helped fix up the boat. They all know I'll be doing that, and it's a short reach for me to use the Church to pass information to my cousin in Boston."

"How will that get to me?" he asked.

"We can set up times for you to call from a public phone. My cousin Paul will pass on your thoughts to me in Havana, without referring to you or using your name. You'll be paid well."

"Like old times," the Cuban said with a laugh. "One thing though, I don't like dealing with amateurs. They make too many mistakes. They get you killed."

"Point taken. I'll try to be very careful and trust no one."

"You're still an amateur."

★

Gordon sat with his feet up in the den of his penthouse apartment, dry martini in hand, and Beethoven's Third bounding through the air around him. It was 8:00 P.M., and Kate Stevens was due any minute. She was becoming a player in his increasing involvement in Cuban-American affairs. He went over in his mind the conversation he'd had that afternoon with the President and her Chief of Staff.

"I promised him a permanent resident visa, Charles."

"That can be managed," the President injected. "This was a bit of luck, wasn't it? Can we trust him?"

"I think so, Rebecca, so far as we've used him to this point. I'm not sure I'd put my life in his hands."

"Yes, make sure you don't," she said. "Is it true he was Fidel's bodyguard?"

"More than that, I guess. He was one of the chief operatives in their Secret Service."

"How did he get here, and why have they let him live? Are we sure he's not a plant?"

"No, we're not sure," Gordon said, "but we don't need to rely on him. What he's told us this far is helpful for a sense of who the really key guys are, and those we might be able to reason with."

"Well, you be careful, Gordon," Charles Black said. "In bringing a person like him into the equation, you open the door to people like this Carlos Diego in Miami and the man's enemies in Havana, of which there seem to be an unlimited number. Maybe we should get the FBI involved?"

"I promised him we wouldn't do that, Charlie. Maybe later if there's good reason. Besides, that would alert the AG, who in turn would tell Diego, the one they call The Orphan. That would be the end of it."

"Alright," Black said. "Madam President, do we have agreement on all issues?"

The President looked to Cox. "Do we, Gordon?" she asked.

Cox had taken that as his cue to go over their plans in some detail. He talked through the gathering of evidence for the Carver family's case, coming finally to the weakest point in the scheme.

"Why would this evidence-gathering mission require the presence of a senior partner in my firm?" Cox said. "Why not a junior lawyer to interview witnesses?"

"Let them think about that all they want," Charles Black responded. "If the Cubans tumble to the fact you've been asked by the White House to go, it may spark some reactions that are helpful. They may find it necessary to take you seriously. I think here in the Capital the fact that the AG has made such a big fuss over your handling this case will put off any close scrutiny as to why it's important that you go."

The President had seemed restless at this point. "Tell him, Charles. This was originally your idea, Gordon."

"Indeed," Black said, as he raised one hand with a finger pointing to the ceiling. "You can give them a scrap. You'll agree to handle the appeals of the three Cubans in jail here for being unregistered foreign agents. You will offer this in exchange for their help with your case. You will intimate that your close connections with this administration will secure their release by Presidential intervention. This will show your good faith, and give this man Hernandez, or Santos if he's the one, something to take away from your first meeting."

"If I make that offer, will you release those men?"

"Yes," said Black.

"That's one hell of a gambit," Cox said, and turned to see the broad smile appearing on the President's face. "So, who goes with me?"

"You're on your own there," the President said.

"To complete the cover, I should probably take the two people I've assigned to the Key West fisherman case. The Cubans probably already know their names."

"Okay, anyone speak Spanish?" the President asked.

"One does," he said.

Gordon would always remember the next few seconds very clearly. The President got up from her desk and walked across the Oval Office. Gordon followed her passage, and Charles Black swiveled his chair so that both men were looking at each other. The President came back and stood over the two of them. She dropped a heavy parchment on the table in front of Gordon. Cox unrolled it as the President walked around the desk and back to her chair. It was a formal Presidential appointment as special ambassador.

"Just so you're not spies, Gordon. There's one in there for Katherine Stevens and Bradford Howe. That would be the team you have in mind taking with you, wouldn't it?" she said with a feminine light in her eye.

Kate waltzed off the elevator, taking in, at a glance, the bachelor accented décor of Cox's apartment.

"Nice place, Gordon. Look at that view. I can almost see my block from here, and the lights around the Kennedy Center. It's brilliant."

"Can I make you a drink?"

"I'll have a glass of wine—white, if you have it." Kate followed him as he led the way through the kitchen to his wine cooler.

"Thanks," she said, raising her glass to his.

As if by habit, Gordon led the way into the well-used room adjacent to his kitchen. He sat so Kate could see a view of the Potomac River over his shoulder.

Kate started speaking to ease her nervousness. She didn't know why she felt so uncertain of herself, but the adrenaline was flowing. She hit hard for the baseline.

"So, Gordon, am I fired?"

"Fired? Good Lord, no," he said, laughing as freely as Kate could imagine. "Is that why you think I invited you here to my apartment? To fire you?"

"Well, it did cross my mind, among other things. I've caused a big stir down in Miami, got Brad and me under threat of death. I think maybe I'd fire me."

Cox smiled, thinking about what her "among other things" might have been.

"Katherine, I'm going to take you into my confidence tonight. I'm going to tell you a few things that only you, and maybe one or two others, will know." He paused when he saw her reaction. "I'm not doing you any favors. You'd be much better off not knowing most of it. And you've got to promise me, the information must be kept in the strictest confidence. Are you game?"

"Absolutely," she said, feeling she was entering his inner world.

"Good. The first bit of news I have is that I want you and Brad Howe to accompany me to Havana."

Kate was wide-eyed.

"Yes," he said, watching for more reaction before continuing. "You and Brad are going to be part of my cover. The world will know we're in Havana only to pursue the fisherman's case. You guys are going to interview witnesses."

Kate blinked.

"How good is your Spanish?"

"My Spanish is fair, but I could take a quick full submersion course," she said, buying into the program.

"Okay, better do that. Have Emily sign you up."

Kate nodded. Meanwhile, I want Brad to go ahead and formally notify the District Court and the Justice Department that we're applying for a visa to take testimony in Havana."

"Ha, that'll stir the pot," she said.

They sat together—the older lawyer and his young summer associate—talking and sipping wine as the evening turned to night. Gordon made scrambled eggs and rescued a day-old salad from the refrigerator. Kate was tipsy by the time Gordon ordered her taxi.

He asked about her tennis career, and why she'd gone out to the coast to attend college. She alternated between the truth and what sounded less psychotic. Was she still playing tennis? *No, it wasn't something she was ready to be relaxed about. The law was enough of a challenge.*

Did she have a boyfriend? *Not really.*

What was her stepfather like? Gordon didn't ask that question, but Kate thought it was what he'd meant at one point. *She didn't know him very well. He seemed nice enough, and was quite rich.*

Had her father remarried? *Are you kidding? The original beach boy with a string of affairs that kept him creative in means of escape? No, absolutely not. She doubted he'd ever marry.*

How about Gordon? After the wine took its course, she intimated that once her mother, Elizabeth, had finished with a man, he might never be good for anyone else.

They experienced laughter of the sort that was close to tears, and a touching of their souls in ways that neither realized was happening. Kate, who was not accustomed to late-night wine tasting accompanied by serious discussion, began to feel tired.

"It's late, Gordon, and I really should go. Are you alright?" she said, for no reason other than it came close to what she was feeling.

"I'm fine," he said, thinking that her looking after him was humorous, but it made him feel good.

"So you, Brad, and I are going to Havana," Kate said, slurring her words just a little. "A dream come true," she giggled.

She climbed off of the couch, feeling the effects of the wine as she stood up. "Now if you'll point me in the right direction, I'm going to use the facilities. Then it's home sweet home for this summer associate."

Gordon took her by the arm to steady her as she got to her feet. She turned into his arms, reaching an arm over his shoulder for support. Her hand moved around his neck, and for a moment she gazed into those blue eyes that made her knees go weak. Then, suddenly, as if awakened from a deep sleep, she released him and bolted for the bathroom door.

SEVEN

Carlos "The Orphan" Diego stood by the back door to his home in Coral Gables as a car drove into the parking area behind the house. The driver had called him from north on Route 1 near Coconut Grove. Carlos waited now, leaning against the doorframe on the small porch attached to the rooms he used as an office. He watched Santiago deChristo get out of the back seat and close the car door.

"Hey, fisherman," Diego called, "what took you so long?"

The visitor needed a shave. "Hello, Diego," he said in Spanish, and walked toward the steps leading to the rear of the house.

"Get us a beer," the Orphan shouted to a woman who was cleaning in the kitchen.

Diego waited until Santiago came up onto the porch level before taking his hand, pulling him close, and giving him a bear hug. The two men disappeared through double glass doors into the office as the driver stood by the limo, lighted a black Cuban cigarette, and threw the match into the patch of grass that passed for a lawn.

"So you see, my friend," said Diego, continuing to speak as he had for the past twenty minutes, "your coming here to this country was for a purpose. You might say you came with God."

"To meet with the devil," deChristo mumbled. It was just the

[79]

two of them in the room, and they were on their second bottle of homemade brew.

"What?" Diego said.

Santiago pretended he didn't hear the question. "When is all this going to take place?"

"It's happening as we speak."

"Why are you telling me?"

"Why am I telling you? You're a funny man, deChristo. Why do you think I saved you from being sent to Guantanamo? You are supposed to be so smart."

"Who will be in the palace?"

"What difference does it make, so long as he is simpatico? So long as we get back what they took from us."

"How will the United States help you do this? It is the Bay of the Pigs all over again, Diego. My father told me about that. You're crazy."

Carlos Diego flew into a rage. A man less agile and less prepared than deChristo would have been cut by the flying beer bottle or the knife that was whisked out from its belted scabbard and thrown at him.

deChristo stood by the door as two of Diego's bodyguards rushed in. Seeing their boss in one of his fits, they wrestled him to the floor and coaxed back his composure.

"Does that happen often?" Santiago asked one of the men as Diego closed the door to his private bathroom. Santiago heard the water run, and he imagined the Orphan splashing it on his face. Diego emerged a few minutes later, drying his hair with a towel.

"Enough of this, deChristo. Let's get down to business. Tell me more about this woman from Washington. She conned you into helping the family of that fisherman who brought the Catholic Church down on my head."

"You could put it that way."

"What else have you been talking to her about?"

Santiago made a puckering, sucking sound with his lips.

"You were trying to screw her? Do you expect me to believe that?"

"Believe what you want," he said.

"In that case, maybe you'd like another chance," Diego snarled.

"Why not?" he said, shrugging his shoulders.

"Didn't she offer you money to work with her boss?"

"No, she didn't do that."

"You're lying. My man saw you with her."

"I made no deal."

Diego wore the look of a man dealing with a liar. Then he said, "Well, I have a deal for you, a good deal."

Santiago knew well enough not to show the slightest interest.

Diego added to the pot. "Lots of money, and a visa."

"What kind of visa?"

"You're interested?"

"Maybe."

"Would you kill that woman if I asked you?"

"What woman?"

"The one in Key West you said you wanted to screw."

"Why should I kill her?"

"If I asked you, would you do it?"

"No."

"For a million dollars?"

"I could get a million dollars from Havana for killing you," Santiago said.

Diego opened the top drawer in his desk and took out a long-barreled .45 caliber revolver. He twirled the cylinder, cocked the hammer, and handed it to Santiago. "So go ahead. Here's your chance to make your first million. Be sure you get it in dollars."

Santiago laughed. He took the piece from Diego, aimed it at the ceiling, and pulled the trigger.

Snap.

"You didn't think I'd hand you a loaded gun, did you?" The Orphan giggled.

Santiago paid no attention. He placed the revolver on the desk.

[81]

Diego grabbed it quickly and fired a live round over deChristo's head.

Santiago didn't flinch. He knew what was coming. He'd used similar tricks many times in the dungeons outside Havana and in the cottages where he interrogated enemies of the Cuban State.

"You're the man for this job, fisherman. I will pay you half a million to go back to Havana for a few days on an errand for me."

Santiago reckoned Diego had sent others on such errands. In the same instant, he knew he would agree to do it, under the right conditions. "So what's the errand, and how do I get there and back?" he said.

"The Dutchman will take you from Key West into Marina Hemingway. From there you're on your own. The Dutchman will stay at the marina for five days. Finish the job and return to the boat, and he'll bring you home."

"What do you want me to do?"

"Your lady friend and her boss have been granted a license to go to Havana to take testimony from fishermen on the docks at the southeast end of Havana Harbor. This is the official story coming out of Washington, but I think more is going on here. You'll follow them closely and report back on everyone they see and speak with."

"Diego, how in hell do you know she's going to Cuba?"

"I know everything that goes on in that case."

Santiago shook his head.

The Orphan continued. "For every bit of useful information you bring back, I will add to your wealth. If I order you to kill either of them, you will do it. If you want to screw the woman first, that's alright with me; just do as you're ordered. That will get you another one hundred big ones. I need you back here before they return. That's why the Dutchman waits only five days. Comprende?"

"I don't want half a million dollars."

"I won't pay more. Are you crazy?"

"I'll take a used Buick car registered in my name, a forty-foot Bertram sport fisherman, also registered to me, an unencumbered deed to a house in Key West that I will point out to you, and fifty-thousand in cash. You give me those four things, and I'll take your Dutchman's boat to Cuba and do your dirty work while I'm there."

"And if you don't come back?"

"I'll be back, Diego. Don't you worry about that. Do we have a deal or not?"

Santiago smiled, and occasionally laughed freely to himself, all the way back to Key West. He was selling the only commodity he owned—his Cuban experience—and getting paid big bucks. He needed to think about the lawyer from Washington, and whether he should tell him and his pretty assistant that he, Santiago deChristo, would be in Havana at the same time they were. He was suspicious of Cox's reasons for going to Cuba. It had to be more important than speaking with fishermen, or The Orphan would not be willing to pay so much. Santiago was sure there would be more opportunities on which he might capitalize. The longer he stayed involved, however, the more dangerous it would become. He'd wait first to see if Diego would make good on his promise of compensation, then he'd pick his time in Havana to contact Cox. He wouldn't be hard to find.

★

Lara Peron walked smartly into the office of José Hernandez, the Cuban Foreign Service officer for North America.

"Hello Lara," Hernandez said, "how have you been?"

"Very well Minister Hernandez, thank you."

"How's your English these days?"

"Okay. I haven't used it much lately, but it's good."

"There is a possibility we'll have three lawyers from Washington, D.C. here in a week." He waited, and seeing what appeared to be a positive reaction, he continued. "They are coming to gather information on a small fishing boat that came in here some time ago to get out of a bad storm. Apparently the boat was stopped by the U.S. Coast Guard on its way home and the crew was arrested. These lawyers are defending the American crew members against the charges. I want you to show them around the docks."

"Yes, Excellency, I will be pleased to do that."

"I'll want to spend some time gathering my own information from these three. You know what I mean. We will extend to them the utmost courtesy, but also be on the lookout for any unusual contacts they make. Keep your pretty eyes and ears open, Lara."

"Yes, Excellency," Lara said, taking her leave, and heading across the courtyard to the Department of Legalities, where she was involved in a project known to very few in the Cuban government. She was one of three legally trained citizens who had been given access to the matter, and Lara's brilliance had quickly vaulted her into the lead position.

"What did that lightweight Hernandez want with you, Lara?" asked the senior lawyer on the research project.

"He's a very nice man, Roberto, and a true patriot. So don't you make fun of him."

Roberto wrinkled his nose as if he'd suddenly smelled something bad. "You are too easy, Lara. He is a nothing."

"Enough of this," she said with a smile, showing it had not been said in anger. "Where are we?"

"You tell me, sister."

"Did you find that case on the Suez Canal?"

"Yes, it's right here, and it supports our position. Even treaties between nations can be declared void if made under threat of force or based upon fraudulent representations. The best part is the United States Solicitor General argued that case for abolition of the treaty."

"But was it before the Court in The Hague?"

"No, but it was in the framework of applying international law to a treaty involving use by one nation of the sovereign land of another."

"Okay, that's good. Let's weave the holding into our brief. Is there any quotable language in the court's opinion?"

"How about this?" the Cuban lawyer said, reading aloud as Lara listened. "It is a well settled matter under international law that the laws of the State desiring application of law to facts at hand can be cited as controlling in cases where international precedent is thin or simply not available."

"Good, so using the laws of almost every state of the United States as controlling precedent, we have grounds to void the lease of Guantanamo Bay to the United States," Lara said triumphantly. I can't wait until Rosalita returns. Did she say when she was coming back?"

"She'll be late. Why don't we go ahead and finish the brief? We need to get it into Eduardo Santos' hands."

Lara was not a fan of Deputy Defense Minister Santos. She suspected he'd been involved in her father's disappearance many years before. His Ministry was well known to favor dealings with Venezuela and China over the United States and other nations within the American sphere of influence. Lara's choice would have been otherwise. She knew Santos' reputation was one of absolute ruthlessness toward anyone who might stand in his way, and that included young women who resisted his advances. The only part of the project that Lara did not like was that it was being done under Santos' command. Nevertheless, she was very pleased to have been chosen for research on a project so hush-hush that not even Minister Jose Hernandez knew of it.

★

The Dutchman had a habit of snorting when speaking and dealing with those for whom he worked. He considered himself an independent special project expert, and resented all authority.

Carlos Diego placed a wad of dollars in his hand, but held onto the money while continuing to speak.

"He will board your boat in Key West next Thursday at 5:00 A.M. You will take him to Marina Hemingway in Cuba and wait for him for five days, no more. If and when he comes back to the boat, you will set out for Key West, but not arrive there. You will kill him while at sea, and toss his body to the sharks. Then come back here to Coral Gables and you'll be paid the other half of your fee," Diego said, and released his hold on the bills.

The Dutchman snorted and began counting the money in his hand. "And if he doesn't return in five days?"

"You leave without him."

"But I still get the rest of my money."

"Yes, when you get back here," The Orphan said. "Do not contact me at any time from Cuba or on your VHF radio."

"What's he going to do in Havana?"

"That's not your business. There may be some fireworks coming from his locations ashore. You stay on your boat at the marina, and you'll be safe. And stay sober," Diego said with a snarl.

★

The two men sat on either side of the screen in the confessional. The church in Havana had been chosen for the Pope to visit during his stay in Cuba years before. The man dressed in Dominican robes was José Hernandez, the Cuban Minister for North American Affairs. The other was an accountant who worked for the largest Cuban owned construction company.

"He's dangerous," the accountant said. "He will compromise our mission."

"It's his natural enthusiasm, but he's too smart to get caught," Hernandez responded. "I like him because he sees all that is possible, not only that which seems difficult."

"I don't care why he's dangerous. He is what he is."

"No, we need him. Wouldn't you rather have a horse you need to rein in than one you need to kick?"

"I don't like horses, and I don't like his relatives. If he does not cause our downfall, they will. Also, he's obsessive about Santos and the Venezuelans," the accountant grumbled.

"I am too," Hernandez said. "If we don't get the job done before Santos completes his deal with Caracas, we are lost, and so is Cuba. Fidel is no longer an infinite presence. Soon they will have a free hand to turn this country into a Venezuelan satellite. We all might as well move to Key West and commune with Santiago deChristo."

"I preferred him to his brother. At least we always knew where we stood with Santiago. Orlando is completely unpredictable. I don't like it. We're not ready. We don't even know what the Americans will do."

"There are three American lawyers coming to Havana week after next. They've been granted permission to nose around the docks and interview fishermen. This may be just what we've been waiting for. I for one do not believe it is coincidence that they are arriving here at the very moment Santos is making his move. It's too good an opportunity to pass up. I think it's about time we took some risks. Come out of the closet."

Hernandez could hear and feel the other man squirming on the confessional bench. "It's too early. We have nothing truly in place. You are a dreamer, and General deChristo is worse."

Hernandez was not put off. "Our information is that the senior lawyer is closely connected to the American President. It is not credible that he is coming down here to interview fishermen as he has requested. Any junior on his payroll can do that. He most certainly has a hidden agenda, and I will attempt to find out what that might be. Perhaps we will also learn something about the American disposition to act in the event of an alliance with that fool from Caracas."

"Does the General know these lawyers are coming?"

"I have not told anyone before now."

"Good, then don't tell him."

"Why are you so obsessed with Orlando? Why should he not know if you do?" Hernandez said.

The accountant repeated his theme. "I don't have a wife whose father is Chairman of the Central Committee and a mistress whose brother is in Santos' intelligence command. That mixture is like a Molotov cocktail. All that is needed is a spark to ignite it."

"Okay, for now I won't confide in deChristo, but he retains our utmost confidence. Is that clear?"

"You are a fool."

"We are all fools. That's not the issue."

★

Passing the small Bertram sport fisherman with the name he'd painted on the transom lifted Santiago's spirits as the Dutchman motored by her slip in the early morning hours. The Cuban threw a kiss at the flying bridge and outriggers of the safely moored boat, as the Dutchman expertly maneuvered his own thirty-five-footer out from the Key West Bite. Once clear of the channel, they turned west toward the Tortugas. In three hours they'd made enough westing to offset the force of the Gulf Stream currents and turned south for Marina Hemingway, some seventy nautical miles distant.

The Cuban had left his newly acquired used Buick in the locked garage of his new house. He gave several thousand dollars of Diego's money to the captain's widow, and left all but a few thousand in a hole he dug in the stone slab under the garage. He took with him enough euros to buy his safety in Havana.

★

Charles Black and Gordon had their final meeting prior to the latter's departure for Havana.

"You understand it was better this time that we meet alone, Gordon."

"Of course."

"So, Kate Stevens is going with you. What happened to the other one? Howe is his name?"

Cox knew Brad Howe was embarrassed by his wife's position and saw no purpose in making things worse. "We needed someone in the office here to support us as questions arose. Kate's not a lawyer, but she does speak Spanish. So we divided up the responsibilities."

Black looked at his friend, and smiled. "What's the plan?"

"We're meeting with the Cuban Ministry of Justice the first morning. They've promised cooperation, and will have any official documentation of Carver's visit available for us to inspect. In return,

I'll make the offer to assist in freeing the three Cubans in jail here. We'll see what that brings on."

"Are you going to use that Cuban deChristo in Key West?"

"I'm not sure. He's been helpful pointing us at the people we'll need to contact. I'm not sure he can do much more. We'll see."

More eyebrows were raised in the halls of the Cox Law Firm than in government circles concerning Kate and the senior partner traveling alone together to Havana. Kate hadn't been at the office long enough to have cultivated many friends. Howe was embarrassed and disappointed that his wife wouldn't agree to his joining the party, so he did nothing to dilute the rumors that were circulating. Kate was attractive. The senior partner was single and known to have a string of angular younger women who paraded on his arm to various Washington functions. Why else would Cox be doing work normally handled by a first year associate? And so it went, until the day Gordon and Kate left for Miami and the chartered flight that would take them to Havana.

★

Eduardo Santos sat in his office on Revolutionary Square in Havana and addressed the man who, until recently, had been Fidel Castro's principal doctor.

"Carlos, how much time is left?"

"Who knows? It could be years, months, or any day."

"Are the effects easily recognized?"

"Yes, his speech is slurred, and he doesn't stand erect as he did."

"So I am second in command?"

"What does that get you? There really is no second."

"But so long as Fidel's situation is less than clear, it matters. Raul can't make it an issue without giving the situation away."

"That's true, but he got rid of me quick enough. You know he trusts no one."

"That's always been the case. But I am not a Santiago deChristo. I will not run."

"At least that one's alive, as far as I know anyway."

"He's alive, but not for long after I'm in charge."

The doctor hunched his shoulders. *Sometimes*, he thought, *Eduardo Santos lets emotion get in the way of his judgment.* "So what can I do?" the doctor asked.

"Nothing right now, Carlos, but stand by please. Do you have the tapes in a safe place?"

"As if my life depended on it," he said, and then considered that it probably did.

★

Marina Hemingway was not at all how Santiago remembered it. There were a few visiting boats flying European and Caribbean flags, some of them quite large. The marina office was freshly painted and the ships' chandlery store had a decent supply of goods, nothing like Key West, but still a big improvement over what had been there five years before. The hotel at the end of the piers looked in good condition, and three of the buildings that Santiago recalled had been used for storing Army vehicles housed a small liquor store, a dive shop, and the harbormaster's office. Twenty or thirty newly built apartments overlooked one of the five lagoons. Santiago supposed they were used by visiting yachtsmen who wanted to get off their boats for a few days. Far from the decaying, morose line of concrete docks he remembered, the improvements were a giant step toward a full service marina.

The regulations set by Washington over the previous ten years under the Trading with the Enemy Act levied large fines on boats from the States caught visiting Cuba. A few American sailors had left their calling cards painted on the cement pier where their boats had been docked. The paintings had the appearance of second grade drawings, and sported the name of the vessel, a drawing of it, the dates of the visit, and the first names of the crew. Santiago was quick to notice that the marina guards were as keen on maintaining the privacy of the visiting yachtsmen as enforcing the State's police rules.

Santiago knew that Marina Hemingway was a thirty-minute

walk from the hotels and shops at Miramar, where Santiago thought Cox and his associates would stay. This convenience fit well with his determination to avoid all contact with taxi drivers, many of whom he knew were Secret Service operatives.

Santiago dressed during the day like a European on tour to Havana: an *Izod* shirt, tailored slacks, colored socks, a camera slung around his neck, and a Cuban cigar clenched between his teeth. He didn't wear one of the ubiquitous American baseball caps, because he knew every man and boy in Old Havana would try to bargain it off his head.

A touch of mascara here and some pale coloring there lowered the odds of a chance encounter becoming instant recognition. His disguise certainly wouldn't pass close inspection, but he'd been out of the country long enough to have been forgotten by all but the country's leaders. Even at the height of his power, his face would not have been recognized by many outside the inner circles of government.

He worried about running into one of his ex-lady friends. He also knew that around every corner, in plain clothes, some perhaps even dressed as he was, were the ever-present Secret Service operatives. Their job was to spot people far less important than he. Discovering that Santiago deChristo had returned to Havana would probably earn them possession of one of the grand homes on the ocean in Miramar.

When the sun went down, Santiago changed to well-worn blue jeans and a dark t-shirt so he could roam the unlighted streets as a local. His biggest problem was where to bed down at night. He considered and discarded the idea of staying with old friends. He wasn't even sure he had any. Even if he did, his presence would place them in jeopardy. Hotels were out of the question. He had no papers. Anyone trying to sleep in the park or on the street was immediately thrown in jail and the key to his cell was lost. He could return to the boat at the marina, but he knew the place was carefully watched around the clock. Sooner or later he'd be stopped. He remembered a small church in the midst of the Old City. It had been boarded up with many others years before when Castro had forced the Church to graduate fewer priests. Some of these churches in the center of town were converted to hotels or small museums and kiosks. Others, like the one he had in mind, were shut up and left to the Almighty's care. He entered and left under cover of darkness, washed up in tourist bars and restaurants, and doused himself with deodorant. He allowed himself an occasional shower back at the marina.

On the second morning in Cuba, Santiago stretched his legs and moved quickly through the pleasant residential neighborhoods of Jaimanitas, Flores, and Nautico. He went through Querejeta, an upscale neighborhood, even by the standards of nearby Florida. He walked by three stately old mansions, their roofs cluttered with satellite antennas, that housed the German, Swiss, and French Embassies. On the rocky north shore of Miramar he saw a hotel that was new since he was last in Havana. This place would be his first try at finding the three persons Carlos Diego had asked him to follow. He'd decide later when and if to make contact with Kate Stevens. The information he'd been given by Diego had them arriving in Havana the following day. He was ready, but he was beginning to doubt that five days was going to be enough time for him to do anything.

EIGHT

Kate had never been through anything like the inspection of her belongings that took place at the Jose Mari airport in Havana. Many garments were taken out, held up to the light, and shaken, as if something could be hidden in a pair of light bikini underwear. The whole process took place in the center of the airport concourse, much to the enjoyment of the many Cubans and incoming tourists that were present. Gordon received no less attention from officials, but his boxer shorts drew less of a crowd than most of Kate's apparel. Her bras were of special interest to the women working in the immigration area.

Following two hours of detailed inspection and light interrogation, a small bus took Gordon and Kate to a large international class hotel. Kate's room looked out over the ocean to the northeast toward Florida. It offered all the conveniences she would expect to find in the best hotels in Washington or California. The service was polite and efficient. She joined Gordon for a swim in the huge, meandering pool, and later they dined nearby in a first class restaurant.

"Why is this place so different than I imagined, Gordon?"

"Tourism is their second largest source of hard currency. They've got to keep their Euro visitors happy and coming back. How's your room?"

"First class. Have you been over to that shopping center across the street?"

"No. What's there?"

"Everything, from Gucci bags to French silk, all kinds of electronic gadgets, and a nice outdoor café."

"See any locals there?"

"Just behind the counters. It's like a non-drinker working in a liquor store. The young Cubans who are employed there have what in the scheme of things is a very, very good job. They are the brightest and the best looking. They all speak English, and I heard them conversing in French, Spanish, and German. The girl at the lobby coffee bar told me she was first in her class at school and that's how she got her job tending bar in the hotel. She failed to mention that she's very cute, too."

"How's your Spanish doing?"

"Okay. It really helps getting them to talk with you. They can speak English, but are obviously more comfortable with Spanish."

"Can they keep the tips they get?"

"I asked that. She said they split them and a preset amount has to be paid to the government each week. But she winked at me when she said it."

"Have you noticed anyone following you?"

"I'm not sure. Maybe."

"Expect it. It won't hurt to be a little paranoid while we're here."

"Are our rooms bugged?"

"That too, probably."

Gordon retired to his room after dinner to make calls to various clients across the U.S., some of whom knew he was in Havana. He assumed the Cubans were listening in, and told his clients as much. Aside from that minor precaution, the conversations were no different than those he would have from his apartment back in Washington.

The hotel lobby was shaped and sized like a football field, with different levels and a large waterfall and fountain in the center. As large as it was, Kate thought it was comfortable and efficiently laid out, with various places to sit or to meet with small groups. At one end overlooking the pool, there was a small bar serving strong coffee and an international choice of liquors.

Kate staked out a comfortable chair between the main desk and the elevator bank. With a magazine in her lap as a prop, she watched people come and go. The parade entailed mostly European tourists, with the occasional Japanese or Chinese business group in animated discussion. There was a tour group of medical people—doctors and administrators—from the U.S. who came in late and were clearly in a party mood, but Kate was mostly ignored. This was a new experience, and it gave her the courage after awhile to take a walk around the hotel grounds.

She crossed paths with uniformed security guards on the perimeters, and she noticed the places where guests still congregated were softly lighted. The hotel staff smiled at her as she walked by. She stopped and spoke with a couple from Germany, and wondered what life was like a few blocks away where no foreigners lived. She was tempted to cross the well-lighted, six-lane main boulevard that passed in front of the hotel and stroll along the pleasant tree-lined sidewalks of the residential community she and Gordon had passed through while driving to the restaurant. In the end, she stifled her curiosity. She'd try it in daylight first.

Kate stayed in the shower longer than usual. She had set her alarm for earlier than necessary and awoke with a slight hangover. The night before, she and Gordon had joined forces after his calls were completed and had stayed up late, sitting outside between the ocean and a noisy waterfall by the pool where they could speak privately. Drinks were served to them there, and the result was an enlightening discussion of everything except what they came to do. At the very last minute, as they were getting into the elevator to go up to their rooms, a hotel clerk handed Gordon an envelope. In it was a list of the persons and meetings fixed for the next day. In one case, the list had changed from low-level lawyers to one of the top officers in the Ministry of Foreign Affairs, José Hernandez.

"Sorry to keep you up so late, Kate," Gordon said as they emerged onto their floor from the elevator.

Kate smiled as an Italian couple on vacation clung to each other on their way to the other wing. Once they disappeared, she moved close to Gordon and planted a kiss on his cheek.

"Good night, Gordon. Thanks for a lovely evening," she said, and strode off to her room.

He stood for a moment, watching her move around the perimeter of the arboretum. She looked back and threw him another kiss as she opened the door and disappeared into her room.

★

They were assigned assistance from the Foreign Affairs Ministry in the form of a young woman lawyer and a much older military type man, probably Secret Service. Over the course of the morning, Gordon came to the conclusion that the bright young woman, whose name was Lara and who spoke fluent English, was one of the new breed of Cuban professionals who saw both the good and the bad in her country's policies. The man, on the other hand, was more like those he'd expected to find: dogmatic, dense, and generally unaware of his own ignorance. Whenever Cox wanted only the young woman to understand, he spoke very fast in English and used as many idiomatic expressions as possible. She usually understood him, but the man would look quizzically at her for an explanation. Gordon enjoyed playing the language game the way it had been played with him on business in Europe and Mexico City.

Their meeting at the Ministry for North American Affairs was chaired by Director José Hernandez, an urbane, well-educated man in his mid-forties who spoke fluent English. Handsome and quite sure of himself in a calm, polite manner, Hernandez could have been the professor at Stanford who'd taught Kate Spanish.

As the Cuban statesman spoke, Cox began to understand the point Santiago had made to him at their meeting earlier in Key West:

that the age of fifty was an important milestone in Cuba. Those born after the sixties had been educated in the revolutionary system and knew little of life before, except the implausible dogma they were taught in school. Their parents had to be careful what they said about pre-revolutionary times. Gifted children were cut out from the crowd and given advanced teaching and special treatment. The young woman Lara, and her boss Hernandez, fit this mold. Cox had seen the same pattern years before when he was in the Soviet Union and the former East Germany.

"Welcome to Havana, Ms. Stevens and Dr. Cox," Hernandez said, extending his hand in warm greeting. "I thought there were to be three of you?"

"Yes, director Hernandez, but Mr. Howe had an important assignment in Washington. We will proceed without him."

"Yes, of course. I applaud what you are trying to do for those fishermen who came here under very difficult circumstances. I will be most pleased, Dr. Cox, to give you both whatever assistance you need."

Kate watched as Gordon nodded, and José Hernandez continued.

"We have assigned two of our best to escort you and assist in your interviews on the docks. How do you wish to proceed?"

"Thank you, Minister Hernandez. Ms. Stevens will go to speak with anyone who comes forward to give us information on the condition of the fishing boat or her crew. I would be pleased also if we could make time to discuss with you another matter that was brought to my attention during the process of getting clearance from my government to come here."

"Of course, Dr. Cox," Hernandez said, visibly lighting up. "Perhaps you could tell me the general subject matter, so I can have the appropriate persons available."

Gordon nodded and looked at Kate as they had rehearsed. "Ms. Stevens, you are the expert on that case."

Kate cleared her throat. "Dr. Cox is referring to the conviction of three Cuban men for failing to register as agents of your government as required by our laws. They are currently serving fifteen-year sentences in federal prison."

Hernandez flushed and coughed uncontrollably for several moments. "Yes, we are all quite familiar with that case, señorita, a gross miscarriage of justice."

Gordon jumped in. "Minister Hernandez, you have been most generous in your assistance to my firm in letting us come here to interview your citizens. If there is any way in which we might assist you in this case, I would be happy to discuss it while we are here."

"How many days will you stay in Havana?"

"It depends on how successful we are, sir, but I think three to five days should do it."

"Good. Stay as long as you want. Give me a day or so to come back to you on your generous offer. In the interim, perhaps you'll allow me to show you around the Ministry. It is not often we have someone here from the United States who is so well connected in Washington."

Gordon thought the last remark was out of character for a bureaucrat operating under a dictatorial regime. Was Hernandez trying to tell him something?

"Cautious hope is always good, Excellency," he said. "Ms. Stevens and I hope to build on your trust."

"Well, sir, assistance in the case of those three innocents is a very good start. Now, Ms. Stevens, Lara will take you to the fishing docks, and Dr. Cox, if you will do me the honor, I will show you around the capital of Cuba."

The tour seemed prearranged. There were various members of Hernandez' staff, as well as more senior men, and a surprising number of women, at each department where the two men stopped. After two hours of apparently offhand meetings and small talk, the Foreign Minister guided Cox to an outdoor café reserved for the most senior officials. They ordered lunch from a table that was remote from the others. Hernandez seated Gordon in a chair with his back to the other tables and sat facing him. He began speaking in normal but subdued tones, stopping only when courses of lunch were served.

"Dr. Cox, how familiar are you with the history of my country?"

Gordon thought for a moment before responding. "Not very," he said. "Certainly not as familiar as I should be."

"Will you indulge me?"

"Of course," the lawyer said.

"You know now that I spent a number of years in the United States before assuming my present post here in Havana. During that period, I learned that much of what I'd been taught about your country was simply not true. I would like to give you a short course in Cuban history, hopefully with the same effect."

"I would welcome that, Minister."

"Good. I promise not to be dogmatic or to propagandize."

Cox smiled and sipped the strong iced tea as the Cuban began.

"I think Cuba always has suffered by its close proximity to the United States. This has had two effects. The first was to make it seem reasonable for your government to take extraordinary measures to make sure Cuba was in friendly hands. This was the case in the war against Spain, and the assumption of the Guantanamo Bay property for a naval base. At the same time, Cuba became a choice spot for anyone wanting to make trouble for the States. Russia is a good example of that phenomenon. Over the two hundred or so years prior to 1958, we have been controlled by Spain, the U.S., and for a while by the American Mafia. The Revolution changed that, although there have been several unfortunate periods where outside forces had the upper hand. Russia was the most obvious and, if one is honest, did a great deal of harm to the psyche of our people, from which we are only now recovering." Hernandez paused while a waitress brought fresh bread and two bowls of fish chowder.

"You have to admit Cuba has done pretty well in spite of your country's fifty-year trade embargo. Yet, I know, as I think you must, that Cuba and the United States are natural trading partners. Even so, many of us have mixed emotions concerning the lifting of that trade prohibition. On the one hand, it will bring the people of Cuba more jobs and a sense of pride in the international community. On the other hand, greed and corruption will increase exponentially."

Gordon started to make a point, but stopped when Hernandez raised his hand. "I know. There are ways to address that problem, but I know Cuba and Cubans, and it would not be easy. In any case, that is not the point I wish to make to you in the short time we have to speak frankly."

Gordon nodded, and waited patiently.

"What some of us fear most are not the people in Miami who wish us dead or under their domination, and not Washington or another Bay of Pigs invasion. What has always hurt Cuba the most is foreign domination by outsiders following their own agendas. Here I speak of two current possibilities: China and Venezuela. True, some would add the United States to that list, but their motives, if not the results they cause, would be more pure."

Cox was anxious to ask questions, but he suppressed his thoughts and continued to listen to words and notions he might not have another chance to hear.

"China may surprise you, Dr. Cox, and I could be hanged for telling you this. Even I am not supposed to know that a move is afoot to argue a case before the International Court in The Hague to force return of Guantanamo Bay to Cuba, whereupon it would be leased to China for the foreign exchange necessary to let this country build its infrastructure into the next century." Hernandez could see incredibility written all over Cox' face. "I know it sounds far-fetched, Dr. Cox, but bear with me. It is only one plan on the minds of some of our people. Don't forget Fidel is not the force he was only a year ago. Others are feeling their muscles now. Best we look at all possibilities or be sadly surprised when the unlikely happens."

Gordon nodded.

"Much more dangerous to my Cuba is the current movement to sell out our sovereignty for Venezuelan oil. You know that Fidel has been flirting with Caracas for years, ever since his attempts to spread our form of government to other Latin countries failed. Make no mistake Fidel is no fool, and very few of us ever thought he would sell us out. But those that follow may be sucked in by the wealth they as individuals would find in their pockets following an alliance with Caracas." At this point, Hernandez seemed exhausted. He paused and drank some of his tea and took a spoonful of the chocolate dessert in front of him.

Cox waited.

Hernandez leaned back in his chair. "I have told you more than I'd intended, Dr. Cox. I hope I may trust in your confidence. In return, I want to know what your President might do if there is fighting in the streets of Havana?"

★

The fishing docks Kate visited were filled with vessels of all shapes and sizes, several hailing from Chinese and North Korean ports. By the end of the morning, which included a pleasant lunch at an outdoor café looking over the entrance to the harbor, she found no one who recalled the Key West boat or the people aboard it.

The afternoon produced two sailors who Kate decided were plants to gain information from her. This meeting was under the direction of their male escort. The bright young lawyer, Lara, seemed embarrassed and kept her distance. Then, late in the day, an older man walked onto the dock off one of the small fishing boats. Kate got his attention and asked him a direct question in Spanish.

"Sir, we are looking for friends of ours . . . fishermen who came here during a storm several months ago from Key West, Florida. Do you recall these people?"

The man looked first at the plain-clothes man and then at Lara. Sensing the coast was clear, he looked back at Kate.

"Sí. I recall them."

Lara seemed as interested as Kate in what the fisherman had to say. She obtained the names of several other fishermen who would corroborate these recollections.

When this bit of news was relayed back the next morning to the Defense Ministry, the word went out: "No more interviews until Deputy Santos has met with these visitors."

★

Kate caught up with Gordon on the house phone to his room.

"Meet me in the lobby in ten minutes, Kate. I'll buy you a cup of coffee."

"Okay," Gordon said as they settled into one of the arranged sitting areas down one end of the immense lobby, "how'd it go?"

"The woman, Lara, is pleasant and very bright. The man is a hard case. I suggest we have her sit in on all the meetings we have."

"She works for Hernandez?"

"She's in the Justice Department. Hernandez apparently asks for her whenever he has need of an attorney. By the way, have you sent any reports back to the White House?"

"Yes . . . 'Nothing to report.'"

"Can we talk here?"

"Let's go out by the waterfall. It's more private."

They walked down to ground level and around the breakfast room to a noisy, man–made waterfall, which poured into the larger of the two swimming pools.

"This will do," Gordon said.

They ordered a drink from a waiter who attended to them immediately, and when he left, Kate picked up her thoughts.

"So nothing has been sent to Santiago in Key West?"

"Not yet. Maybe tomorrow."

"Want a suggestion?"

"Sure."

"Why not send something through now when it doesn't count—a smokescreen, sort of?"

"Why?"

"I don't know, just an intuition."

"I never ignore a woman's intuition. Your mother was brilliant in that regard."

"Really?" Kate said, blushing at the reference to her mother and Gordon's long lost relationship.

"Sorry, that embarrassed you, didn't it?" he said. "I didn't mean it as a clever remark. It's true, her precognition was remarkable."

"It's okay; you just surprised me."

"In any case, I will honor your intuition. We'll put a report through tomorrow whether we need it or not. How about another glass of wine?"

★

It wasn't difficult to recognize the car that came to pick up Kate and her boss at the hotel. Santiago had ridden in its front seat more than once. As dusk descended on the city, he watched it head west from the hotel and travel along the oceanfront until it was out of sight. He walked across the street, and went in and out the other side of the shopping center. The heavy seawall gave him a place to change into his night garbs. Santiago followed along the street Kate's limo had taken. It was a little under a mile from there to one of the many casas used to entertain important visitors. Three other limos were parked nearby, a clear indication that the dinner guest list was small but prestigious. One of the cars displayed the markings of the Ministry of Defense. This was a high level meeting for sure. *Perhaps worth a half million dollars to someone*, he mused.

★

Gordon and Kate entered the marbled foyer of a magnificent building by the sea. The night lighting bathed the outside coral and marble terrace in a tropical moonlight that was accented by flashes of lightning moving by in squalls out in the Gulf. The house looked to have in excess of 10,000 square feet of space. Dual spiral staircases ascended from the entrance foyer to an ornate balcony and wide hallways on the second floor.

"Apparently some are more equal than others in the Cuban form of communism," Kate whispered.

Gordon had witnessed the same paradox years before when visiting Soviet Russia with his Boston congressman, but with half the splendor evident here.

A dark eyed young woman approached and led the way to a pair of brightly varnished double doors, two stories high.

"Good evening, Ambassador Cox and Ms. Stevens. My name is Maria and I will be your interpreter this evening. Please come with me. The Ministers will join us in a few moments."

The huge doors opened as if by magic. They walked through and down two steps into a large formal area that looked like the lobby of a five-star hotel. On the far end were large glass doors, which opened into a dining room that looked out over the sea. The long table was set at one end with places for six people. A well dressed young man approached and offered them both light rum drinks that Maria called mojitos. Gordon did not hesitate to accept, and Kate followed suit.

"Gracias," Kate said to Maria, raising her glass.

"Oh, you speak Spanish, Ms. Stevens," she said.

"A little," Kate answered.

At that moment, three men came into the room from the direction Kate and Gordon had entered. Kate watched as the first and clearly senior minister approached. He was lean and flashy in a dark pinstriped suit and conservative tie.

The second man was bright-eyed and overweight. He wore a formal white shirt loose at the waist, reminding Gordon of the shirts worn by Malaysian and Philippine diplomats in Washington. The third, who either chose or was relegated to stay inconspicuous in the background, was the man with whom Gordon had met, José Hernandez.

"Welcome to Havana," the flashy one said in perfect English. "My name is Eduardo Santos, Ms. Stevens. I am Second Minister of Defense. I believe you know Dr. Hernandez, and this is Commander Mendosa, my attaché." Turning to Gordon, he said, "And how are you this evening, Ambassador?"

"Very well, thank you," Gordon said.

The aide, who was giving Kate a good looking over, held out his hand to her in greeting. She shook his hand, but had to pull hard to get it back.

[104]

Santos escorted them around the marbled patio, pointing out the paintings of Cuban artists that covered the walls. Once in their seats at the dinner table, he nodded in Kate's direction, and addressed Gordon.

"It's interesting to me that it is necessary to defend a fisherman in your courts merely because he came to Havana to escape the loss of his vessel. What does your President think of her friend, Gordon Cox, taking a position against her government?"

"Our President is well versed in the rights of individuals under our Constitution," Gordon said. "She would have no problem with my undertaking to defend a citizen's rights."

"What about non-citizens who are in your country? Do they also have the same rights?"

"Except to vote in our elections, yes. If they are there legally, they have all the same rights."

"Not apparently if they are Cuban."

"What do you mean?" Gordon said.

"José has told me of your offer in the case of three of our citizens who were legally in your country, and who are now in jail because they were accused of being spies by those terrorists in Miami."

"You're referring to the three Cuban nationals who were accused of acting on behalf of the Havana government without having registered as foreign agents?"

"They were accused of spying," Santos said.

"Maybe accused, but I think they were convicted of failing to register as agents of a foreign nation. It's true that they were accused of working to subvert the activities of an organization in Miami formed to promote the overthrow of the government here. Unfortunately, the lawyers for the three men admitted in papers filed in the Federal Court that they were in the United States legally as representatives of Cuba. Those admissions sealed their fate, because they had not registered. From there it was just a question of sentencing. I should point out," Gordon said, "that the sentences were arguably harsher than similar convictions in other cases."

Kate studied the urbane Santos to see if Gordon's comments mollified him in any way.

"Our lawyers asked for the case to be tried outside of Florida where they might get a fair trial," Santos said. "This request was refused."

The discussion of this case went on for some time while two courses of shrimp and a soup, which Kate thought was the best thing she'd ever tasted, were served along with appropriate wines. The discussion reminded Kate of the give and take during a class at law school. She watched Gordon's restraint, admiring his ability to keep the issue in doubt while not making too much of a fuss. She imagined Gordon at Harvard, giving the assistant professor and his fellow students all they could handle in classroom debate. She was good at it too, which made her admiration of Gordon's abilities all the more honest.

Santos seemed pleased to be having a reasoned discussion, which pointed at the three men's American lawyers being at least partially responsible for the negative outcome of the case. Gordon waited until the right moment to do what he and Charles Black had discussed.

"Minister Santos, your people have been helpful to Ms. Stevens in gathering facts for the case we're working on. As we mentioned to Minister Hernandez, I would be willing, if you think it would do any good, to have our people look into the basis for an appeal of these convictions. It appears on the surface there could be grounds for some optimism, though I can't guarantee anything. If you can arrange to get us appointed to represent them, we'll do what we can."

Santos looked at Hernandez, whose expression conveyed a *See, I told you so* kind of look. Commander Mendoza remained intent on Kate, who gave him a timid smile and then ignored him.

"That's an interesting proposal, Dr. Cox. With your firm in their corner, we might get honest justice."

"You understand, Minister, that I'll not be used for propaganda. If we look into the matter and discover that these three men haven't had their day in court, we'll be more than happy to seek any remedies they might have. If we think they received a just sentence, we'll tell you that, too."

Santos seemed to weigh the good and bad of Gordon's remarks. He looked around the table at his own men, and then turned to Cox. "Your firm is prestigious, Dr. Cox. I don't see any downside to your taking on such an assignment. What would be the cost of this endeavor?"

"If we were to take this on, we'd do it in exchange for your help gathering evidence here. I cannot know whether we'll act on their behalf until I have studied the matter more fully. You understand that."

"So, you will take what we give you while you are here and then back away when you get home?"

Kate wondered what Gordon's reaction was going to be to that bit of mischief.

Gordon laughed genuinely. "If you think that, Minister Santos, then we'd best go home tomorrow, because nothing good is going to come of this visit."

"But you ask me to trust you. Why should I do that?"

"Trust is a two way street, Minister."

Santos paused for what seemed to Kate an eternity, and then turned to José Hernandez. "You will give them the help they need."

Santos waited until after the dessert course was served to bring up the subject that Gordon had been expecting.

"Those cowards in Miami, Ambassador, they do not terrorize you, but they commit such acts here in Cuba, and they manipulate your President."

"Do you really believe that?" Gordon asked.

"It's true," Santos insisted. "These activities do not make it onto your television news stations, but they happen regularly. Mercenaries from Central America, who were paid by Miami, blew up a school outside Havana last month, killing a young teacher and several children. This wasn't an isolated act of violence. It's an ongoing course of crime against the Cuban people."

"How do you know they were acting on instructions from Miami?"

"They were Nicaraguan. We caught some of them. They told us who hired them."

"How do you think these people you call terrorists manipulate our President?"

"The President is a friend of yours, Ambassador, so perhaps you don't want to hear this."

"Yes, the President is a friend of mine, and that's precisely why I do want to hear it."

Santos nodded respectfully. "Certainly you are aware of the voting records in Florida. Is that not what you call a swing vote in your elections for President?"

"It has been an important state, and I'm sure it will continue to be. But the Cuban dictatorship and the Embargo are only two of many questions that drive its people to vote."

Santos seemed to contemplate continuing the argument, but instead moved the subject back to the timing and agenda for the next day's meetings.

"Dr. Cox, I suggest we pick up this discussion in the morning, say about ten-thirty, while Ms. Stevens continues her interviews on the docks."

NINE

Santiago deChristo had a piece of unfinished business to attend to in Havana. When he'd departed, there'd been no time for goodbyes. His mother probably didn't suffer as a result of his absence from a high government position. After all, his younger brother was a ranking officer in the Cuban Army. Although they were once very close, his brother became his sworn enemy upon Santiago's defection to Florida. The word went out. His brother Orlando would kill him the next time they met. Santiago would have said the same had his brother been the defector. Whether the man really meant it or not remained a question. In any case, Santiago would chance his mother turning him in.

He walked through streets without shadows a block back from the main thoroughfare running along the ocean in Miramar. His route was intended in part to satisfy his curiosity about parts of the city he hadn't seen in many years. He walked east into the Old City, stopping at a small outdoor cantina near the harbor entrance to have a late-night beer. From there he roamed the dark honeycomb of streets and rows of once stylish buildings constructed in past eras and still housing most of the city's inhabitants.

Clear of the harbor side, there were no lights and few people on the streets. The ones he met looked straight ahead as they passed. He was careful not to overtake anyone. He felt one man turn and look at his back before moving on. He made no contact with others.

The tenement stood five stories high, about the limit for the old buildings in Havana. He slipped into the open doorway at street level and climbed familiar stairs to the third floor. A gentle knock on the door solicited no response. There were no empty apartments in Havana. He waited, took a deep breath, and opened the door. He crept through the darkness to an alcove closed off by a curtain. The figure on the small cot shifted as he pulled the curtain aside.

A young woman stirred and came awake, wide-eyed with fear at the sight of a strange man at her bedside. Santiago stifled her scream with his hand and put a single finger to his lips, telling her to be quiet and that he wouldn't hurt her.

He spoke quietly to her in Spanish. "I'm sorry. I'm in the wrong place. I didn't mean to frighten you. Do not scream when I remove my hand. It will bring the police and I'm sure you don't want that."

She nodded, and he relaxed his grip on her jaw.

"Go away," she said.

"I will leave, señorita, but first I must ask you a question."

She looked terrified, but again nodded her head in consent.

"Do you know the old woman who used to live in this apartment?"

The young woman studied him more carefully before answering.

"No," she said. "I do not know her."

"Do you know what happened to her?" he pressed. "How long have you lived here?"

His last question unsettled her. She looked past him, expecting other companions, seeking a means of escape.

"I won't harm you," he said in the softest tone he could manage. "The woman who lived here several years ago is my mother. I'm looking for her. That's all."

"You are her son? No, that's impossible. She has only one son."

As she said the words, the truth suddenly hit her. A rush of adrenaline gave her the strength to push Santiago onto his back. She leapt over him and ran out the door.

He caught her before she could get to the top of the stairs at the end of the hall, but the noise they made wakened the people in the next flat. He dragged her kicking and squirming back into her apartment and shut the door. Only then did he realize she was naked. He held her wrist tight with one hand and grabbed the blanket off the bed with the other.

"Here, wrap this around yourself," he said. "What's the matter with you? I said I wouldn't hurt you."

"Let go of my wrist."

He did as she asked, ready to grab her again if she tried to run.

"What did you mean by 'She has only one son'?"

"You're Santiago."

"You know me?"

"I know your brother, Orlando. He gave me this apartment when he moved her to Habana Nuevo."

The light went on in his brain. The girl was his brother's mistress.

★

The fisherman's eyes darted around the room as he took a seat near the end of the long conference table. Deputy Minister Eduardo Santos was in charge of the meeting, and he wasted no time in getting started.

"Is this the man?" he asked the Secret Service officer seated opposite the fisherman.

"Yes, he is the one who spoke with the Americans."

Santos looked at Lara Peron.

She nodded her head.

"What is your name?" Santos said to the only person in the room not dressed for business.

"Pablo," he said.

"So tell us what you saw," Santos said.

"They were fishermen. The captain was an old man who had fished all his life. His boat was old too, and it had sprung a leak forward at the waterline. We helped him repair the damage well enough for him to prepare for sea. The captain gave us some of his catch to pay for our assistance. We also gave him some rum."

"Why didn't you report this to the Harbor Control?"

"It was reported. The captain filed his papers with the Seguredad."

"Did the Frontera conduct an inspection?"

"I don't know. If so, it was before we started work on board."

Santos looked around the table. One of those present passed to him a thin file containing no more than three papers. Santos gave these a glance and turned to Lara Peron.

"Lawyer Peron, were there others on the docks that the Americans spoke with?"

"Yes, Minister, as many as fifteen, although I did not keep an exact count."

Santos looked back at the fisherman.

"So when did you see this other man?"

"When I went below to help fix their leak," the fisherman said.

Santos picked up the file in front of him, and took from it one of the papers. He studied it for a moment and addressed the one who had given it to him.

"Only two crew are listed. What are we to conclude from this? That the American captain filed a false report or that he came into Havana to pick up someone and take him to Florida. Which shall it be?"

Santos looked around the room from face to face. In the silence that followed, the door to the conference room opened and a woman walked to the Deputy Minister's side. She said something to him and handed him a sealed envelope.

"Please close the door as you leave," Santos said to her as he opened the letter and read its contents. Finished, he placed the note in the inside pocket of his coat. "Would anyone like to know the identity of the man stowed away on that fishing boat?" he said, with a sardonic smile across his face.

No one spoke or moved.

"No?" he said. "Well then this meeting is over. Go back to your business. José, you stay if you please," he said to Foreign Minister Hernandez.

★

The two men met in the confessional for the second time in two days. Of the two, the accountant was the most nervous.

"We are breaking our carefully thought out rules. This is too much contact. We will be discovered," he said.

Hernandez spoke in carefully modulated tones. "That is a chance we have to take. The news I have for you is too important."

"Get on with it then, José, and be quick. No one has so many sins to confess."

Hernandez cleared his throat and spoke in hushed tones. "Don't use my name, not even in this confessional." The Minister paused. "You know the American lawyers came here to prove their clients— two fishermen—had to enter Cuba to save themselves."

"Yes, yes, you've told me that."

"Well apparently there were three on board when that boat left to return to Key West."

"Of course, what should the government expect? It was too good a chance for someone not to take the risk. Is that all?"

"No, that is not all," the other said, his voice rising in frustration.

"Shhhh," the accountant dressed as a priest continued.

"The man on board was Orlando's brother, Santiago."

Now it was the accountant's turn to raise his voice. "How do you know that? You mean he has been in Cuba all this time? No, we know he was in Key West. Are you saying that fisherman was a spy?"

"Santiago was on board when they arrived. They may have intended to carry out some act of sabotage. Or they merely were trying to keep Santiago out of sight so he would not be arrested. We know from the American lawyers that they were intercepted by the United States Coast Guard leaving here, and Santiago, if that really was him, was arrested. He could be in Guantanamo right now."

"How did you learn it was Santiago deChristo?"

"We know he was taken off the boat by the U.S. Coast Guard. Santos will speak to the Americans this afternoon for corroboration."

"They certainly should know who was on board."

"Yes."

"Aren't you happy now we didn't tell Orlando about their visit?"

"We need to tell him now."

"Why? That would be too dangerous."

"But he will find out. It is not such a well kept a secret anymore."

"But we can play down the importance. It changes nothing really. We continue to lie low. You will have more meetings with the Americans. What are they really doing here? That's what I would like to know."

"So would Eduardo Santos," José Hernandez said, and came out of the confessional making the sign of a cross with his right hand.

★

Santiago couldn't trust the young woman to keep his presence a secret. He didn't want to hurt her, but she had to be isolated. He could take her with him to the marina and let her go after they passed the breakwater. Or he could tie and gag her and hope his brother didn't pick tonight to come for comfort.

"What's your name?"

"Ana."

"I can't let you speak to anyone."

"I won't. I promise."

"I'm sorry, but I can't take the chance."

"Are you going to hurt me?"

"You'll come with me to a place near Jaimanitas. There we'll go on a boat. I'll let you off as we leave the harbor." He could see she didn't believe him.

"Orlando says you are a very cruel man. You killed many of us. You'll kill me, too. I know it."

"If I were going to kill you, I'd have already done it. You'll be safe. Now put on some clothes and we'll go."

He took his eyes off her for only a second as she pulled on a t–shirt and long pants. This time, she was out of the room and down the stairs so quickly, Santiago had no chance to stop her.

It was over three miles to the Havana Harbor entrance or the National Hotel, the closest places to get a taxi to Marina Hemingway. He might cover the distance to the taxi stand in twenty-five minutes. That would get him to the marina in maybe forty-five minutes. The cell phone he saw near her bed was gone. He swore under his breath at how careless he was. The police would be after him within minutes.

Ana did not stop running until she had covered several blocks in the darkness. She waited to see if Santiago had followed. Only then did she use her cellular phone. She was under strict orders never to call Orlando. Instead, she called her brother.

"Ernesto, this is Ana. I'm sorry to wake you. May I come to your apartment?"

Ernesto didn't like Orlando deChristo, and he didn't like his sister living as she did. But the General was a very powerful man, so Ernesto kept his opinions to himself. "What is it? Did he throw you out?"

"Please, Brother. I'll tell you what happened when I see you."

"Alright, but don't ring the chimes. I'll leave the door open. When will you be here?"

"In five minutes," Ana said.

Ernesto Legra was twenty-one, five years older than his sister. He did well in school and worked for the Ministry of Defense as a research clerk in the intelligence section while continuing his studies. This made him eligible for a one-bedroom apartment in a respectable and clean, if antiquated, building. Ana arrived there exactly when she said she would. The two sat together in the corner, where he made food.

"Orlando's brother?"

"Yes, it was he. He said he was her son, Orlando's mother's son."

"Where is he now?"

"He said something about taking me to a boat that was waiting near Jaimanitas, but I ran out."

"That would be the marina. What else did he say?"

"He said he'd take me with him and let me go when they left."

"This is a big problem, Sister. If we call Orlando, it will get you into trouble. If we don't, there'll be hell to play if he finds out. Did anyone hear you?"

"I don't know. There was noise. The neighbors must have known there was someone in the apartment besides me."

"Will they tell Orlando?"

"I don't think so, but you never know."

"When will you see him again?"

"Probably tomorrow. Sometimes he comes in the morning and brings coffee and a cake."

Ernesto Legra had grown up with the legend of Santiago deChristo, and a scheme to get Ana away from his brother once and for all began to take shape in his mind.

"Here is what I think you must do, Sister."

Ernesto loved his sister Ana enough to make up for the loss of both their parents. She was smarter than he, but she had no patience. Until the age of ten, she thought he walked on water. At thirteen, she was pretty enough to be taken for seventeen. And taken she was, by the local police chief. Ernesto was away on military service when it happened. She had no one to protect or console her. She retreated inside herself, deciding that next time, she'd get more back than was taken from her.

He'd hardly recognized his sister when he returned to Havana. She used tough words and behaved in a worldly manner that made her seem much older. They drifted apart after that, because that was what Ana wanted. When Ernesto heard she'd become Orlando deChristo's woman, he went to the park overlooking the harbor entrance at Este Havana and got very drunk. The hangover that followed provided him with moments to see and accept things as they were. Still, as the head of what remained of her family, there was nothing he wouldn't do for her.

Ernesto's evolving plan had two parts. The first involved an attempt to coerce Orlando into leaving his sister. The only tunnel through which Ernesto could communicate with a man as important as Orlando deChristo was located on the keyboard of his computer. He knew the lines of command within Defense. He knew the committee men and women who tended to business, as well as those for whom political maneuvering was the route to success. There were two times each day when he could make the communication he wanted to make. The best was already passed by the time he arrived in the office. The next would be immediately after lunch.

The more important part of the scheme involved Santiago. Ernesto knew of Santiago through the stories he heard. The man lived a charmed life during the time the Russians were in Cuba. He heard stories of Santiago being targeted for elimination by the KGB, but in each case, the man turned the tables on those who had him in their sights. When the Russians left Cuba, Santiago was promoted to the top Secret Service job at Fidel Castro's right hand. He was Fidel's personal choice over the several chosen by Raul Castro, the Minister of Defense. This didn't please Raul, and Santiago eventually fled Cuba for his own safety. Now, he was back, and Ernesto needed to meet with him.

The more Ana's brother contemplated his idea to use Santiago's presence in Cuba as the key to her freedom, the more impressed he became with himself. It was a brilliant plan, he decided, and he began the process of implementing it.

★

Gordon and Kate went into the Old City of Havana, the most popular stop on the Euro tours. It was also a place where they could talk without fear of being easily overheard. They lunched at an outdoor café that could have been in one of the nicer parts of Buenos Aires or in Old San Juan. The music was live and the food excellent.

"I don't want to leave," Kate said.

"You like it that much?"

"I like the feel of the place. I know what we see here isn't the real Cuban life. You can see it in their eyes, and men like Eduardo Santos give me chills. It's as if sitting here now, I'm playing a part in an old movie classic. Nothing is real, it's all images and walk-ons." Kate smiled and reached out for Gordon. "I like having you to myself, too, Gordon Cox. You know, my mother warned me about you."

"Katherine . . ." he began.

"Just kidding."

Gordon waited while Kate leaned back as if pondering some profound thought.

"The girl in the hotel bar told me there's a great dance club here in one of the big office buildings. She gave me the address. Will you take me there tonight? It doesn't open until ten."

"Sure, we can go."

"You don't sound overly enthusiastic."

"Young lady, I'll take you dancing anywhere, anytime."

"Tonight?"

"You bet."

Kate took a sip of the Cuban pass-off for Coke she had ordered, and gave Gordon her best *come hither* look. "Did you and the President ever . . . ?"

"Ever what?" he asked, laughing.

"You know. I mean you two have spent a lot of time together, on the road, campaigning, and eating and drinking together."

"No, she and I never, and that's a very impertinent question. Maybe I *should* fire you after all," he said with a wide smile.

"Not until we get back, please. I want at least one more night in Havana. And may I pose one more impertinent question?"

Gordon was still smiling. He didn't want their time to end either.

"Did you bring me down here so we could get it on?"

He'd asked himself that same question. "Absolutely not. You're the only person who speaks Spanish and was up to speed on the case. You fit the reason for the trip. Besides, we're doing this for the

President and she likes you. And, young lady, it wasn't my decision that caused Brad Howe not to be here."

Kate smiled and touched his arm with her outstretched hand. "What we're doing is exciting. Havana is exciting. And you're exciting. If there's anything left of us, I'd like to come back here with you some day and see what we missed." Kate stopped talking as she saw Lara coming across the square. "She's giving me the complete transcript on the case of those Cubans in Miami. She also wants me to meet her brother. She says he's very handsome." Winking at him, Kate turned to greet their guide.

"I'll be back at the hotel by five." She waved to Cox as the two women strode off.

Gordon watched them walk across the square. *An American and a Cuban lawyer in Havana,* he thought, *going off together to analyze transcripts in a case against three Cubans convicted of a crime in Miami.* "Who would have thought?" he said to himself.

Five minutes later, reality returned. The Cuban agent arrived to escort Gordon to his meeting with José Hernandez. That was not where they went. There had been a change in plans. Eduardo Santos wanted to speak with Gordon concerning Santiago deChristo.

★

Kate and the young Cuban lawyer, Lara, finished working through the transcripts of trial and the resulting federal convictions of the three Cuban men in Miami. At Lara's suggestion, they walked a few blocks to the University of Havana, where they had coffee and Cuban pastry in Lara's favorite outdoor café adjacent to the campus. The sun was creeping below the line of the University Tower when they finished talking, and they headed back to pick up their papers at Lara's office in the Ministry of Justice. Kate gathered up her things and got into the limo to be driven back to the hotel. Halfway there, she suddenly realized the notebook in her lap was not hers. Panicked, because her book contained many of Gordon and her thoughts on the subject of Cuba, she asked the driver to return to the Ministry. On the way back, she looked into the notes she'd carelessly mistaken for her own, and stared down at the legal brief Lara had written on recovering the Guantanamo Naval Base from the United States. Shocked by the revelation, she closed the book quickly and sat on it.

★

Gordon's arrival at the Ministry of Defense for the first time caused a stir. He felt all eyes on him as he walked the length of the third floor into Santos' office.

"I thought we should meet alone, just the two of us, Dr. Cox. I trust that's alright with you."

Gordon nodded.

"I think the time has come for you and me to drop all pretenses. I want to know what you are really doing in Havana."

"What do you want me to be doing here, Excellency?" Gordon said.

Santos smiled. "You lawyers are all alike. Answer a question with a question. That must be the first thing they teach you at the Harvard Law School." He raised his arms in mock surrender. "Okay, I want you to look me in the eye and tell me the truth about why you came to Cuba. I don't think you came here to gather facts that you already had. You came to talk political business, to test the temperature of the waters in Revolutionary Square, or to meet with those people who do not have the best interests of Cuba in their hearts. Which will it be, Dr. Cox?"

"The other night at dinner you said you would speak with your superiors about meeting with me . . . and you, to discuss the subjects brought up that evening."

"You are a man of the world, Dr. Cox. You can appreciate taking that action will put me at some risk. If you turn out to be a wolf in sheep's clothing, I will be embarrassed. If I can reach a level of confidence that you are here to be reasonable and not to cause trouble, we can proceed as you wish."

"Minister Santos, we are what you see. I can tell you this much. Our President would like to end fifty years of antagonism. I will not

[120]

embarrass her anymore than you will those to whom you are responsible, but nothing is gained without risk."

"Can you tell me that you have the authority to deal on behalf of your President?"

"To deal? No, but to talk and bring home a sense of what is possible? Yes."

"Do I have any assurance your President will look at your work here as a starting point for further discussions, perhaps at a higher level?"

"I can give you that," Gordon said.

"Good, very good, but first I need your help on a small matter. The crew of that fishing boat you came here to help, how many were on board?"

Cox played chess. His mind raced through the possibilities. He decided there was no downside to telling the truth. It had all passed. There was no one left in Cuba to be harmed by the honest answer. Perhaps it was the breakthrough he'd been looking for, his ticket to the Ball. "Three," he said.

Santos nodded. "The captain, and who were the other two?"

"I know one of them was arrested by the Coast Guard as a suspected Cuban national. I don't know who the other one was."

"Do you know his name, the Cuban I mean?"

"No. That information was not part of the indictment, or the arrest report. Only a criminal charge that the captain was transporting a Cuban to Florida for money."

"Hmmm, you don't know if that man was sent back to Guantanamo Bay by the U.S. Immigration authorities?"

"No, I don't," but Cox decided to throw some bait in the water. "Would you like me to make an inquiry? It must be important."

"No, that won't be necessary, Dr. Cox, but it's interesting that this third man's name was not on the manifest filed with our Harbor Authority." Santos squinted to neutralize his astigmatism and see if his comment caused any reaction.

Cox was too good a poker player to show any interest. "I believe the Coast Guard has orders to send Cubans picked up at sea to

Guantanamo Bay for repatriation to Cuba, as you suggested. I guess whoever it was will be back here soon enough."

"Yes, but it's interesting. Why would a Cuban who had left for Florida voluntarily return, except to do mischief?"

"If that boat came in here in a storm, and they were sinking, then I guess it wouldn't have been a voluntary visit. But what makes you think this person originated in Cuba? Is it because our Coast Guard assumed that he did?"

"Not entirely, Dr. Cox. We have information that this particular individual, a wanted criminal, was employed by your client on his fishing boat. Wasn't the captain killed following his return to Florida?"

"Yes he was. You don't think the captain's death was at the hands of that Cuban man, do you?"

"No, I think the criminals in Miami were the more likely perpetrators."

"I have no reason to think that, Dr. Santos." Gordon decided to chance some confrontation. He didn't like playing cat and mouse when he was the mouse. "Political or social?" he said.

"Pardon?" the Cuban said.

"The crewman whose name was not on the manifest. Was his crime here political or social?"

Santos cleared his throat. "In Cuba, Dr. Cox, there is often no difference."

"I see," the lawyer said. "Nevertheless, if you would like me to inquire in Miami or Washington concerning the name of this individual, I shall be pleased to do so."

"That will not be necessary. His name is Santiago deChristo. We know who he is. I thought perhaps you did as well."

★

Kate tucked the Guantanamo brief under her arm and walked through the door to Lara's office. The young Cuban lawyer was nowhere in sight. In fact, the two rooms Kate had been in earlier were both empty. She took a careful look around for her notebook, but did not see it. In desperation she decided to take a chair near the door between the two rooms and wait for someone to appear. More as a prop in case someone other than Lara showed up, she passed the time reading the brief. An hour passed, and she could see a cleaning person down the hall, working her way toward where Kate was sitting. Afraid of being accused of stealing classified information, and with no Lara around to defend her, Kate got up from the chair and walked matter-of-factly out to the waiting limo. She was afraid to leave the brief out on one of the tables in the office, and took it with her.

Kate dreaded having to tell Gordon she'd misplaced her note-book. With a crazy mix of loyalty to Lara and guilt for having read her secreted work, Kate wrestled with the question of turning over the Guantanamo brief to him. In the end, she decided Gordon had to be informed on both counts.

★

Eduardo Santos, fresh from his meeting with Gordon Cox, stalked the conference room used for the most secure meetings in his Ministry. Lara Peron's senior lawyer, Rosalita, spoke, and her other assistant, Roberto, paged through the documents he'd collected in support of their position.

"And Lara Peron," Santos said, turning on his heels in full stride and facing her, "what are your thoughts on how long this process will take from start to finish?"

"Two years, Excellency."

"Is there nothing that can be done to speed things up?"

"No, and my estimate assumes no unusual delay, which is diffi-cult to rule out."

"But time is not critical," Rosalita said. "Once the complaint is filed and the issues are drawn, you will begin the process of making demands and following up with negotiation in the world of public opinion. That will be sufficient for the Chinese."

Santos, who looked tired, plopped down into the chair at the head of the table. "Will the world take us seriously?"

"It's a very strong case," Lara said. "Maybe at first people will be amused, but once they understand our grounds, they will have no choice but to take us seriously."

Finished speaking for the moment, Lara moved to the credenza behind Santos' chair to check a reference among her notes.

★

Gordon and Kate sat in her room while she translated the Guantanamo brief from Spanish to English. It made interesting reading from the standpoint of the legal points made, some of which were brilliantly argued. But the key for Cox was the fact that it corroborated what Hernandez had told him. They were about to retire to their secure table next to the waterfall on the hotel grounds when Kate's phone rang. It was Lara Peron, calling from the lobby. Kate could tell she'd been crying. Her tone of voice was lacking its usual melody.

"Did you take my notebook by mistake? I have yours."

"Yes, I have it."

"May I come up and get it, Katherine?"

"I'll bring it down."

"No, no, please, let me come up."

"Alright," Kate said and shooed Gordon out the door and around the corner to his own room.

Lara insisted that she and Kate talk in the hall outside Kate's room, but also close to the wall and out of sight of anyone walking around the rotunda of the arboretum, around which all the hotel rooms were lined. She spoke in hushed tones.

"I must ask you, Katherine, if you read what is in my notebook."

Kate and Gordon had decided that question should be answered truthfully, with no acknowledgement of the brief's importance.

"I looked at it. Why?"

"Nothing, I just wondered if you'd taken the opportunity to read it?"

"I read enough to know it wasn't mine. I went back to return it to you and pick up my own book, but no one was around. I thought it best not to leave it out on your table."

The expression in Lara's eyes approached abject fear. "Yes, thanks. Here's your book," she said, making the exchange. "I have also read some of your notes. In fact, I would love sometime to answer the questions you raise about my country." Lara stepped back and looked tentatively at Kate. "Our notes are private. I hope you agree that we should both keep it that way."

"I'm not sure I can do that, Lara. I can't pretend that I don't know what you've written. Knowing the subject gives me a terrible conflict with my loyalty to my own country."

Kate could see from Lara's expression and silence that she was facing up to what she'd expected.

"But I don't see why it can't wait," Kate said, pausing for a second before continuing, "until I return to Washington, if that helps you any."

Lara's reaction was immediate. "Oh, yes, that would help. Thank you so much, Katherine. You don't know how much that means to me. I would lose my job and my career if news leaked out on this subject before we are ready. Can you really wait? Have you told Dr. Cox?"

"Yes, it can wait until then," is all that Kate said. "Will you do the same for me and the embarrassing notes in that book of mine?"

"Your notes are not embarrassing. We all have those same thoughts," the Cuban lawyer said, and her attempt at a smile resulted in a grim expression as she backed away and turned to leave. "Hasta mañana, Katherine, and gracias."

"Hasta luego, Lara."

The Cuban woman stopped before taking more than a few steps toward the elevator bank. "Katherine, if I give you some advice, will you promise to keep it between us and no one else?"

Kate nodded.

Lara took a deep breath, which accentuated the concerned look on her face. "Do not trust Eduardo Santos," she said, turning and moving quickly down the hall to the elevators.

Kate, to be extra careful, waited five minutes before calling Gordon. He came out of his room, and took the elevator down to the lobby. Kate joined him and together they went out to the terrace by the waterfall, and ordered drinks. Kate told him what had transpired with Lara Peron.

"So what do we do about that brief?" she asked when the waiter was gone.

"Nothing right now," Gordon said, having decided not to tell Kate of the substance of his meeting with Hernandez. "It's an interesting concept, and frankly, one that has some merit. In today's atmosphere of anti-Americanism I wouldn't be surprised if their position provoked a good deal of sympathy around the globe."

"Does she have the facts right? Did we really threaten to use force if Cuba didn't grant us the right to use the Bay for a base?"

"I'm not sure it matters whether we did or not. The issue is whether the treaty, drafted the way it is, could ever be held to grant perpetual rights over the sovereign land of another country. If it had purported to be an outright grant, such as the Louisiana Purchase, or the assumption of rights to southern California from Mexico, then it could have accomplished what might have been intended. The theme of this treaty is one of arrogance. It's not a lease, not a grant, yet it purports to be eternal. There was no substantial consideration for the rights granted, only a statement of friendship—a state of affairs that has not existed for over forty-five years, and may not have been true at the time of the grant."

"How strong is their argument that our use of the Base as a prison is *ultra vires*, or constitutes abandonment, and voids the grant?"

"That's a creative position; not as powerful as the points on perpetual transfer of interest, but worth considering nevertheless."

"Our friend Conner Omega will have fun with this, won't he?"

Gordon laughed. "Yes, but it will be a matter for the Solicitor General, not the AG."

"What about Lara's warning about Santos?"

"She must have had something specific in mind. From what I

can see, no one trusts Eduardo Santos. Does she know something that's in the works? Maybe it involves Santiago deChristo. He was certainly on Santos' mind this afternoon."

"We never sent that message to your cousin in Boston, did we?"

Gordon blushed. "No, I completely forgot about it, but now we have a subject to discuss with him. I'll make the call tomorrow."

Cox finished his drink and pointed in the direction of the ocean. "Katherine, can you hear that live Latin beat coming from the ocean terrace to our left? Care to check it out? Maybe you can find a young man or two to whirl you around the dance floor."

TEN

Eduardo Santos had finished reading his intelligence reports on the visiting lawyers before going to breakfast in the Room of Ministers. "Is it true they were dancing together last evening at the hotel? Did they retire to the same room?"

Gordon handled the Latin beat better than Kate when they began to dance, but she improved quickly and managed to follow his steps better and better until the hotel band hit the Tango. They sat this one out.

"Where'd you learn to dance like that, Gordon?" she said, as they sat down at their table next to the dance floor. Giggling as she watched the Tango being danced by two who knew what they were doing, she said, "You've got to teach me the Tango, Gordon. That's the sexiest thing I've ever seen."

They danced every dance after that, and sipped rum punch between breaks in the music. The last sets were slow and the mood romantic. Kate was tucked into Gordon's shoulder, with an arm stretched up and her hand caressing the nape of his neck. Gordon's large right hand held her low at the waist, his other hand clasping hers. The rhythm of their dance continued for several moments after the music stopped for the last time. Their arms entwined, the dancers turned and applauded the band from the middle of the dance floor.

"What time is it?" Kate asked as they emerged from the elevator on her floor.

As Gordon turned his wrist to look at his watch, Kate took his other arm and placed it around her waist, moving closer as she did. Their kiss was long and sweet, unlike any that Kate had experienced before that moment. She wrapped her arm around his and kept it there until they were outside the door to her room. She handed Gordon her key, and held onto him while he opened the door.

★

The hotel buffet breakfast room was full of an assortment of Europeans, with a sprinkling of Asians, as Kate entered and found a table for two on the ocean side. The walls she'd built up to guard against male advances had come tumbling down in her room the night before. Nor were there any regrets to complicate her life.

She watched as Gordon strolled across the lower lobby. Her heart jumped a beat when she saw he'd spotted her. She took a deep breath and gave him a cheery, "Good Morning, Gordon."

They ate a leisurely breakfast, enjoying each other's company. They were on their second coffee when Kate hit for the baseline. "Gordon, last night . . ."

"I have no regrets, Katherine, but I wouldn't blame you . . ."

She reached across the table. Her finger touched his lips and he stopped talking.

"I was about to tell you that only my politically induced paranoia keeps me from leaping into your lap right now."

"Kate . . ."

"No. I mean it."

"I'm sure you—"

"I've led a pretty sheltered life, you know. I'll tell you about it sometime. Now, it's back to the docks for me," she said, getting up from the table and moving around to Gordon's shoulder. "I should be back by five. Are we still on for that dance hall down in the old town? It's a late place. I don't think it opens until ten or eleven."

Gordon smiled and nodded. He was not looking forward to another late night, but he'd promised.

★

Santiago, as he moved through the city, saw no activity in all the places he knew would be mobilized if the guard or police were under orders to apprehend him. Instinct told him not to compound one error with another. Running scared was the worst thing he could do. He knew the marina was heavily guarded at night. He could enter the area during daylight hours after changing back into his tourist clothes, but to get in through the gate alone in the hours before dawn was too risky. He had euros. He decided to go to one of the nightclubs that officially didn't exist, and drink beer until the sun came up. He'd have good music and pass the time by watching people dance. He paid a twenty-euro entrance fee, which eliminated the need to show identification. As he pushed through the unruly crowd milling around the entrance to the club, he bumped into Gordon Cox as he and Kate were leaving. This time, she recognized him.

"Santiago, is that you?" she said, attracting little attention from the crowd of locals standing around outside the bar, hawking cigars, cocaine and, in some cases, their girlfriends.

He moved close to her, speaking English. "Hello, señorita. Enjoying Havana, I see."

"What are you doing here?" she said in a low voice, grasping Gordon's arm for support.

Gordon moved between Kate and the Cuban. "Can we go somewhere and talk?"

"Do you have your papers with you?" the Cuban asked.

Gordon nodded.

"Then we'll go to the marina. The boat I came on is berthed there. We can speak there without being overheard. But you will have to get us through the gate."

[130]

★

Ana prepared herself. When Orlando arrived, she looked quite beautiful in the dress he'd given her. He made her happy by not rushing into things. It was almost possible to believe he truly loved her as he spoke his most ardent expressions of passion. Usually, he left quickly when they finished, but on this day Ana had some information for him.

"Your brother Santiago is in Havana," she said as Orlando was on his way out the door.

He turned and stared at her. "What did you say?"

"He's here, Orlando. I saw him."

"How do you know? You've never met him."

"He was here, looking for your mother."

"When? What did he say?"

"He didn't know me. He asked me if I knew the woman who used to live here. He said she was his mother."

"Does he know you and I . . . ?"

"No. He left when I said I didn't know his mother."

"Did he tell you where he's staying?"

She lied, as her brother instructed. "No," she said.

Orlando looked at Ana, his eyes questioning.

She stared back at him. It was easier to lie when someone else had told you what to say.

Orlando took a pen from his uniform pocket and wrote something on a small pad of paper. He handed it to her.

"Call that number if he comes back. Ask for Vivian. Just tell her my package is ready. I'll get the message." He wheeled around to leave, but stopped and turned back to her. "Speak of this to no one," he said sternly. "Understand? No one."

★

The President put off meeting with the Attorney General as long as possible. As others in her Cabinet made the rounds on the Hill, building support for removal of the Cuban Embargo, Conner

Omega caroused around Congress, subtly taking issue with the Treasury Department for granting Gordon Cox a license to visit Cuba and dropping hints of illegal dealings with the Cubans in Havana. Charlie Black began to receive calls from his friends in the House, informing him that Omega was making a mockery of the President's proposals regarding Cuba.

"She'll see you now, Conner. Come on, we'll both go in."

Black escorted the AG to a chair at the large coffee table that doubled as her conference center. The President, engrossed in her work, didn't look up.

Omega cleared his throat.

"Have a sore throat, Conner?" she said, without lifting her eyes from the papers in front of her.

Charles Black put on his best poker face. Omega sat still and tightlipped; the forefinger and thumb of his right hand twirled in tight circles like he was sewing an invisible garment.

The President stood and addressed her Chief of Staff. "Charles, where is that paper from London?"

"The one on Venezuela?"

She nodded. "Yes, that one."

"Bessy has it."

The President called her administrative assistant on the intercom. "Bessy, can you bring in that piece we received on the Venezuelan takeover of Cuba? Charles says you have it handy."

Satisfied, the President walked across the room to the two men, who stood as she approached.

"Hello, Conner. Thanks for coming," she said, taking her seat at the table.

Charles Black took the Caracas paper from the President's secretary, confirming with a quick glance that it was the right document.

The President browsed the paper, speaking to the Attorney General as her gaze stayed focused on what was in her hand. "Conner, are you cozy with the regime in Havana?"

"I'm not sure what you mean, Madam President."

"Yes, perhaps I could have chosen a better word than 'cozy.' Are you comfortable with the present government of Cuba?"

"You know I'm not."

She looked up at Black, who spoke on cue. "So what's kept them in power for all these years, Conner?"

His first reaction was an audible grunt, which made the President's face muscles tighten as she tried to stymie a smile.

Conner avoided looking directly at either of them, responding, "It's a goddamned dictatorship. Guns and fear have kept them in power."

"What was the purpose of the Embargo, Conner?"

"To bring them to their knees."

"Who? To bring who to their knees? The poor people of Cuba?"

"No, Fidel and all his cronies."

"And has it done that?"

"No, because every other country in the universe has not honored it."

"And why do you think they haven't?"

"Because they're after the buck."

"Oh, I see, you mean because they're business people taking advantage of an opportunity?"

"Because our government has not been tough enough."

"What do you want us to do?"

"Tell the Europeans and the Asians to stay the hell out of Cuba."

"Or what, Conner? What do I threaten them with?"

"Or we'll take measures."

"Yes . . . ?" she said, waiting expectantly with her tongue protruding from inside one cheek.

"Look," Omega said, "the Embargo has put a lot of pressure on the people down there. Why do you say it hasn't worked?"

The President, unable to stay seated any longer, rose up out of her chair.

"Because they're still there, Conner. The same people, doing the same things, are still there."

"And you think you can remove them by lifting the Embargo?"

"It might be a start. It will take away the only excuse they've had over the last forty years for all their failures to provide a good life to their people. I have to tell you, Conner, the ruling party's done remarkably well in spite of that damned Embargo. They have pretty good medical facilities. The people are poor, but they're not as desperate as some other places in this hemisphere. The upper crust, which includes not just politicians, but also star athletes and other celebrities, live as well in Miramar, Havana as they do in Malibu or Miami Beach. You and Fidel Castro's disciples appear to have the same interest. Keep the people poor so you can control them. Give them the light of day and all will be lost. It's a very small world today, Conner. Nothing happens anywhere that people don't know about. Propaganda works to a point, but its bitter enemy is sunlight and information."

"What about the Cubans who lost everything when Castro took over?"

"What about them?" asked Black, taking back the initiative.

"Well, shouldn't they get compensated?"

"By whom?"

"By Cuba."

"That's an interesting concept, Conner. You want the people of Cuba to pay the other Cubans who fled fifty years ago the value of what they lost. Can you tell me why this country should encourage one Cuban to pay another under such a circumstance? Do you have any precedent for that notion? Besides, isn't it your theory that the Cubans who went to Miami are a lot better off than those who stayed? Isn't that why people leave Cuba every chance they get? Because they want what the people in Miami have? Why should those who stayed home give them anything?"

"They want freedom."

"So how does keeping the crowd in Havana in power advance the cause of freedom?"

"That's why . . ."

"What?" Black demanded, losing his patience. "That's why you want to continue an embargo that's been in place for almost fifty years with no discernable effect on the power structure it was designed to topple? Come on, Conner, give it up. It's time to let Cuba have a stake in its own future. You know the President's plan. If you've got a better solution, let's have it. Meanwhile, better get on our side, and stop undercutting the administration that you're part of."

"Bravo, Charles," the President said, taking her seat again. "What do you think, Mr. Attorney General? It's time to choose sides. You're with us, or you're against us. I don't see any middle ground here. You need to make up your mind, and you need to do it right now."

★

Kate and Gordon sat with Santiago in the enclosed cabin of the Dutchman's sport fisherman. The air smelled of rum and stale cigars. Kate went around opening ports and hatches as Gordon and the Cuban spoke. Then she took a seat on the steps near the open hatch to the deck, as her eyes became accustomed to the dim lights in the cabin.

Santiago was surprised not to find the Dutchman on board when they arrived. It looked like the man had left in a hurry. The Cuban took several minutes to clean up the rum soaked table and put away the bottles. He spoke to them as he worked.

"This is a poor country, Dr. Cox, but the people don't know how poor they are. They're told all their problems lie at the feet of the United States and the Embargo. You must understand there's a whole generation here that knows nothing else. If someone gave them a real job tomorrow they wouldn't know what to do with it. The intelligentsia works for the government. There is no such thing as profit. They understand very well the concept of cash flow, but ask them tomorrow when you go to the Ministry the meaning of *return on investment*. You'll see."

"How is it there's never been a revolt or any kind of insurrection?" Cox said, thinking Santiago's snapshot of Cuban economics was pretty good for a fisherman.

"There've been a few. The government's spies are everywhere. We always knew when things were cooking. It's been a combination of education and fear. Most of the upper class—and understand that there are different classes here—most of them believe in the system. They also know if they step out of line, they're dead, or worse. Look at the way the government has handled AIDS."

"How's that?"

"They put any person with HIV in quarantine until the cure is found. They handle the disease like leprosy was addressed a century ago. Those poor devils are isolated and left to die. They use them to experiment new drugs, telling them the medicine will help and maybe cure them. Meanwhile they tell the world that there's no HIV in Cuba, because there's no drug use and no promiscuity. And that, if you haven't noticed, is a laugh."

"Is the fact they treat AIDS in this way generally known outside of Cuba?" Cox asked.

"Apparently not, but it may not be such a bad idea when you look at the high rate of AIDS elsewhere in the Caribbean."

"So what happens if the Embargo is lifted?"

Santiago nodded, as if to say it was a good question. "At first, not much," he said. "Eventually, the people are not going to be kept out of the world's economic party. I don't know how well you know Cubans, Dr. Cox, but they're a talented and achievement oriented people. Look at Miami. The Cubans who went there turned that city around. They've done the same in parts of Puerto Rico. Everywhere they go, they push to succeed. They're also hated for their ambition and success. Why do you think Fidel's efforts to foment revolution elsewhere in Latin America failed so miserably? Do you think Che Guevera would have failed?"

Gordon knew it was a rhetorical question, and waited.

"It was because Cubans are not well liked in those countries," he said, answering his own question. "Remember, Che was not Cuban."

Santiago walked over to the small refrigerator and took out three beers. He first offered one to Kate.

"I don't think you like beer, señorita, but it's all we have."

"Thank you," she said, taking a can and setting it on the table beside her chair.

Gordon opened his as the Cuban continued speaking.

"You have been driven through the areas between here and your hotel. What is your general impression?"

"Very upmarket," he said.

"For Cuba or for other places?"

"I don't know the rest of Cuba, but from an American perspective, these neighborhoods wouldn't be out of place in the better suburbs of any of our major cities."

"Did you stop to think who owns them?"

"I did," said Kate.

Santiago and Gordon both looked at her.

"So, don't keep us in suspense, Santiago," she said. "Who lives there?"

"The government's friends live there; the loyalists, the celebrities, and foreign embassies willing to pay the steep rents in hard currency. It's just like in the U.S. The baseball and television stars have the luxurious homes. But here it lasts only as long as you are in favor."

"So the government owns all of them?"

"The State owns every piece of real estate in Cuba."

In a moment of reflection by the two men, Kate asked the question that had been on her mind since they first crossed paths with the Cuban.

"Santiago, what are you doing here? You told me you'd never come back."

He was about to say something more about life in Cuba, but stopped at her question. He looked briefly at Gordon before answering. He was on his turf here at the boat, and it made him comfortable enough to risk confrontation.

"You and Dr. Cox are here to meet with the government. I'm here to see my mother one more time before she dies."

"Is that what you were doing when we met?" Kate asked with a touch of irony in her voice.

"I was discovered going to where she used to live. I needed a place to hide. No place is better for hiding than one that doesn't exist."

Kate glanced at Gordon. He could see she didn't believe him either. "Santiago," Gordon said. "If you're here at all it must mean there is more freedom to move about than I would have guessed."

Santiago greeted Cox's question with contempt. "I know my way around Havana. I play the odds."

Kate broke in. "And you'd risk being caught just to see your mother?"

The Cuban's eyes softened. "She is a very wonderful person, señorita. If you'd like to meet her, I'll take you there."

"Santiago, I don't believe you. What are you really doing here?"

Before the Cuban could say anything more, a line of blinding lights came on at the far end of the pier. Santiago bolted past Kate and up onto the deck. Cox scooped up Kate, following the Cuban topside. The two got as far as the side of the cement pier before they found themselves peering down the barrel of an automatic rifle. On the trigger end was a Cuban soldier, a uniformed compatriot on either side.

A young man in civilian clothes seemed in charge of the three military types. Standing by the gunwales of the boat, he pointed a finger at Santiago.

"Captain, sir, stay where you are. Please do not move, or these men will shoot you." He jumped onto the fishing deck next to where Santiago stood, and spoke rapidly in English, "I know who you are. It is not my intention to turn you in." Returning to Spanish and shouting, he commanded, "Take me below and show me your papers." The two of them went down the companionway, and closed the hatch.

"What's going on?" Kate whispered to Gordon.

Cox hunched his shoulders, studying the three soldiers. They appeared more frightened than threatening, but frightened soldiers with guns made Gordon nervous. Moving slowly and making no overt gestures, he escorted Kate to the far side of the boat deck. They sat down in the glare of the floodlights blazing from the gate-house. He saw lights flickering on in the apartment complex behind them. Otherwise, there was no movement off the boat.

Down below, Santiago spoke first. "How do you know me?"

"We are almost family. Ana, your brother's mistress, is my sister."

Santiago was quick to react. "The men with you, I take it they don't know who I am?"

"They think we're here to check on boats staying at the marina without proper papers."

"So you were following me?"

"We've been waiting here for you to return. Ana told me you threatened to take her out to sea. This was the only place."

"What do you want?"

The young man lowered his head and nodded. "I will get right to the point. I want you to take my sister to the United States. I don't want her being your brother's house pet. She's only sixteen. She's a very intelligent girl and needs a good life. It's the only way."

Santiago smiled inwardly. "You are an enterprising young man."

"Ernesto," he said. "That's my name."

Santiago nodded. "What makes you think I can take your sister out from under my brother's nose, get her aboard this boat, and take her to Florida?"

"I'll get her here. The rest is up to you."

Santiago thought for a moment before responding. "You're counting on my brother not coming after me, aren't you?"

"With my help you'll be in Key West before he realizes she's missing."

"What are your reasons?"

"It's a risk. The alternative is worse."

"So you'd place your sister's life at stake rather than have her be my brother's mistress?"

"I know you're a clever man. I'm counting on you to save your own life and, in the process, Ana's."

"Maybe I'll just trade her in for my freedom."

"No. We both know none of us could ever agree to that."

Santiago smiled. "How old are you, Ernesto?"

"I have twenty-one years on this earth."

"Let me tell you something. If it were me instead of my brother, and this scene was in reverse, I would not hesitate for one minute to destroy both your sister and my brother."

Ernesto looked at him.

"Well?"

"I don't know you, but I know Orlando. He would not."

"What about the Americans?"

"Those two?" Ernesto said, pointing up on deck.

"Yes."

"That depends. How do you know them?"

"I don't know them. We met at the dancing club. I speak English. I was curious as to what they were doing here. I invited them to come back here and have a drink."

"What are you doing here, Santiago?"

"I came to see my mother. Didn't Ana tell you that?"

"And take her back with you?"

"No, she's better off here. I just wanted to see her once before she dies."

"When will you leave?"

"I would like to go as soon as I have seen her."

"I'll post a watch on this boat, and if you try to leave before I can get Ana here, you'll not get far, I promise you. I will give you thirty-six hours. Tell one of my men you need to see me when you are ready."

"What about those two on deck?" Santiago asked.

"I know who they are. I will keep your meeting with them in confidence so long as you agree to take Ana to Florida in this boat. If you do not cooperate with me, your friends will be at risk. Maybe I'll use the old trick you used with the Russians, and have the man swim with the sharks. The woman would be a big hit in the AIDS colony on Pablo's Island."

"Be my guest." Santiago said. "The Americans are nothing to me."

"It doesn't matter. I'll act as I've said."

"I'll need to see your papers," Ernesto said to Gordon and Kate.

The only light was coming from the normal lights on the guard-house of the marina. They turned out the flood lights when Ernesto gave the signal and walked away with Kate and Gordon in tow, leaving the Dutchman's boat in Santiago's hands and two unarmed soldiers on the dock.

Gordon handed over his passport and visa. Kate scrambled to get hers out of the small belt wallet she wore. The long black Russian made car they were in had no markings.

"You should be more careful with whom you associate, Mr. Cox," the young Cuban said, leafing through the pages of Gordon's passport. "Your visa does not give you permission to be in places like this."

"I wasn't aware of that," Cox answered.

"How do you know that man?" he asked, looking at Gordon and then Kate.

"We met him at the nightclub," Gordon said. "He invited us back to see his boat and join him for a drink."

Ernesto turned his attention to Kate. "You're a lawyer, too? Many of our lawyers here are women. My sister was going to study law," he said.

Kate nodded, but said nothing.

The Cuban handed them back their passports. "My men will take you back to your hotel."

ELEVEN

Orlando deChristo spent as little time as necessary in his home. His wife was the daughter of a member of the Council of Ministers. She was more of a communist than Karl Marx. Even her father joked about her ideological extremism. His children were being brought up to hate their father. No one, including Nurris his wife, would believe that if he told them, but it was true. The time he spent with Ana renewed his soul. She was very bright and her youth insulated her from the system of pedagogy he thought surrounded him in other places. His friends would have laughed at that observation. "You want her young body," they'd laugh, but that was only part of it.

He wished his older brother hadn't run away. In a real sense, Ana had taken his place. She was almost as smart. Orlando was not so stupid with women that he did not understand that she was using him as much as he used her. It was more of an even bargain than he had with his wife, Nurris. His father-in-law was worse. He was an old fool. She was just a fool.

Orlando was never going to be head of the Cuban State, but he intended to play an important part in the next succession. His position as a general was firmly rooted in the Communist Party, if not the Council of Ministers. Everyone knew that the Council, headed by his father-in-law, kept the politicians busy with so much nonsense they didn't have time to develop dangerous ideas. Orlando's power came from his control of the most modern divisions of the Army. They were the best paid and the best equipped of all Cuban military forces, and they owed their elevated status to him. He also cultivated support among well-positioned patriots of his own age who believed Cuba should reestablish itself in the Western Hemisphere and not seek support from outside forces. They all saw what happened when reliance was placed on outsiders, who could leave as quickly as they came when things became difficult. A half century ago it was Batista's alliance with the American Mafia, then Castro and the Russians. Both alliances were a disservice to Cuba, and the current leaders of the middle ranks were sure others were capable of worse.

These men and women, under the age of fifty, did not carry the intense emotional baggage that burdened their older comrades. Fidel Castro was neither their god nor a devil. He was a man for his time, and that would be his legacy. Orlando and his compatriots focused their concern on the future of Cuba, a future without any form of foreign domination and a lowering of the obstacles to international trade and investment. To be self-supporting, Cuba needed liberalized trade and foreign investment. Those Cubans too closely tied to Fidel's legacy, as well as the old men who long ago left Cuba, would be isolated and, if necessary, eliminated.

His new guard had to lay very low for now. When the time came, they would be ruthless in establishing a new order, based on rejoining the trade of nations and eventually producing more choice for the people of Cuba. Cuba's resource was its people. The wheels of State had become rusty, and fixing it would take time. It would work if they could keep the Americans out until they were ready.

Orlando didn't believe any of their plans would be opposed by a rational government in Washington, but he and the other leaders of his group worried about miscalculation and the propaganda they could expect from adversaries in Miami as well as Revolutionary Square, Havana. The apparent power held by the Cuban expatriate community in Miami was both a mystery and a source of frustration. Those in Havana who liked things the way they were could be silenced and neutralized, but the activists in Miami were out of reach. His group had tried to infiltrate the expatriate community in Miami to learn how they managed to exert such influence on the United States government in Washington. The effort had landed those patriots in U.S. Federal prison.

Orlando feared the activists in Miami would be able to talk the American President into military intervention when shots were fired in the streets of Havana. He felt his group needed better information. Cuban intelligence was not their friend. Six of the ten officials Orlando counted as needing elimination were old school Cuban intelligence officers. He thought for months about his brother, and what information or misinformation Santiago might be able to provide now that he lived in Florida. Suddenly, Santiago was in Havana. It was an omen.

One thing bothered him about Santiago's suddenly coming to Havana. Why did his comrades not pick up on his presence? Did José Hernandez know he was in Cuba? Were Santiago's old enemies just waiting for Santiago to make contact with others? Did they follow Santiago to Ana's apartment? He needed to proceed with great caution, until he understood completely what was going on. He knew that not all those in his conspiratorial group liked or trusted the military. Was he being kept out of the loop? If so, his position was precarious.

★

Santiago slept until the sun came up. Only when his thoughts cleared did he start visualizing his escape from the tight corner in which he now found himself. Start the engines and make a run for it? Not likely. Assuming the guards didn't shoot him, he might get to the end of the channel coming into the marina, maybe even a mile or two offshore, no more in daylight.

Waiting for Ernesto to play out his childish game would accomplish nothing, and probably get them all killed. Santiago refused to sit around on the Dutchman's damn boat and wait to be taken to the Palace of Pain or shot on sight. He had no idea what had happened to the Dutchman. Drunk and probably whoring his way around Havana, he'd have to fend for himself. If the Dutchman had been arrested, Santiago felt sure the police would long ago have come to seal up his boat.

Santiago ate a bowl of dry cereal, and put on his loose fitting night-time garb. The solution to his predicament surfaced while he shaved in the boat's galley sink. It was a big gamble, but the alternatives were far less promising.

He walked purposely down the marina pier and out through the gate along 5th Avenido. Cars, motorbikes, and buses on the streets created fumes of leaded gas that made his eyes water. Was it this bad when he was growing up in Havana? Or had he just become accustomed to the cleaner air in Key West?

He set a fast pace toward Old Havana. Ernesto's guards, armed with the ubiquitous cell phone, both followed, one on foot and another on a bike. He half expected one of the old Russian police vans to roll down the street, sirens blazing, to take him to the Palace of Pain. He didn't let himself look over his shoulder, but he knew the guards were following.

He went straight to the apartment where he'd met Ana. It was the only safe house for him. Ernesto could not send the police there without involving his sister. Santiago gambled that he'd find Ana alone. If he was wrong, the gambit could turn out badly.

★

Ernesto Legra's plan to have Santiago save himself by taking Ana to Key West did not seem to be working out. His men reported Santiago's movements, and that they had followed Santiago to his sister's apartment, where they waited outside. This was not good, but Ernesto had little choice but to hold off. Perhaps the older deChristo was setting the stage for following his orders. If not, he'd deal with him later. Ernesto did not want to take any action that would place his sister in danger. She was going to be angry with him if Santiago told her what he'd asked him to do. He knew he could handle that part of the problem. Why should she believe the traitor over her own brother? But what was Santiago up to?

"I didn't think you'd come back," Ana said without any show of emotion. "It won't do any good for you to kill me. I told Orlando you're in Havana. He knows."

They sat on two wooden chairs in the corner of her one-room living space. Nothing separated them but the differences in age and outlook.

"Life is full of surprises, child. When will my brother come?"

"He doesn't keep to a schedule, you know. He likes to surprise me."

"Well today you're going to surprise him." He handed the girl her cell phone and said, "Call him."

"I can't. He doesn't want me to call him. Besides, I don't have his number."

"Look, there are two Defense Department guards outside this building. They work for your brother and they followed me here. They do not—"

"You don't know my brother. You're lying."

"Your brother's name is Ernesto. He is twenty-one years old. He and I met last night to discuss your situation."

Ana's face went white and her balance wavered on the old wooden stool. If she hadn't been seated, Santiago was sure she would have collapsed. He placed the phone in her lap, pinched her nipples tightly, and looked severely into her eyes.

"Call him."

"What are you going to do?"

"You'll find out soon enough, but it will be much better for you and your brother if you do what I ask. Now, call Orlando."

"I need to call another number and leave a message."

He pressed the phone into the palm of her hand. "Make the call."

"Please tell Orlando his package is here," she said, and waited a moment before saying, "Thank you," and signing off. "He will know

now that you are here with me," she said, placing her phone into Santiago's outstretched hand.

★

The two guards following Ernesto's instructions were standing in the shadows of the veranda in front of the crumbling but still gracious apartment building when General Orlando deChristo's car drove up. Without getting out of the car, the General opened the back window and addressed the senior of the two soldiers.

"What are you doing here?"

"We're instructed to keep a foreigner under surveillance," the one on the bike answered in a voice that showed more than a little apprehension.

"Whose instructions?" Orlando demanded.

"An officer."

"Who?" Orlando said in a voice that made the soldier wish he were some other place at that moment.

"He is with the Ministry, sir, in the intelligence section."

"You are not attached to intelligence."

"No, sir, we are regulars."

"Then you are under my command. Go back to your units and stay the hell out of here . . . on the double, and I won't ask for your names."

Both soldiers, who were only boys—maybe seventeen—moved quickly and were down the street in seconds. The one on foot was faster than the one on the bike.

Orlando came to this place often. His impressive looking car being there on this morning aroused no special interest among the three or four ladies hanging wash on the narrow balconies outside their apartments. He directed his driver to go to the usual place for a coffee, got out of the car, and strolled into the building.

He moved quickly up the stairs to Ana's apartment. Without a moment's hesitation and with his pistol drawn, he burst into her room. Ana was in his field of vision, but he saw only his brother. He stopped a stride inside the open door, making sure the unarmed man was Santiago. Only then did he look at Ana.

"Orlando," Santiago said, "thank you for coming."

Ana thought Santiago had made a joke. She laughed so hard, both men thought she was crying. When they realized how out of context the remark was, they laughed with her.

"Santiago," Orlando said, "you're as foolish as ever, I see."

Santiago raised both arms with his hands palms up. "And you are as prompt as ever. We don't change much, do we?"

Orlando looked at Ana. "Go for a walk, my pet, but do not call Ernesto or speak with anyone. Leave your cell phone here."

"Please, do not involve Ernesto. He—"

"Do as you're told. My brother and I need to talk."

"Who are you really? And what are you, Brother?" Orlando asked as soon as Ana was out of earshot.

"You forgot a more fruitful question. And do you mind putting the gun away?"

Orlando slid the pistol into its leather holster, but didn't snap the buckle. "You mean what you're doing here?"

"Yes. That's what everyone else wants to know."

"Who are the others?"

"Her brother for starters," Santiago said.

That explained the presence of the two guards Orlando met downstairs. "Who else?" the General asked.

"The two American lawyers, allowed in by the Foreign Ministry and now chummy with the Second Minister of Defense."

"Say that again, Santiago. What two Americans do you talk about?"

"I am surprised you don't know, Brother, a man in your high position. There are two lawyers from Washington here. They've had meetings with Eduardo Santos and José Hernandez, both formally and at the Miramar Casa."

Orlando was stunned at the mention of José Hernandez. If what Santiago was telling him was true, Orlando's fears of being left out of the loop had become reality. "How do you know this?" he said, looking closely at his brother.

"That comes close to your other two questions."

"You're working with the American government?"

"No, but I've met the two lawyers. One is a young woman who came to me in Key West to ask for my help in assisting the family of the man I fished with. The other is her boss."

"What are they doing in Havana?"

"She's been interviewing fishermen on the docks to gather evidence for a matter involving the family I mentioned. The boat I was working on sought refuge during a storm last year. The U.S. Coast Guard stopped us on our way back to Key West. They assumed I boarded here, and arrested the captain. Transporting passengers from Cuba to the U.S. is a serious matter these days. The captain of the vessel also lost his boat, torn apart as they searched for drugs. The Church was helping them and hired the lawyer to fight the government's case. They're here gathering evidence, but the man also has had at least three meetings with the Ministry of Defense."

"How do you know all of this? Did they tell you?"

Santiago shrugged. "I guess they must have. How else would I know?"

"Who do they see there?"

"I told you."

Orlando paused. "What were their dealings with Santos?" he asked.

"How do I know?"

"Can you find out?"

"From whom? The two Americans?"

"I don't expect Santos will tell you."

"No, I guess not," Santiago said as he laughed. "If those two are here on official business, I doubt they'll tell me either."

"Say again, who are they?"

"The man is a lawyer in Washington. The woman works for the same firm. She's attractive and much younger. You know how that works, Brother," he said, a knowing smile crossing his face.

Orlando ignored his brother's visceral jab. "What happens if I take them for a little ride in the country?"

"I think a little sugar might work better. Anyway, if you get rough, it might allow Santos to do some things you wouldn't want."

Orlando was silent. He thought it might serve his compatriots right. They trusted him so little. He would teach them. "I want to speak with these two. Can you get to them?"

"You scare me sometimes, Orlando. What do you have in mind?"

"First tell me whose side you're on."

"You know me," Santiago said. "I don't take sides."

"This time you'll have to. Much has happened since you ran away, Santiago. Do you not hear rumors in Miami?"

"Rumors are rumors. I pay no attention."

"You said you were taken by the U.S. Coast Guard. How did you avoid being sent back here if you are not working with the Americans?"

"The usual. They let me repatriate."

Orlando seemed to realize suddenly that he was still standing. He moved a few feet to one side and took a seat near his brother. He spoke in a soft voice. "Santiago, what would the United States do if there was an armed revolt taking place in Havana?"

Santiago looked caustically at his brother. "Don't you have any beer around here?"

Orlando pointed behind the curtain at the rear of the room. "Back there. Get me one, too."

Santiago brought out four Mexican Coronas at room temperature. "You live well, Brother," he said, carefully opening two and handing one to the General. He put the other two on a small two-legged table, which was leaned against the wall to keep it upright.

"So what would they do?" Orlando repeated.

"I don't know. In Miami, there's a man called The Orphan. He's well known to Eduardo Santos' people. He has connections in Washington. He would probably try to get the U.S. to come in on the pretense it will be an anti-American *coup*. Then The Orphan would try to angle himself into the mix. Other than that, I don't know what the reaction would be. Our American lawyer friend might have some views on that question."

"Can you ask him? Feel him out?"

"I can if you'll get Ana's brother off my back."

"What do you mean?"

Santiago knew his brother well enough to realize he held Ernesto's life in his hands. He paused, considering his words carefully. "I've met him," was all he said.

Orlando thought again about the two soldiers guarding the building. "She told him, didn't she?"

"It's not a problem so long as Ernesto doesn't decide to become a hero of the revolution and turn me in."

As if on cue, they heard Ana's light knock. Orlando walked over and opened the door.

"Are you still at it?" Ana said, looking up at her middle-aged lover. "I need something from the box in the back."

"Come on in," Orlando said.

"Oh," she said, spotting the bottles on the table. "May I have a beer?"

"You're too young to drink beer," Santiago joked.

"But not too young to fuck your brother, eh, Santiago?"

Santiago nodded and raised his beer, acknowledging Ana's adroit comeback. He watched as she took one of the Coronas off the table, opened it, and walked over and sat on his brother's knee. She clinked her bottle against Orlando's and raised it to Santiago.

"It looks like you're friends again," she said, turning her shoulders to face Orlando.

"Ana, what have you told Ernesto?"

She turned and looked fiercely at Santiago, as his brother lifted the sixteen-year-old and turned her in the air to face him.

"Answer my question. What did you tell Ernesto?"

Ana sighed as if resigned to telling the truth. She knew Orlando would know if she lied. She'd tried it before on less important issues.

"I told him Santiago was here looking for his mother. I was

scared that night. I had no one else to go to. He won't do anything about it."

"Apparently he already has."

★

Ernesto kicked the wastebasket in his cubicle halfway across the station that housed a dozen of the junior intelligence officers at the Ministry. He'd been so confident that the trap he laid for Santiago would work that he'd given the man too much room to wiggle. Santiago had made a bold move, using Ana to get to Orlando. So the scheme to transport Ana to Florida was compromised. He needed to learn how much of this plan had been revealed to Ana before implementing the first part of his final idea to rescue his sister from the General's debauchery. He waited until he was back in his apartment before calling her cell phone.

★

The Dutchman's whore had taken her money and some of his, and left in a hurry after Ernesto and the soldiers had arrived at the marina. The two of them had ringside seats from the apartment the Dutchman had rented to entertain and bed the woman. They watched Kate and Gordon being held in the cockpit at gunpoint. When the floodlights were turned off, and while Kate and Gordon were being interrogated by Ernesto, the woman silently made her exit.

Since then, the Dutchman had been afraid to go near the boat. What he wanted was to get the hell out of Cuba as fast as possible. In desperation, he risked a call to Miami from the pay phone in the marina office. He was smart enough not to use Diego's name on the call. Both men spoke cautiously, assuming they were not alone on the line.

"Why hasn't he called me?" Diego demanded.

"I don't know where he is. The soldiers came the other night. Maybe they took him away. Anyway, I'm getting out of here today, with or without him."

"Wait one more day."

"Why?"

"Just do it. Did he tell you whether he found them?"

"No, but he was following someone, and he went to some hotel several times. I know that."

"Do you know what the woman looks like?"

"Generally."

"I want you to find him and tell him to take the woman like he contracted to do. I want it done exactly as we discussed. Tell him when he returns to call on the ship's phone. Why aren't you using it?"

"It's been disabled. All the wires were ripped out."

There was a long pause while Diego collected his thoughts and his patience. "Did he do that?"

"Maybe the ones who came in the night did it. Anyway, they don't let you use it from here."

"Call when you're offshore. Call through the Key West operator. Now find him and tell him what I said," Diego said.

The Dutchman knew he wouldn't do what The Orphan asked. It was too dangerous, and he didn't sign on to this voyage to die in Havana. Departure documents had to be filed before he could leave. He paid his bill for the apartment at the marina office, and returned to the boat. His ship's papers were not where he always kept them. "Damn Santiago," he mumbled through his teeth every few minutes, looking in vain for the pieces of sheepskin that were his ticket out of Cuba.

★

At first, Kate didn't recognize the composite of European tourist with dark glasses and large cigar promenading toward them across the expanse of the Melia Habana Hotel lobby. He was close to their location at the small open bar down one end of the lobby when she whispered to Gordon, "Don't look now, Gordon, but here comes Santiago."

Cox turned to the Euro fashion plate as he sat down next to

him. "Didn't we meet in Madrid last year?" the loud-voiced tourist said with a contrived Spanish—not Cuban—accent, for benefit of the young woman attending the bar. "Sam Delgrado is the name. What's that you're drinking?"

Kate was having a hard time keeping a straight face as Gordon said, "Madrid, Spain? No, I don't think so."

"Give my friends a drink, señorita," he said in Spanish, hoping his speech didn't sound too Cuban in its dialect. "And I will have a brandy."

The woman looked at Cox, and he shook his head. "No thanks."

When she turned to attend to Santiago's drink, he whispered to Cox, "We must talk."

"Santiago," Gordon said in a low voice as the three of them sat by the Melia Hotel pool waterfall in the semi-darkness, "I need to know what you're doing in Havana before I can address any part of what you've just asked us."

The Cuban looked at Kate, then at Cox. "It makes no difference why I came back here. What matters is why I went to the club where we met. I found a young woman in the place where my mother used to live. You met the girl's brother. He was the one who came to us on the boat. That night, he demanded I take his sister to the United States. I think you can see that this puts me in a difficult position. I decided to take action rather than sit around waiting to be arrested or shot trying to leave with or without this young girl. I went back to the apartment and arranged for the girl's brother to join us there. There were others with him who knew of my past, and that I would return to Florida. We negotiated. If I can provide them with intelligence of the sort I have asked you, they will not turn me in or insist I take passengers to the U.S."

Santiago's eyes shifted to all points of the compass as he spoke. Kate thought he looked like a caged lion, continuing with his long but fascinating answer to Gordon's question. Cox was no less enthralled with the Cuban's story, which he instinctively did not believe.

[154]

"Did you mention our names to these people? Do they know what we're doing here?"

"Yes and no. Yes to your names, but I don't really know what you're doing here, so how could I tell them?"

Gordon shook his head and shot Kate a raised eyebrow.

Santiago laughed quietly, "I gave them your party line, and they think, as do I, that a Washington lawyer such as you will have a good idea what reactions would be to a scuffle or two in Havana."

"You're asking us what our President would do if blood were to flow in the streets of Havana. You still haven't told me why this information is so important to you right now."

"Okay, okay, what if . . . a group of young Cubans in fairly high places were to take over the administration of this country?"

Gordon looked sharply at Kate, who was thinking this was what they came to Havana to scoop out.

"You mean a *coup d'etat*?" Cox said.

"Call it what you want, since there's bound to be some fighting. The bullets won't be flying for very long."

"Any help from outside the country?" he asked, looking at Kate again, as if making sure she was getting it.

"No China, no Venezuela, no USA—just Cubans."

"Just native Cubans?"

"Yes, none of the Miami crowd."

"And your question is what would Washington do?"

"Yes."

"I don't know, Santiago. I'd need to know more."

An expectant but deflated Santiago said resignedly, "What would you need?"

"What's your role in this? Kate and I thought you were working for the Miami interests. Is this their business?"

"No."

"Then whose?"

"I can't tell you that. Anyway, you don't want to know."

"I need to—"

"No," Santiago said, anger in his voice. "It's my turn, Dr. Cox."

Cox and Kate focused on the Cuban's face, lighted in the reflections coming off the pool.

"You are not here to interview fishermen. You've been in meetings with the infamous Eduardo Santos, the number-two man in the Defense Ministry. You didn't get in to see him without something more important to discuss than the old captain's case. Santos is the most dangerous man in Cuba. He's a man who owes his position to cruelty and oppression. Whether you know it or not, he's the sworn enemy of the United States and the future of Cuba as well. It would be quite easy to satisfy the expatriates in Miami. Just give them some of the money Fidel Castro took from their fathers. But Santos will not be satisfied until he's buried you, your friends, and all you stand for. So tell me, what are you doing here?"

Kate looked at Gordon, fervently waiting for him to work his magic.

"It appears we have a standoff, Santiago. You know why you're here, and we're beginning to doubt why we came."

Santiago showed his frustration by blowing a burst of air through his lips. "Well I think you have friends in high places, Dr. Cox. Otherwise, Santos would not have bothered with you. Take my advice. Do not trust him."

"Trust is a word I know something about, Santiago. I know it has to be earned. You can earn our trust by telling us what you're really doing here. If you can do that, we'll try to earn yours."

★

Ana met Santiago as he came to the top of the stairs outside her apartment.

"He's in there waiting for you," she said, and skipped down the stairway like the teenager she was.

Santiago pushed open the door to Ana's room and saw his brother sitting in the corner next to a lighted candle. He held a Corona in his hand and placed another on the small table next to him. Santiago walked matter-of-factly over to him and took the chair next to the open beer. They exchanged jokes, like they used to do as young men, before Santiago got down to the issue at hand.

"The lawyer Cox poses an interesting idea, Orlando. He claims to personally know the President. I tend to believe that, from my dealings with the woman. I think Santos has that on good intelligence or he wouldn't be spending his time with them."

Orlando seemed distracted, but Santiago continued without asking his brother what was wrong.

"The man, Cox, will ask the President to remove the Embargo. If that action is taken, it will be a signal to you that a Cuban uprising, clear of any foreign involvement, is welcome by Washington."

"Does that mean they'll stay out?"

"He made no promises other than what I've just said."

"You say he knows the President? Did she send him here?"

"It's possible. He doesn't seem very interested in interviewing fishermen."

Orlando turned to take papers from a small case on the floor next to him. When he shifted his weight, the chair collapsed.

"Why don't you get the girl some decent furniture?"

"Why don't you mind your own business? Do you want to see Mother? Ana can take you there when we're finished."

Santiago raised his hand in a salute as his brother gathered the pieces of the chair and piled them in the corner.

"What you've said is interesting," Orlando said, "but I have a more pressing problem." He stamped around the room.

"Ana's brother?"

"On my computer this morning there was a coded message. It referred to my relationship with Ana Legra. It warned me to discontinue or be disclosed for plotting against the regime."

Santiago knew the drill, but said nothing.

"Of course, it's Ernesto," said Orlando.

"He knows?"

"I don't think so. This is the kind of threat that's always made. Don't you remember? Being in the intelligence branch, he knows they look into these things whether there's truth or not. He's stumbled onto it. It's simple. He's just a kid."

"Are you certain you haven't let on to the other kid?"

"Ana? I don't think so."

Santiago didn't want to have all this information. It reminded him of why he left Cuba.

"So, my brother," Orlando continued, "you will take Ernesto to Florida instead of Ana." Orlando cleared his throat, acknowledging the irony in his order.

"Shit," Santiago said, clearly not pleased. "How do we get him on the boat?"

"I'll handle that. You just be ready to go."

So he was back where he started. Orlando's attitude seemed almost demented. He was allowing Ernesto Legra to dictate his actions, and Santiago thought this was very dangerous. His brother had been aware that Eduardo Santos had caused him, Santiago, his place at Fidel's side, and he seemed sure that Ernesto was just doing Santos' bidding. On balance, he'd rather take Ana to Florida than her brother. But he wondered absently what Carlos Diego would pay for a young Cuban intelligence officer delivered to him in Miami. It would make up for his not following up with The Orphan on Kate's innocent activities.

★

"Now you know what good lawyers get paid for, Kate," said Gordon.

"Judgment?"

"Sound judgment."

"Are we on the same square?" Kate asked.

"I don't know. Everything is below the surface. Who do we trust?"

"Yes, I know. Santiago shows all the signs of being between a rock and a hard place. I don't think we can trust him. What about Hernandez?"

"He's a mystery. Why would he tell me about the Chinese and

the Venezuelan conspiracies? I thought at first it was to gain my confidence. But why would he take such a risk? It really doesn't make sense."

"Well, no doubt about Santos, anyway. We know where he stands," said Kate.

"True, but in a way that makes him the most trustworthy. He gains from the action we take freeing those three Cubans from federal prison, and from the press release we issue when we leave. He even gains some false comfort from our cooperative approach. Maybe we've made a mistake not being more aggressive."

"How would that help? You've been no pushover. He knows exactly where you stand, and he can paint the President with the same brush. Is he the one making goo-goo eyes at Caracas?"

"He's behind the recovery of the naval base and leasing it to China for big bucks. I wouldn't doubt he's in the group looking at Venezuelan oil as well. But none of that requires a *coup*. The takeover is probably already set for the day Fidel kicks off," Gordon said.

"What did Hernandez say about Fidel Castro?"

"Only that his presence is not the force it was. I think the man's had a stroke or something. No one has seen or heard him in public in months, but he's not dead. I'd bet my pockets on that."

"So what are we missing?"

"There's an undercurrent here. Santiago said it. Hernandez hinted at it. Even Santos seemed worried about it. Not all his looking over the shoulder is focused on Miami. That's red herring. I think we need another session with Santiago. Do we know where he is?"

Kate hunched her shoulders. "He'll show up eventually. He always does."

TWELVE

Kate's mind was moving like fast water around a big rock as she tried to keep up with the rapid Spanish echoing through the meeting room. They'd been working for hours on a draft of the joint press release on which Santos had insisted. The Cuban ministers and their assistants were running words together and throwing in so many idioms that Kate understood less than a third. Cox had been in similar situations, and Kate watched as he turned his own lack of understanding into advantage.

Communications between the Americans and any member of the Cuban group were translated, but the real substance of the Cuban position lived inside their own language and the comments and arguments they thought were hidden from their English-speaking adversaries. Following this routine, whenever a consensus was reached among the Cubans, they'd deal with Gordon through the interpreter. Gordon, as a tactic, interrupted this process by focusing on one or two of the Cuban officials who obviously differed in their points of view. Years of experience allowed him to distinguish those who were the hard-liners from the ones who were disposed to make a deal. He could see it in their eyes and mannerisms without needing words to convey precise thought. Rather than let them reach common ground or allow Santos a basis for a position, Gordon interrupted in English with questions every time he saw a disagreement surfacing. He committed to memory each of the Cuban names and their titles. He addressed only Eduardo Santos, but he always used one or more of the other names to make his point. Then he watched carefully as what he said was translated into their language.

At first, they thought he understood Spanish after all, and as the discussion progressed they began addressing him directly with their points, usually too fast for the translator to keep up. Gordon seemed to know what they were saying without really knowing. In this manner, he obtained agreement on most of the points he and Kate had worked out in advance. Finally, Santos ordered the final draft to be prepared in both languages. It was at this point that Kate's knowledge of Spanish would be important.

While they waited for the draft to be typed, Santos asked to speak privately with Gordon.

"Dr. Cox, I have received information you might be interested in having. You know that we think here in Havana that your client, the fishing captain, was in fact killed by those who would rather you did not pursue his case."

Gordon nodded. This was the second time for the Cuban to make this point, although he still produced no evidence to back up his assertions.

"Now we have information that those same terrorists have sent someone to Cuba on a mission. That person is none other than the infamous Santiago deChristo."

Eduardo Santos let this sink in, and watched for a reaction before continuing.

"And do you know what deChristo was sent here to do?"

Gordon adopted his best poker face, waiting for the answer he knew would come.

"He was sent here to find out what you and Ms. Stevens are up to . . . and to kill you if necessary."

This information came very close to Charles Black's latest note to Gordon, delivered through the Church as they had agreed. Either this intelligence was being confirmed, or the Cubans figured out how Gordon and Kate received messages and intercepted the last note about Carlos Diego's plot against Kate. Gordon resisted the impulse to join forces with Eduardo Santos in an all-out campaign against The Orphan. Cox felt alone and isolated, and it was tempting to make such an alliance, but he needed more facts.

"Are you telling me, Minister Santos, that there is a man in Havana who is, as you say, infamous and bent on harming Ms. Stevens and me, and you have not apprehended him?"

"That's exactly what I'm telling you."

"So arrest the man," Gordon said, calling Santos' bluff.

"As you North Americans have found out, it is not always easy to find an individual. They can hide, sometimes right under your nose."

A few minutes later Gordon was back in the corner of the conference room where Kate was waiting. He told her what Santos said about Santiago, and that he again hinted that The Orphan killed the fishing boat captain.

"You know, Gordon, I believe that's exactly what happened. I believe those people were responsible for it. How surprised are you that the Cubans have that kind of solid intelligence in Florida?"

"If that's where they got the information, I'm impressed. Knowing that may be worth the price of this trip. But it's also possible they intercepted Black's note."

"Then why did he tell you?"

"He may have been showing off, or he might be telling us to stop messing about in things we don't understand. Then again Santos might have been making a down payment on the pardon of those three men."

"What's your guess?"

Gordon blew air out of one side of his mouth, and cocked his head. "You know, my bet is it was mostly just showing off, and trying to reel me in as an ally on this joint press release. What about the reasons he gave for having the captain terminated, that it would derail our case?"

"I would agree," Kate said, "absolutely for those reasons."

"Do you think Conner Omega was in on it?"

"No. I agree with you that Diego is a lone wolf. Maybe he does things expecting Omega to bail him out, but I don't think the Attorney General would be involved in murder or its cover up. What about Santiago?" she said, showing no apprehension at being his or anyone else's target. "What are we going to do about that?"

"Nothing, if we're lucky. The real question is whether Eduardo Santos has been giving Santiago enough rope to hang himself, along with these others he's been talking about. It's not credible that Santos doesn't know we've been meeting with deChristo. If he knows he's here on the island, he surely had him followed around the clock."

"You might be wrong about that, Gordon. Santiago has been in this game a long time. Don't you think he'd know if he's being followed?"

"Maybe he does know, and he's just using it for his own purposes. The mouse can play with the cat if he's very careful and gets the timing right. In any case, we've still got a problem."

Kate waited. "Which is?" she said when Gordon seemed lost in thought.

"Whether to continue playing along with Santos, or give Santiago's compadres, whoever they are, some encouragement. I think our use of the Church to send messages has been compromised. I think maybe it's time to go home."

★

José Hernandez excused himself from his guests at dinner in the newest hotel on the north end of the Guayaquel Beach. Many of the German, English, and other European tourists seated in other parts of the large dining room had heard the speech he gave an hour before, and they smiled and greeted him now as a local celebrity. When he reached his destination at the bathroom for caballeros, he looked to see if others were present before choosing a stall at the end of the toilet.

"The General knows," the voice from the next stall said.

"Yes, and he also is aware that the lawyers have made some kind of deal with the Ministry."

"Do you know what that deal was?"

"I do. It's what we thought."

"So we better have that meeting."

"Not right now. There's a witch hunt on."

"Santos?"

"No, actually it began with one of the junior officers in the group," and the speaker paused as if to summon courage for what he was going to say. "You're not going to like this."

"What is it? Speak up."

The speaker flushed his toilet as he heard sounds of another person in the bath. He opened the door and went to the wash basin. When the European had left, he moved to the stall where his companion still sat.

"The young officer is Ana Legra's brother. I think he has Orlando in his sights. I'll keep you informed. I should go and speak with Orlando, but I'm afraid he's being watched. If so, it would give us all away. We made a great mistake not taking Orlando into our confidence when we had the chance."

★

The taxi let them off behind three other cars in front of a ranch style house that would have been at home in nice sections of Miami or Santa Barbara, California. They followed a winding stone path up to and around a small courtyard bathed in indirect light and flowers of every color. Four or five couples sat at tables, drinking and quietly enjoying themselves. The scene posed a stark contrast to Kate's expectation of having dinner in some poor Cuban's kitchen.

They continued down a flight of stone steps into a backyard covered with straw hatch. It was a garden with tables and Japanese lanterns that hung from the rain-vulnerable woven straw roof. They were taken to a table in the corner, which was dimly lit, more for a romantic effect than for secrecy. On the table were two bottles of Beringer Champagne. One sat in a cooler, the second bottle wrapped in a towel at the ready. A note said, *All checks must be paid in euros.*

"I don't believe this," Kate said.

"Do you remember what the agent man who's been taking us around told us on day one?"

"I know he couldn't have recommended this place, because it doesn't exist."

"He said there's no lobster in Cuba. He said taking lobster is against the law and punishable by several years in jail. I don't recall how many."

She nodded. "Yes, he did say that."

"So how about a lobster dinner that doesn't exist, in a place that doesn't exist? Sound like Alice in Wonderland?"

"Maybe we're not really here either."

This was what Kate always thought it would be like. A romantic dinner on an island somewhere in the Caribbean with a man you could actually spend the rest of your life loving. One thing was missing. She had not disclosed her feelings to Gordon. It would probably shock him to death. Maybe he'd do to her what her mother had done to him. *Better come down to earth, Katie baby*, she thought to herself after the fourth glass of champagne. *On the other hand, a good start might be to tell him how you feel.*

She excused herself before dessert and the coffee to which she'd become addicted. Showing some effects from the champagne, she slid out of her chair, sidestepped to Gordon, leaned over, and kissed him with enough passion to raise the hair on the back of his neck.

"You've made the last few days the very best of my life," she said. "I'll be right back, so please hold onto that thought."

Kate never made it to the ladies room. She didn't hear or see the man who came up behind her as she moved from the lighted dining area through the overhanging bougainvillea. Her arms were pinned behind her back so firmly that one of her breasts popped out of the low-cut blouse she wore. A wet cloth was stuffed into her mouth as a second man seized her kicking feet and scooped her off the ground. He tied a quick loop of rope around her ankles like a calf roper in the rodeo. A heartbeat later, and without any more sound than her muffled cry and a pocketbook dropping to the pavement, her abductors hauled Kate out of the place and into a waiting car less than thirty meters away.

★

The note was pushed under the door to Gordon's hotel room between the time he finally dozed off and eight o'clock in the morning, when a call from the lobby phone awakened him.

"It's Lara, Dr. Cox. I'm here to drive you to Minister Hernandez' office."

"I'll be a few minutes, Lara."

"No hurry, Doctor. I'll be here when you're ready."

Gordon didn't spot the note until he came out of the bathroom.

Go home lawyer. Stay out of Cuba's business.
Your assistant will be returned to you in Miami,
if you go now.

"I'll need to speak with Dr. Cox alone," Hernandez said to Lara when she delivered him to the Foreign Ministry.

The young woman nodded submissively and took a seat down the hall near Hernandez' secretary.

José Hernandez seemed angry. At first, Gordon thought the man's enmity was aimed at him, but as they talked, he seemed as upset about Kate's abduction as Cox. Hernandez' concern focused less on Kate's welfare, and more on a breakdown in the system.

"This is the work of those criminals in Miami, Dr. Cox," he said, pounding his fist on the desk in front of him. Cox watched as the Cuban took a deep breath and his tone became more measured. "Of course you are welcome to stay in Cuba as long as necessary," he said, looking not at Gordon, but rather out the window as if trying to summon help. Then, suddenly back in Gordon's world, he continued with less truthfulness coming through in his voice. "Eduardo Santos has assured me his people are doing everything in their power to gain her safe return."

Gordon stood and placed both hands on Hernandez' desk and leaned over him. "I am putting in a call to Washington now. I will tell my contacts there everything I have learned while here, and that includes what you told me the first day at lunch. Everything is relevant now and I'm going to tear this place apart until we find Katherine Stevens."

Hernandez looked up into Gordon's face. His demeanor was steadfast and he didn't blink. "Does it occur to you, Dr. Cox, that this is exactly the reaction these people are looking to create?"

Gordon stood straight, not letting his focus move from the Minister's face. "I think you better explain that."

"You and Ms. Stevens have made more of an impact here than you may realize. There is no political force on these islands, or I suspect in Miami, which does not know you are here and involved in more than gathering evidence on the docks. Let me go down the list. It includes my Office; the Ministry of Defense; the Justice Department; all those in Miami who take too keen an interest in what happens here; and the Chinese and Venezuelan Embassies, who have been extraordinarily active in recent days, speaking with Caracas and Beijing. Not to mention any persons who might be planning some insurrection of their own, like are constantly the source of rumors in Havana. Let's think about this for a moment, you and me, and see if we can make some sense out of it. Who indeed would want you to leave?"

Cox stood erect and squinted at Hernandez. "Please go on," he said after a moment.

"Well, I don't think any of our Ministries had anything to do with it. This press release you and Santos spent so much time on was going to elevate his status within the party, as will your undertaking to assist the appeals of those unfortunates in your prisons. Although

I doubt his friends in Caracas like your being here as an emissary of your President, it is not a direct threat to whatever they may have on the table, or under it. No, I think the most likely source comes out of Miami."

Cox let the Minister's words sink in. He thought about the threats made before he and Kate had left Washington and the recent note from Charles Black, along with Santiago's completely unexpected appearance in Havana. "What you say makes some sense," he said to Hernandez, but his mind was stuck on deChristo. Santiago was involved in Kate's disappearance one way or another. If Gordon could locate Santiago, maybe he'd find Kate.

What Cox feared most, in spite of Hernandez' continued assurances to the contrary, was that the Cuban government would act without regard to the well being of the victim. Their priority would be to teach the culprits a hard lesson, not to save Kate. If the kidnappers were making a political point, tolerance levels would be even lower. As much as he hated to admit it, the best hope for Kate's safe return might be Santiago deChristo. Gordon held onto the hope that the man wouldn't let anything truly bad happen to Kate if—and it might be a big *if*—he could help it.

Gordon flopped into the chair in his room back at the hotel. He'd put it off as long as he could. It was time to face the music, and call Elizabeth and Bob Stevens. It was early in Los Angeles, so he called Kate's mother first.

"Hello," Elizabeth answered.

"Elizabeth, its Gordon Cox." He waited for the long pause to end.

"Gordon, what's happened?"

"We're still in Havana, Elizabeth. Kate's missing. She was abducted last night while we were at dinner."

"Oh, my God."

"I've been with the Ministries all morning. There's a ransom note telling me to leave Cuba, and she'll be returned to us in Miami. The police here think they'll have her back within a day. They seem to know who did this, but I'm not so sure. I'm sorry. I wish it had been me they took."

"Why did they take her?"

"We've been in talks with the government here. There are people here and in Miami who would rather we didn't do this. But the truth is I don't know, and the police don't seem to either. I'm pushing these people to do everything possible."

"What about the note? Are you going to leave?"

"Here's the problem. There's no way in hell the kidnappers can get her out of the country without giving themselves away. I just don't think that's going to happen. If they let her go here, there's too much she can tell authorities. I'm afraid my leaving is not going to help."

"So you're going to stay."

"I'd rather stay and keep the pressure on. That's my current plan. If I was half sure for a moment that my leaving would free Kate, I would do it in a second."

"I'm coming down there."

Gordon recognized the Elizabeth he knew in that voice. She'd never been able to bully him, and this time was no exception. "And do what?" he said. "Besides, you'd need to get a permit from both the Treasury and Commerce Departments to travel here."

"Will you keep me in the loop?"

"Of course."

"Have you called Robert?"

"Not yet. I'll do that in a couple of hours."

"No, get the lazy bastard out of bed."

Gordon laughed to himself. That was Kate's mother through and through. "Okay, Elizabeth, I'll call now."

"No, don't bother. He won't answer the phone before nine. I'm sorry, but this is so distressing."

"We'll get her back. I promise you I'll do everything under the sun to make it happen."

"I believe you, Gordon. Kate idolizes you. You know that, don't you?"

The call to Kate's father lasted only a few minutes. Then Bob Stevens called back, and the two men spoke for over an hour.

Cox was exhausted. Both parents had taken the news hard, but had shown amazing strength in the positive, almost optimistic, belief that things would turn out well. Gordon wished he were so well disposed. He felt responsible for not seeing something like this coming. He was surprised, more than relieved, that neither of Kate's parents had placed the blame where he, himself, would have.

★

The guards were dressed in casual, almost makeshift, clothes. They took everything that Kate wore, and gave her a hospital gown to wear. She was kept barefoot to make escape more difficult. The guard who brought her food stayed to ogle and watch her eat it. They brought her water by the glass, and stood around until she drank it. The latrine was not out in the open, but that was all the good she could say about it. There was one small sink with water the color of *café con leche*.

No one gave her any idea by whom or for what reason she'd been abducted. There were one or two more prisoners she could hear down the hall. She asked to communicate with Gordon, to let him know she was alright. This request was denied with a raucous laugh when they finally understood what she'd asked. She slept fitfully. Men came in and went out at all hours. No one touched her, but the threat was always there. The only ventilation was in small louvers at the top of the side walls of the room, which meant she could hear what was going on in the rooms on either side of her. Those sounds were most disconcerting. Kate didn't want to believe what she was hearing.

★

The man on the fishing boat was not Santiago, but he clearly seemed to belong there. He was shirtless, and his shoulders were draped in circles of frayed wiring. Unable to fix whatever he was working on, he cursed and threw things around. This was no happy boatman, whoever he was.

"Do you take people out to fish?" Gordon asked, to get the man's attention.

The boatman ignored all questions that were put to him. Frustrated and angry, Gordon leapt over the rail onto the fishing deck of the boat and walked toward the man.

"Hey! Get the hell off my boat."

The man was broad shouldered and husky. His arms were muscular, but his belly rippled as he shouted. Gordon, who towered over him, stayed just out of the man's reach.

"Where is Santiago?" he demanded.

The man looked quickly at Cox, then for an avenue of escape. Seeing none, he came to terms with his situation. "I don't know anyone by that name."

"The hell you don't," Gordon said. "You're the Dutchman. You brought Santiago to Havana, and I know who paid you to do it. Now tell me where he is, or I'll turn you over to the Cuban police. When they find out you're working for Carlos Diego, they'll treat you as a spy. That won't be pretty, my friend. So what'll be?"

"Who are you?" he said, sputtering through the phlegm gurgling in his throat.

"Never mind who I am. You've got two seconds to tell me where Santiago is, or I go to the police."

"I don't know."

"You're testing my patience, Dutch. Do you think I'm stupid, or are you just plain dumb?"

"He hasn't been here in three days. I'm leaving today. I don't know where he is."

"Okay, have it your way. The only place you're going today is into what Santiago calls the Palace of Pain." As he turned to walk away, the Dutchman swung the pliers in his hand at the lawyer's head. Gordon anticipated and easily dodged the blow. The force of the Dutchman's swing cost him his balance, and the assailant fell to his knees. Strengthened by the rage and frustration he felt, Cox kicked the man in the face as he labored to get back to his feet. The boot snapped the captain's head back and he lost consciousness. Cox dragged him below deck, threw a glass of stale water in his face, and waited for him to revive.

"I need a drink," the Dutchman muttered as he regained consciousness.

"I need answers. Where is he?"

"Okay, but it's true, I don't know where he is. All I know is he left here night before last. There was a car waiting for him up by the gates, a nice car, not one of those old Chevys. I thought he'd be back, but he hasn't shown his face around here since. Maybe they caught up with him. I don't know."

"When was the last time you talked with Diego?"

The Dutchman eyed him suspiciously. "How do you know Diego?"

"You don't get it, do you? I'm asking the questions, and you're going to answer them or be arrested as a spy. Which is it going to be?"

"Okay, okay. I talked with him three days ago. I told him I was leaving. He said to wait another day, the sonofabitch. Now, I can't leave. They tell me if two came in, two have to go out."

"Santiago?"

"He's got to leave, too."

"Has Santiago been in touch with Diego?" Cox asked.

"Not so far as I know. He hadn't as of three days ago. Diego was pissed."

If true, that seemed to eliminate The Orphan as a suspect in Kate's kidnapping, but Santiago was still the best bet.

★

Ernesto Legra had ready a five page manifesto on the activities of General Orlando deChristo, the origin of which was vague and illusive. He knew what type of factual allegations tended to trigger aggressive response within the Cuban intelligence community. He'd seen their officers go after highly placed individuals alleged to have lined their own pockets at the expense of the State, or plotted against the Party or Party members. The truth was often clouded or buried under hate and resentment. Ernesto knew Orlando was not well liked within Ernesto's Department. Of all the regular Army generals, deChristo was considered too smart and far too arrogant for his own good. There was the added point that his brother, Santiago, was not trusted by the Ministry of Defense and had fled to the United States.

Ernesto painted a picture of subversion and intrigue. He used Orlando's dismissal of the two soldiers posted in front of Ana's apartment as proof of the General's attempts to hide Santiago's whereabouts. He pieced together a plot between the two brothers, which was driven home by the fact that Santiago returned surreptitiously to Havana. Ernesto's document embellished this part, suggesting a conspiracy with the infamous Carlos Diego in Miami. He tied in the abduction of the pretty American lawyer, concluding that this had been managed by persons loyal to the terrorists in Miami. Finally, Ernesto called for the immediate arrest of the boat captain who had brought Santiago back to Havana. Under interrogation, the captain might have some interesting facts to reveal. Everything was falling into place. Not even Santiago deChristo in his heyday could have done any better.

★

Santiago was surprised that his usual means to cross paths with Gordon Cox or Kate had not worked. Hanging around the Melia Hotel for long periods was bound to get him reported. He decided to take one more stroll through the grounds of the Melia in hopes of finding one or both of them. Time was getting short. He could almost feel the walls closing in on him. He stood behind a large palm tree to let two of the hotel security guards pass. He heard part of their conversation.

"Yes, the pretty one, up on the eleventh floor. She's missing. They think the terrorists took her."

"When did it happen?"

"I'm not sure, but she hasn't been seen around here since yesterday afternoon."

Santiago did not go back through the hotel lobby. He walked out the lower floor and crossed the street to the small shopping mall that was located nearby to attract tourists staying at the Melia.

He decided it was time to depart Cuba, and moved quickly through the shopping street and then to Marina Hemingway. As he approached the guardhouse at the entrance to the Marina Hemingway, two police cars made a fast exit, the way he used to drive when he'd made an arrest. As the second car sped past, he recognized the Dutchman sitting in the back seat between two policemen in all black uniforms. They were the Secret Police, Santos' men.

THIRTEEN

The President and Charles Black took lunch alone in the Executive Room near the Oval Office. It was one of the few places that allowed her complete privacy with one of her staff.

"How's he taking it?" she said.

"He's a trooper. I know he's absolutely devastated, but he's staying cool and rational."

"How was the note delivered?"

"He said it was slid under the door to his hotel room."

"Who does he think took her? In whose interest is it that they leave now?"

"That's the question. Miami is no longer at the top of his list. He thinks it might have been something unintentional. He said he's been amazed at the amount of information and misinformation that goes back and forth at all levels. The Cubans are quite outspoken about their knowledge of what happens in Miami and Washington."

"So, someone or several someones, who don't want us to let the current government off the hook have taken Kate Stevens with the intention of bending me to their will?"

"That's about it. The irony is that these may be the very people that we'd like to work with."

"Do you think they're smart enough to know we'd think that? Assume for the moment this is true. Suppose they understand the importance of abolishing the Embargo to the current government, but they want to communicate with us. How could they do it? They can't pick up the telephone, send an e-mail, write a letter, or fill up a diplomatic pouch, can they?"

"No, Madam President, they cannot."

"So how do they get in touch?"

"They could have talked with Gordon."

"Could they? Our whole plan down there was to turn him into an absolute red flag to the current powers that be. You can be sure those people have been following the two of them every step of the way. Should we expect they'd not notice this new group or person making contact?"

"Probably not."

"That's what I think. Please pass the salad dressing, Charlie. More water? So now what do we do?"

"Your scenario may be right, but there's also the outside chance that these are the men tied in with the Diego crowd in Miami."

"Well, that's certainly a possibility. It's more logical and less of a stretch."

"I can see you don't buy it, Rebecca. Why not?"

"I can't see the Miami hard-liners playing their ace on the first trick. This smells to me like a gambit from deep in the forest. Persons not used to playing with a full deck. Why don't we try it on for size? Tell Gordon to fly over to Nassau for the day, and let everyone in Havana think he's complying with the kidnappers' instructions. Arrange his flight over, and more important, the one back to Havana."

"He won't like that."

"Just for the day. Tell him we've got an idea, and that you'll meet him in Nassau near the airport. Take that scruffy FBI man with you. The one Conner doesn't like."

★

Lara Peron eliminated all the logical suspects in Kate Stevens' disappearance. She had come to respect the visiting law student, and the fact that she'd been kidnapped embarrassed her personally. She decided to look into the corners of her own world to learn what she could. She went first to one of the women who worked at the "home" restaurant where Kate and Gordon were having dinner the night she was taken.

"Maria, this young woman is a friend of mine, and I know the Foreign Office is concerned with her safety. It was my responsibility to see she was safe at all times."

"I cannot get involved in this."

"You don't need to. If you saw anything that you can tell me, I will not mention your name or act directly on the information. Did you see any of it?"

"There were three men. Two of them grabbed her and the third covered her face. Jorge, who works in the kitchen, was taking garbage out the back. He saw them putting her in the car. It was one of those long black Russian made cars."

Lara frowned. This was surprising news. Only the highest ranking officers of the government were allowed to use the three or four of those big cars. She was frightened by this news, but determined to follow the trail a little further. "Are you sure?" she asked.

"Jorge drove such a car when he served in the Army. He said the driver, a fourth man, was in uniform."

"Have you told anyone else about this, Maria?"

"No, of course not, and Jorge will kill me if he finds out I told you. You know we are allowed to run this restaurant for tourists. It is all unofficial. They will shut us down if there is any notoriety. My father's supporters will be most unhappy with us. You know what can happen."

"I will not tell anyone, Maria. Thank you for trusting me. Have the police been here?"

"The woman's friend, the man who was here with her, had us call the police. They have not returned."

That did not sound like the intense search that Minister

Hernandez said was being conducted to find out what happened to Kate.

Lara's next stop was the operations office for the Army car pool. She showed the card identifying her as a member of the Ministry of Justice.

"Do you keep a record of the vehicles charged out after sixteen-hundred hours each day?"

"Yes," the woman in a sargent's uniform behind the counter told her.

"How many car pools are there in Havana?"

"Ten," the sergeant said.

"I need information on one of the Russian staff cars, like you make available to my Ministry. One of our VIPs left a small case in the back of the car. He said it was driven by a man in uniform."

The woman looked at Lara sympathetically. "Why do we women always get these assignments picking up after the men?"

Lara smiled. "Yes, I know. They all need their mothers helping them."

"I'll see what I can find."

The sergeant returned after several minutes with a paper, which she handed to Lara. There were three Army Units and the Defense Ministry noted, along with the name of the officer to whom each vehicle was checked out. Lara immediately recognized the name of the young Ministry officer, fourth on the list. She thanked the woman and left.

Lara's first impulse was to take the information she'd uncovered to Minister Hernandez. He would know where to go from there. She was sure she'd found the connection. The more she thought about it, the more worried she became that her friend Maria and the nice woman at the car pool would be implicated and placed in a danger-ous position. She decided she needed to get one step closer to the culprit before going to Hernandez or anyone else in official capacity.

★

The first policeman laughed. "This is no fun. He told us everything without our even taking down his pants."

"Maybe he's not telling the truth. We better twist his parts a little," said the second.

Ernesto received a transcript of the Dutchman's testimony
answering all the questions that the junior officer had given the
implementers. "It was easy, eh?" Ernesto said as they handed him fifteen pages of typed text and a voice tape of the sessions. "Good job.
I'll see you both get a commendation for this."

"What do you want done with him?"

Ernesto hadn't thought about that. "Hold him for further questioning until we have checked out his story. Don't let anyone in to
see him, and he's to be kept in solitary until further notice."

The police guard nodded, and Ernesto left.

★

*Why does he always have serious meetings in beautiful places like
Nassau?* Charles Black asked himself as he and the agent arrived at
the hotel where he rented a suite of rooms. It was early afternoon,
and Gordon was already at their rendezvous.

"I need to call her mother and father, Charlie," Cox said as their
talks got started.

"Can you hold off until we see if this idea works? It will certainly help Katherine's position if it does."

"Okay, Charlie, let's move on. I'll hold back for now."

Black nodded to the agent with him, who took two notebooks
out of his case and gave one to Gordon. "Take a minute to read
through it. Then we'll bat it around."

Cox quickly read three pages of an outlined proposal. The
President's plan boiled down to her telling the world that Gordon
and Katherine Stevens were in Havana on a diplomatic mission, and
that the Cuban/American relationship was under review at the
White House. She would make a point of extending a hand to all

Cubans, regardless of who they were or where they resided, a clear signal that she was not dealing with those currently in power.

When he finished reading, Cox tossed the book on the table. He shot a questioning look at Black.

"The idea is they'll know to contact you again," Black said.

"Doesn't that depend on who 'they' are?" Cox asked.

"Maybe," the agent, Mason, interjected. "We're betting it's all a ploy by the current regime to squeeze more out of us."

"But you're betting with someone else's life," Gordon said, looking only at Charles Black.

The FBI agent belatedly introduced himself. "Mr. Cox, my name is Bill Mason. May I respond to that?"

Cox knew it wasn't an honest question. The man was just trying to ingratiate himself. Gordon looked at him.

"Okay, well, once we understand Ms. Stevens' life is being used as leverage to make a point, we can move from there to getting her back safe and sound."

Cox said nothing, but it didn't discourage Mason.

"We see two possibilities. One is she was taken by a terrorist group to embarrass the Cuban state, and the second by the existing government to make it look like Miami was involved."

Cox looked at Charles Black. "That's out of sync with what I've just read."

"You're right. The President believes this is the work of a subversive group in Havana who want things to stay as they are until they are ready to pounce. The idea is they'll find a way to contact you if she issues that press release."

"And if they do, don't you think the Cuban government will take immediate action? Where will Kate be then? If these people don't kill her she'll get caught in the crossfire."

"That can happen in any case," Mason said, again injecting himself into the conversation between Cox and Black.

Gordon was starting to show signs of frustration. Charles Black knew the signs as he watched Cox take a deep breath.

Turning to Black, Gordon said, "Is that all you've got, Charles?"

"Have you been able to relocate Santiago?"

"No, that's the whole problem. If I knew where he was, I'd know what to do. We might even salvage this thing and get Kate back at the same time. But this plan of yours is dangerous. You want me to go back to Havana and sit around waiting for them to contact me. I don't think the government is going to do that either, and if I don't cooperate with this man Eduardo Santos, he's not going to play it my way."

"You trust the Cubans too much, Mr. Cox," said Mason.

"They are all Cubans, Mason, the men you want to trust as well as the present government. Anyway, it's you I don't trust."

"Gordon," Black said quickly, "do the Cubans in government know Santiago is in Cuba?"

"Yes. Eduardo Santos himself told me. But they don't have him in custody. At least I don't think so."

"Could he have returned to Key West?"

"Not likely. The boat he came on is still at the marina."

"So he's in hiding?" asked Black.

"I suppose, but I really don't know. He may even be the one who had Kate abducted."

"Can we get to him through the FBI's contacts in Havana?" Black asked Mason, who was sulking after Gordon's remark about not trusting him.

"No, we can't compromise that group," Mason said, making the point firmly.

"See!" Gordon said, coming out of his chair. "You see now why I don't trust you people. You sit here with your little crystal ball, giving me bullshit that will probably cost my friend her life, and when you're asked for real help, you punt."

Mason responded, "Look, they took her as the way to get our attention."

"Well that was the wrong way to do it," Gordon said. "Besides, if it was an insurgent group that snatched Kate to stop us from dealing with those in power now, that makes them terrorists in my book."

"So what do you want to do, Gordon?" Charles Black said, recognizing Cox's upset determination. "What do you think?"

"What do I think?" Cox leaned back in his chair with a look on his face that Charles Black hadn't seen before. "I think this plan is dangerous and stupid."

"What do you suggest we do?" Black said, unable to disguise the apprehension that Gordon's facial expression evoked in him.

"Pray," Gordon said. He got up from the table and stalked about the room.

Black and Mason watched in silence as the lawyer roamed the room. The mood continued for several minutes until Gordon returned to his seat at the table and looked across at Charles Black.

"Tell her I'm going along for thirty-six hours. Then I will deal with the existing Cuban government, such as it is, with all its defensive aggression and misguided nonsense. I think the kidnappers, whoever they may be, are no different than any other terrorist organization." Gordon walked toward the door, looking back at Charles Black. "And now I'm going to call her parents. You guys do what you need to do. Then, I'm going back to Havana and see if I can find Kate."

Black nodded and said, "I'm sorry, Gordon. Good luck. Keep in touch as best you can, and let me know if you want me to do anything."

★

Cox hung up the phone after his second call from Nassau. Bob Stevens was becoming increasingly agitated, which was no surprise. Father and daughter had a close relationship. What surprised Cox was how cool and reasoned Elizabeth's reaction was. Her questions were right on the money. She counseled Gordon not to blame himself for Kate's situation. She only wanted to know what was being done to effect Kate's rescue. She ended their conversation by telling Cox he was like every other lawyer she'd ever met, long on confidence and short on promises.

★

Ernesto's motive had been to gain his sister's freedom from

General deChristo. He didn't realize how close to the real facts his trumped up charges were. The first strike he'd engineered was to haul in the Dutchman for questioning. To Ernesto's amazement and delight, with some urging from the secret police, the Dutchman not only established Santiago's presence in Cuba, but also revealed both of them really did have connections with Carlos Diego in Miami.

Armed with this information, generated about the time Cox returned to Havana from Nassau, Ernesto's next step was to obtain permission to bring in the General himself for questioning. This request, dispatched up the chain of command to the highest level of the Ministry, landed on Eduardo Santos' desk minutes before his meeting with Gordon Cox.

★

The two men met again inside the confessional.

"How did you find out?" the accountant asked.

"Santos called to tell me both the deChristo brothers were involved in the American woman's kidnapping. He ordered me to inform the lawyer, Cox."

"I told you he'd spoil everything."

"It was our fault. When he found out the lawyers from Washington were dealing with my office, and I hadn't informed him, he came to the conclusion we were hanging him out to dry. The clincher was when he found out his brother was in Havana, and we'd not told him that either. Anyway, what's done is done. We need to deal with it."

"Easier said than done. He's got to be killed or shipped out of the country. We can't have him spilling his guts to Santos' goons."

"That's right. I'll make arrangements to get him to Honduras."

★

Santiago's means to return to Key West was under police guard at Marina Hemingway. The Dutchman was in police custody. He'd have to make a try to take the boat, and make a run for it. One thing bothered him, more than any thoughts of failure, and that was Kate

[183]

Stevens' abduction. He thought about the first time he'd met her, and the innocent questions she'd asked him about himself and Cuba. He decided he owed it to her, and to himself, to find out what had happened to her.

Santiago had not yet made contact with any of his old comrades in Havana. He'd heard that several of them did not survive his own departure by more than a few months. Raul Castro had proceeded to clean house, a project in which Eduardo Santos was only too pleased to lend assistance. Still, there was one place he might be able to obtain information on Kate Stevens' location, and whether she was even alive at this point. He'd take it one step at a time. If he were careful, it wouldn't make his own situation much worse than it already was.

He knew only that she'd been taken in the evening, away from the hotel. He figured it had to have been outside the Old City because too many people would see and hear, and there was no buzz going around the way there always was when something like this happened.

Santiago called the concierge desk at the Melia Hotel, in the manner he had done many times in his previous life in Havana. Only the name of the hotel and the time were different.

"Your desk made the reservations for Dr. Cox. Look through your records and tell me where you booked them for dinner three nights ago."

His path from there was similar to that forged by Lara Peron. His methods were different, but equally effective. When he too had the description of the car involved in the kidnapping, his knowledge of the dark side jumped him well beyond where Lara's quest could have taken her. Santiago knew immediately where Kate must have been taken. If she was still there, and had not been transported to the AIDS camp as Ernesto Legra had threatened, he would find her. If she was in the old leper colony, getting her off the island would be almost impossible, and God help her.

FOURTEEN

The thirty-six hours that Cox had promised Charles Black were up. He went to meet with the Deputy Minister of Defense.

"Come in, Dr. Cox," Eduardo Santos said, walking from behind his desk to shake Gordon's hand. "I understand you went over to Nassau. That's one of my favorite cities. Have you been there before?"

Gordon had assumed they'd followed him. "Once or twice, Dr. Santos," he said, "on business."

"As it was this time, unless I'm mistaken."

"You're not mistaken. I met with an old friend."

Eduardo Santos nodded. "Yes, of course. Please sit down, Dr. Cox," he said, as a waiter came into the room with coffee and small cakes. "Please join me in a cup of coffee."

Gordon took a mug of the strong Cuban coffee. "Thank you for seeing me this morning."

"No problem, Dr. Cox. I understand you have some news to share with us that might help in our search for your associate."

"I hope it helps." Cox described their original crossing of paths with Santiago in Florida, and their surprise to suddenly see him in Havana. He said Santiago came to see them the night before Kate was kidnapped and sought his opinion on matters involving Washington. He ended by admitting he'd gone to the marina to look for Santiago. Cox left out the meeting with Ernesto and direct mention of the people Santiago said wanted the information from him. He ended by saying, "So there you have it. I'm sorry I didn't get this information to you earlier, but frankly I didn't think any of it significant at the time."

"What you say is very interesting, Dr. Cox. Were you aware that Santiago deChristo has a brother here in Cuba?"

"No, I didn't know that," Gordon said honestly.

"Yes, well, his name is Orlando, and he is a high ranking officer in the Cuban Army."

Gordon connected the dots.

"You will recall I spoke to you of Santiago deChristo when we last met," he said, showing annoyance at having been toyed with by Cox at the time.

Cox nodded affirmation, and Eduardo Santos continued.

"Unknown to me then, one of our bright young intelligence officers had Santiago under surveillance. Had we known this earlier, we might have avoided this unfortunate business with Ms. Stevens."

I wonder who the bright young officer could be, Gordon thought ironically. Then he asked, "Do you think both deChristos are implicated in Kate's abduction?"

"No doubt. I have signed an order to have Santiago found and brought in dead or alive. The General is to be held for questioning. It seems from our talks with the captain of the boat in which Santiago came to Marina Hemingway, who is no friend of yours I might add, that they were also working in collaboration with the terrorists in Miami. Kidnapping your dear friend to obtain political leverage was an act of terrorism, was it not?"

"Minister Santos, I would like to be with your men when they go to rescue Kate."

"That will not be possible, Dr. Cox. I'm sure you understand how difficult it would be for our people to have someone along who is untrained in such matters and does not even speak the language."

"But . . ."

"I assure you we will take every precaution to safeguard Ms. Stevens. I do not want her hurt. The element of surprise will help us get to them before they can harm her. Leave it to us, please."

Gordon left the Defense Ministry with a sickening feeling in the pit of his stomach. Now that the Cuban police had the Dutchman's testimony implicating Miami, it was not in Santos' interests to make sure Kate was not hurt. Her rescue had become unimportant. Gordon's worse fear was they'd make sure she was killed, along with Santiago. Then the propaganda machine would roll out, making his diplomatic venture to Cuba a disastrous failure. He felt helpless to do anything for Kate. He had a call to make to Charles Black. Before doing so, he decided to pay a visit to José Hernandez in the Foreign Office.

★

Santiago gained entry in the darkness through a confined space with a small opening near the ceiling that let in light and provided a minimum of ventilation. He walked in the shadows, and listened for something familiar to point him in the right direction. He heard voices coming from a cell at the end of one corridor of the small building, and smiled in the glow of some very good luck. He recognized the sound of Kate's broken Spanish. The other voice seemed to belong to one of the guards. He spoke in rapid Spanish, detailing the fun the two of them were going to have before he killed her. Santiago could tell from Kate's replies that she didn't understand anything of what the man was saying.

Santiago hid and watched as a single guard made his rounds. He paid close attention to his interaction with Kate, and in which arm he held his gun.

Kate awakened from a nightmarish sleep to see Santiago standing over her.

"Come on, get up, señorita. Quick, before more of them come."

She scrambled to her feet, and followed Santiago and the man he held at gunpoint out the door of her room. He threw her a weapon, which she caught out of reflex.

"Use it if you have to, and stay close to me."

She ran barefoot along the outside of the building and into an underground tunnel. Kate heard a commotion behind them, and knew her escape had been noticed. Their hostage slowed them down, but Santiago was in no hurry to let him go. A few hundred feet later they came out of the tunnel and into a grove of trees with a courtyard beyond.

Santiago knocked the guard unconscious with a well-aimed blow to the back of the head. He led Kate through one of the main buildings adjacent to the courtyard and out the main gate to the compound. In three minutes Kate and Santiago were out of sight down the road and across a series of natural ditches. The next order of business was to find Kate some clothing.

They didn't need to look far. Santiago climbed up the brick facing of a nearby apartment building, and threw down to Kate everything he could quickly take from the line of laundry hung out to dry overnight. They stopped next at a fountain in a nearby park, and Kate washed off as much of the accumulated dirt as she could.

"Where are we going?" she asked, wiping her face with fountain water and an unstained corner of the sack she still wore as a shirt over her new pants.

"Key West." said Santiago. "Can you run in bare feet?"

He took off before Kate could answer or question him further. She wanted to get back to the Melia Hotel, but she had no idea where they were or whether Gordon would be there. She ran hard to keep up.

They found a motorbike in front of a half-restored building. Santiago quickly hot-wired the bike. He motioned Kate to get on the back as he revved up the motor. They careened down side streets in Santiago's mad dash for Marina Hemingway. Twenty minutes later they reached the guardhouse in front of the marina. Santiago turned hard left and sped along the pier until they arrived alongside the

Dutchman's boat. No one was on board. As Santiago jumped onto the fishing deck, Kate saw a figure with a flashlight in his hand running along the farthest pier from their position. She assumed it was the night watchman, who was doing his rounds when they came in through the main gate into Marina Hemingway.

Kate fell to her knees as the boat's two engines roared to life. Santiago quickly cast off the four lines securing the boat to the pier. He threw the gears into reverse, turning the craft in its own length to head out of the harbor. Kate struggled to stay upright as Santiago guided the boat at high speed through the labyrinth of channels leading out of the marina. The night watchman began firing at them, and Kate ducked below the combings on the deck.

Once clear of the narrow harbor channel, Santiago took a straight course out through the opening in the breakwater. A ground swell coming in from the northwest made the ride uncomfortable at slow speed. Santiago passed close to a stake marker on the west side of the channel. He couldn't see the marker to starboard that he knew was there. A few minutes later, clear of the narrow channel, he pushed up the RPMs on both engines. Only then did he risk a nervous glance astern for activity onshore.

The night watchman would, of course, inform the Frontier Guard that a boat showing no running lights had left the harbor without clearance. Escape hinged on getting far offshore while it was still dark. Vectored-in patrol boats and MIG jets with air-to-surface radar posed an overwhelming threat. No doubt he'd been linked to his brother's activities. If not, he was still at the top of their *Most Wanted* list. The authorities would pull out all the stops to find and terminate him. A quick glance at the fuel gauges revealed that the Dutchman hadn't refueled. Santiago cursed, wondering how far they'd get.

★

General deChristo received a message from the man he had most respected within his group of conspirators—the man who, in his mind, would be the next head of the Cuban State when they were successful. The message directed him to an armed vehicle parked in the courtyard of his headquarters and to a phone inside. The man sat nearby on the other end of a closed circuit.

"Orlando, they're coming for you. The intelligence section has asked the Defense Ministry's authority to pick you up for questioning. The Boeing 707 is fueled and ready at Santiago de Cuba to take you to Honduras. A small cargo plane is ready at Havana to take you down there. You better get moving. God be with you," and the man disconnected.

Orlando called Ana. There was no answer on her cell phone. It was that damn Ernesto. He should have known something was in the wind. He took a car himself and went to Ana's apartment. As he expected, she was sitting in her room and was dressed to go out. He dragged her into the car. They found the first plane fueled and ready to fly east when they arrived at the military end of the runway at Havana airport.

Ana Legra was not at home when the police came looking for her. Her brother didn't reckon with the fact that Orlando's mistress was considered a cancerous cell within the upper echelons of the Cuban Communist Party, particularly with Orlando's wife and father-in-law. As such, Ana would be a delicious source of information. The security branch of the government's police couldn't wait to get their hands on her.

Orlando took Ana with him as much to spite her brother and his wife's family as to provide himself comfort. Their plane headed east for Santiago de Cuba, the de facto headquarters of the rebel group, because it was next-door to an escape route into the U.S. Guantanamo Bay Naval Base, should their planned insurrection go badly. Orlando and Ana landed there about the same time Santos' teams raided the General's headquarters near Havana.

Orlando's only regret was leaving his brother to their mutual enemy. Santiago would be dealt with harshly. There was a lot of hate stored up at Revolutionary Square, waiting for Santiago to unleash it.

On the runway, already fueled and cleared for departure to

Honduras, was an old Boeing 707 that had been bought by Castro from the Mexicans. Orlando and his coconspirators had secretly modernized it with all the latest electronic gadgets and a fully stocked bar and lounge where the first class passenger cabin had been. There were beds, lockers, and a place to show movies and similar forms of entertainment.

Ernesto's stage play had combined to force Orlando into exile until his friends were ready to act. Until then, he would live an expatriate life in a friendly country. But he was not going to Honduras. At this point, he was suspicious of everyone. Once airborne out of Santiago de Cuba, he ordered the pilots, at gunpoint, to take them to Mexico City. He'd be available to American intelligence there, for a price, and still close enough to Cuban soil to return in a matter of hours.

★

Gordon was in a desperate mood when he arrived at Hernandez' office.

"Here's some of that coffee you like, Dr. Cox," the Cuban said.

Gordon took the offered cup. "Minister Hernandez, isn't there some way I can be with the police when they go after Kate?"

"I know you are distressed, Dr. Cox. I don't blame you, but please listen to what I need to tell you. Then you will know as much as I do."

"I've been listening to what you've told me for over a week. For what? For nothing."

"Let me finish, Dr. Cox."

"Go ahead," he said.

"It seems Ms. Stevens is in the custody of the man you know as Santiago deChristo."

"Where? You know where they are?"

Hernandez used his hands to try to calm Gordon down. "They are being sought, and no doubt will be found, hopefully in her case, alive."

Cox was stunned. He'd been sure Santiago was the key to finding Kate, but he didn't expect him to be directly involved.

"This is all I know at present, Dr. Cox. I will keep you informed, and you are welcome to stay here as long as you want."

★

Santiago urged the sport fishing boat ahead at full throttle heading NNE at twenty-seven knots. It leapt from the crest of one wave to the next with bone-jarring abandon, leaving behind a wake of brilliant phosphorescence. He knew that wake created a giant Magic Marker, highlighting their position from three hundred yards astern. It made their position brilliantly evident from the air on such a clear night. But he needed to run at top speed to get far enough offshore to widen the search pattern. Only then could he chance shutting down the engines and drift until daylight. Every yard made good increased their chances of survival. The longer he avoided being spotted, the better the odds of reaching Key West in one piece.

★

Lara was called to the Foreign Minister's office. She waited for thirty minutes until Hernandez finally called her into his quarters.

He said nothing at first, as if searching for the words to address her. Finally he broke the heavy silence.

"Lara, I am happy you are alive. Next time you decide to become a Secret Police person, please let me know so I might dissuade you."

Lara nodded, but said nothing. There were too many things that didn't add up. If she'd learned anything from the actions she'd taken, it was to keep your mouth shut until you were sure you knew those who were friends and those who were enemies.

"Now the criminals who made this abduction have escaped," Hernandez continued, "and the woman Kate Stevens is still not accounted for. I fear the worst for her well-being."

Lara could not believe what she was hearing. Hernandez seemed to be saying that it was her fault. But how did the Foreign Ministry find out Kate was being held incommunicado by persons who had to be associated with the government? And who authorized the American's release? She wanted answers to these and other questions, but not so fervently as to get herself killed. She knew she'd had a close encounter with extreme sanction.

"You will need to attend to Dr. Cox as you have been doing. We will keep him informed as this all plays out, and it will be your job to look after him. But please no more of these heroics."

★

Santiago raced on for an hour and a half, while Kate searched the spaces below for more suitable clothing. She replaced the prison garb with an oversized sweatshirt she found tucked away up forward where the Dutchman had bedded down.

Santiago began to think they might make it all the way to Key West when the first MIG came in high from the south. He cut both engines and the boat slowed abruptly to five knots, then two. Within a few minutes, they were drifting and no longer leaving a trail of plankton glowing in the turbulence of their wake and marking their position.

With the roar of the two engines reduced to a purr, the Cuban heard the drone of a small gunboat off to the south. They were looking for him further inshore. He resisted the temptation to renew his high-speed course, even though he thought time was not in their favor.

"Why'd we stop?" Kate said.

"You saw the light behind us in the water. It gives us away from the air."

"But won't they catch us if we stay here?"

"That is our . . ." he searched for the English word.

"Dilemma," Kate said.

"Yes."

Kate saw the problem. She waited, wishing she were back in the Melia Hotel with Gordon, and wondering why she'd trusted this man.

The Cuban's commanding voice brought her back to the

moment. "Go below," he ordered. "Pick up everything you can see that we can eat or drink. Bring it up here, and be quick. No lights."

Kate went down and rummaged around where she'd seen things earlier, collecting all the items she could find.

Santiago dragged the life raft out from its canister and inflated it. He checked the contents of the abandon ship bag encased inside. It contained a handheld VHF radio with batteries, a search light, flares, a small hand held water maker, a reflecting mirror for signaling, a compass, a GPS receiver, some fishing gear, canned food, and a repair kit for the raft. Kate added two jugs of water, some packaged food, and two six-packs of beer, which brought a thumbs-up response from the Cuban. He added an emergency radio beacon and some fishing lures.

He launched the raft from the stern of the drifting boat and tied it off with a light line. He put a loaded revolver in his pocket, and left the other weapons on deck. He was in too much of a hurry to push them over the side.

Kate was next. Santiago told her to trust him and do what he said. He pushed her through the open slat in the boat's transom and into the life raft. Kate held on for dear life as the fishing boat rose above her, bucked over the top of a wave, and then dropped below her in the seaway.

Santiago took the line to the raft in his hands, put the sport fisherman on autopilot, set the course at NE and the speed at twenty-five knots, and jumped overboard. The boat shot forward on course as Santiago pulled himself to the raft with the line. He timed his move with the top of a wave and somersaulted inside, coming to rest alongside a wide-eyed Kate.

From Gordon's lap, to prison, to a life raft in the middle of that Gulf Stream that had stood out so brilliantly in the opening sequence of her film, Kate's life was moving in the wrong direction. She leaned back on her elbows and blew a strand of hair from her right cheek. She'd managed many times to come back from oblivion on the tennis court. She'd do the same now in the middle of the damn ocean. She wondered if the NASA satellite was taking their picture.

Santiago caught his breath, and took stock of their situation. The seas were running at two to three feet, there was a warm breeze, and at least one of the life raft's occupants was in his element.

He rambled through his thoughts as they came to him.

It would be daylight in a few hours. Meanwhile, the Gulf Stream current carried their bright orange raft at close to three knots on a course offshore Key Largo, and close in to the Keys as the Gulf Stream current bends slowly ENE and finally north around the Florida peninsula. The currents would take them close in some 180 nautical miles away. They would make the trip in five to six days, assuming a Cuban gunboat or the United States Coast Guard didn't spot them in the interim.

Surviving that amount of time in the open ocean with nothing but a small life raft between her and the bottom of the sea, seemingly miles below, was more than Kate could imagine. Santiago pointed out that the raft was well equipped. He reminded her that he knew how to catch fish. Kate wasn't sure of anything but the rubber boat she sat in. That was enough for the moment. She'd take it one point at a time, and learn to survive at sea the way she often had been forced to do on the tennis court.

★

Twelve nautical miles to the northeast of Kate and Santiago, the MIG flight wing leader decided not to wait for the hour it would take to get a gunboat into the area. By that time, he would be recalled to base and would miss all the fun. He radioed his wingman, and the two went in for a strike. He came around in a low altitude turn, following the phosphorescent wake right up to the speeding sport fisherman. No need to waste one of the few air-to-surface missiles the Chinese had provided his air group. This would be good gunnery practice.

As he fired, he watched the bullets walk up the path of the boat's wake and tear huge pieces from the flying bridge. He idly wondered if he'd hit any of the people on board. Apparently not, as the boat sped on into the night. As he pulled up to make another run, his wingman followed in on the same line. The second MIG pilot got lucky. His bullets penetrated one of the fuel tanks under the aft deck, and the boat exploded into a mushroom cloud of orange flames and black smoke.

★

Kate looked at the Cuban, alarmed by the noise and blinding flash from the distant explosion of the boat's gas tank.

"Santiago! How far away was that?"

He didn't answer her question. "That was our boat, señorita. They'll stop searching for us now."

★

"Scratch one traitor," the wingman signaled his commander. The two jets formed up, made one final pass over the burning vessel to make sure the job was done, and headed back to base.

★

The Cuban government driver took Gordon to the Ministry of Defense. Gordon recognized the entrance to Eduardo Santos' office. He tried to redirect the driver. Señor José Hernandez was with the Foreign Office, not the Defense Ministry. The driver shook his head. He didn't understand English.

As the car pulled up in front of the large building, Gordon was surprised to see Lara Peron waiting by the entrance.

"Dr. Cox, please come with me. Minister Hernandez is with the Deputy Minister of Defense. He will see you shortly."

Gordon waited impatiently. His antennas were transmitting nothing good. Lara seemed worried in the extreme, and avoided eye contact. Ten minutes passed before Hernandez arrived.

"I'm sorry to summon you here, Dr. Cox," he said, "but I

promised to let you know what's going on." Then, turning to Lara, he said, "I will speak with Dr. Cox alone, Lara."

"I'm afraid the news is not the best," Hernandez said as soon as they were alone. His voice seemed heavy with anger and disgust.

Gordon braced himself.

"Unfortunately," Hernandez continued, "Santiago, with Ms. Stevens as his hostage, managed to avoid the police at the Marina Hemingway, where he took a boat. We are quite sure she is with him, and we are searching for them now. I will keep you informed."

"That's it?" Gordon said, his tone demanding more information.

"I'm afraid that's all I can tell you at this moment. We're conducting a full-scale search offshore. We believe Santiago is heading for Key West. Last we knew, Ms. Stevens was alive," Hernandez said.

"Who abducted Kate?" Gordon demanded.

"Dr. Cox, you have come here at a time when certain forces are at play. I can't identify exactly the people who abducted your associate, but I can tell you that my government, not Ms. Stevens, is their target."

"Who took her?" Gordon repeated.

"We will find them, and deal with them."

Gordon vented his frustration. "I don't give a damn what you do, Mr. Hernandez. Your Ministry of Defense knew these forces, as you call them, were a threat to Kate, and did nothing to protect her. I hold you and this government responsible."

"You have your terrorists too, Dr. Cox. Whom do you blame for their activities?"

Those who knew Gordon Cox would recognize intense anger in the man when he lowered his voice by several octaves and spoke very slowly, enunciating each syllable, as if about to administer a *coup de grace*. "I blame my government," Gordon enunciated, "when they ignore all the signs that are there, as you have done."

Hernandez' eyes grew large as Gordon rose out of his chair and moved to the edge of the Cuban's desk. The lawyer pounded his fist on the desk surface and used his height to lean over so that he was almost nose-to-nose with the Cuban. "You are not telling me all you know, Hernandez," he said, purposefully using the man's last name. "And you can tell your friend the Deputy Minister for me that—"

"You can tell me yourself," Santos said, entering the room from behind Cox.

Gordon turned as he would in court to address an opponent who attacked him personally. "And I shall," he said, turning his back on Hernandez and looking squarely at Eduardo Santos. "I want to know the identity of the ones who kidnapped Kate Stevens, where she is now, and what your government is doing to guarantee her safety."

Santos smiled, and motioned with his hand. "Please sit down, Dr. Cox. I will tell you everything we know," he said, casting a sideways glance at Hernandez as he took a seat in the remaining chair.

FIFTEEN

The car taking Gordon to meet his Washington arranged flight to Miami pulled up in front of the hotel as he gave his and Kate's luggage to the doorman. The young woman, Lara, was in the back seat. She jumped out, as if surprised to see that he was ready to depart. She greeted him with more warmth than when last they'd met in Hernandez' office.

"Dr. Cox, I am here to take you to the airport. If there is anything I can do . . ." she said, seeing from his listless eyes that he'd had little sleep.

"No, Lara, everything is taken care of, but thank you for coming to escort me through the last mile."

"I'm happy to be able to do that," she said, and directed the doorman to secure the bags in the trunk of the car.

"Lara?" Gordon asked. "May we stop by the Marina Hemingway for a couple of minutes?"

"I thought your flight was at three o'clock," she said, implying their time was short.

"The American pilot will not leave until I am present, Lara. I'd like to depart Cuba with an image of that marina fresh in my mind."

"I will instruct the driver, Dr. Cox."

The police were everywhere. The Dutchman's boat was not at its berth alongside the pier. Many of the visiting boat people congregated at one end of the marina near a small café. A cup of coffee and some friendly smiles from Gordon's escort yielded comments about a Dutch powerboat that left port early in the morning without proper clearance. The police took up the chase, as contraband or some other criminal activity was suspected, but the boat wasn't brought back. One man commented on MIG fighters screaming across the sky during the early morning hours.

"We're getting the hell out of here today. There's a revolution coming, sure as shit," one of the boatmen told Gordon.

Another described an armed search helicopter that landed in the marina before heading off on a course NE out into the Gulf.

"They either sank it, or escorted it into their naval base down the coast," he said. "Probably more of that rebel activity we've been hearing about on our SSB radio."

Lara called Hernandez' office from the airport, at Gordon's request.

"No, they have not found them," she reported. "They might be in Key West by now."

Gordon didn't like the sound of her offhand comment about Key West. It was the first time since arriving in Havana that he thought the young woman might not be leveling with him.

"You'd tell me the truth, wouldn't you Lara, even if it wasn't good news?"

"Dr. Cox," she said, sadness in her soft voice. "You mustn't tell anyone."

"It's alright, Lara. I'll tell no one. What's happened?"

"The boat was sunk last night by jet fighters. There were no survivors."

Gordon's lower lip trembled. He turned away for a moment, regaining his composure. When he faced her again, he placed a hand on her arm. "Thank you for being honest with me, Lara," he said. "I won't forget it."

Tears formed as the young woman struggled to speak.

"Apparently the boat did not stop when confronted by the pilots," she explained. "They fired on the boat and it exploded. It was very dark after the explosion. There could have been survivors in the sea, but it seems unlikely. Maybe their report was wrong about that." Finally, she added, "I'm sorry. I liked her very much."

★

The news of the destroyed boat reached Carlos Diego at the breakfast table. The good news was that he wouldn't have to pay the Dutchman for his efforts. With Santiago gone he could foreclose on the purchase money liens he'd filed on the toys given him. He was unaware that anyone was with Santiago, and was still waiting for the report on the two lawyers Omega told him were in Havana. "Plenty of time for that later," he reasoned. He had more urgent business. The news about the Dutchman's boat was combined with rumors of an attempted revolt among the Cuban Army Officer Corp. Diego began calling all the people on his list.

★

In the gray dawn just before sunrise, Kate saw that they were in no immediate danger of drowning. They sat deep inside the bulbous orange floats that formed an octagon. The raft had a canopy to provide protection from the tropical sun. At daybreak, Santiago rolled half of it back, explaining, "We need shade, señorita, but I need more open space to fish, and the rain squalls, when they come, will give us a bath. We will close it down if we get into bad weather, or maybe at night."

She nodded. What he said made sense, and he was in charge. She wondered idly what he would do if she objected to anything.

She tried to imagine what adventures the next few days would bring as the sun peeked over the horizon to the east. She wasn't frightened, but certainly felt apprehensive to be out of sight of land in such a small floating space, alone with a man she knew had a ruthless side. There was no point, Kate thought, in trying to maintain any sense of privacy. She and the Cuban were both dressed for the beach.

"Santiago, we don't seem to be moving much. It's hard for me to believe Key Largo is only three or four days away."

"We move with the ocean, señorita, not through it. You do not think we are moving through space either, do you?"

She understood. "What will happen if there's a storm? This is hurricane season isn't it?"

"A hurricane would not be good, but this raft is made to survive most storms at sea. We'll be alright," and Santiago went back to work setting up his fishing gear.

As the sun lighted up the early morning sky, the dragons of the night disappeared. In the early light the scene was quite beautiful. The sky was a deep azure, laced with tropical cloud formations that hung over the Gulf Stream. The ocean was a clear greenish-blue, and looked crystal clear as it lapped against the side of the raft in small wavelets formed by a moderate southwest wind. Sea birds flew in close, drawn by movement on the ocean surface. She watched Santiago prepare his fishing line, and it gave her an idea.

"Santiago, may I borrow your knife?"

"Sure, but be careful not to cut the raft." He passed the knife to her, handle first.

She sawed off the sleeves of the sweatshirt at her shoulders and her pants just above the knees. "Any use for the rest of these rags?" she asked, returning the knife.

"Yes, I can use it to clean the water maker," he said.

"Santiago?"

"Yes, señorita?"

"Is it alright if I go over the side and clean up a little?"

"Yes, but wait another hour. The sun will be bright on the water but still low in the sky. It will allow me to see better and keep a look-out for sharks."

Her bath could wait, she decided. Santiago's matter-of-fact mention of sharks unnerved her. "What's going to happen, Santiago?" she asked. "How are we going to survive out here?"

"We are on a slow boat to Miami, señorita. It's called the Gulf Stream, and it will take us right up along the Keys. When we get in close to Largo, or somewhere around there, we'll swim ashore. It may be four or five miles. I hope you're a good swimmer."

Kate wondered what she'd do for a bathing suit, but that seemed the least of her problems at the moment. She dragged her hand through the water, and was pleased to find it quite warm.

"This is the Gulf Stream," Santiago said, noticing her test. "It's probably eighty degrees Fahrenheit."

Kate looked at him, blowing a curl away from her right cheek as she did.

★

The first call Cox made once on U.S. soil was to the United States Coast Guard. He intended to follow up later by getting the White House involved. Gordon needed to be personally involved in trying to find Kate. He considered how to answer all the questions the Coast Guard would ask, while not revealing too much about their time in Cuba and their mission for the President. The petty officer on duty put Gordon's call through to the Command Duty Officer.

"I'd like to report a possible missing sport fishing boat, which I'm told left Marina Hemingway in Cuba bound for Key West, Florida a day and a half ago . . . Yes, of course, my name is Gordon Cox, and I'm calling from Miami. Here's the number of the hotel where I'm staying tonight . . . No, I don't know the name or home port of the boat, but I believe it was of Dutch registry . . . Where did I hear about it? My cousin is a priest in the Catholic Church. He knew I was coming to Miami. He helps refugees coming into the U.S. I guess they received a call from someone in Cuba . . . Yes, of course I know my cousin's name . . . Yes, at least one of the persons believed to be on board the vessel is an American citizen . . . No, I don't know what she was doing in Cuba. Just visiting, I guess. That's not against the law, is it? For Americans to visit Cuba? . . . Yes, of course, you can call me. Let me give you my office and home addresses in Washington. Please take this call seriously. There may be people out there who need your help . . . Yes, I'm sure you do get a lot of calls that are bogus. Check me out. I am a lawyer in Washington. You have my address. I'm sorry I cannot give you more information on this boat . . . Well do the best you can . . . Yes, I know it's a big ocean, and they've probably been at sea for several days now. Please do what you can, and we'll let the good Lord handle the rest."

He called the White House next. "Gordon, let me call you right back," Charles Black said. "Is the phone secure?"

"No, it isn't."

When Black rang back, he had the Director of the CIA on the line. "James Callaby, Gordon Cox," Black said.

The Director was anxious. "Mr. Cox, what can you tell me about the insurrection that's underway in Havana?"

"Hold on, James," Black interrupted. "Any news, Gordon? Have you found her?"

"Not yet. Look, Charles, before we go any further, can you contact the Coast Guard brass and get them on the case? I filed a missing vessel report a few minutes ago. It would help things greatly if you could lubricate the process."

"I'll do it right now, Gordon. Fill James in on the situation in Cuba while I'm on the other line."

Gordon started with Kate's abduction and took Callaby through to the time Santiago rescued her. "She was taken hostage by our friend trying to get out of Cuba. The Cuban Air Force went after the boat night before last. It's possible they sank it. The situation didn't look good when I left Havana."

"We have reports of aircraft activity off Havana two nights ago, and several explosions," Callaby said. "I don't have the satellite pictures yet, but we know something went down out there . . . Sorry, that was a bad choice of words."

"That's okay," Gordon said. "I've chartered a plane to go look for her, soon as I hang up," Cox said, as Black rejoined the call.

"Mr. Cox, I would advise you not to . . ."

Charles Black interrupted. "Good luck, Gordon. Anything you want me to tell the President?"

"You can tell her the current government was clearly in full control of things when I left. Now, if you'll excuse me, I've got to find Kate. Don't forget to follow up with the Coast Guard."

Cox called the Boston Archdiocese to warn his cousin that he'd played fast and loose with the facts. He told him to expect a call from the Coast Guard. Then he took off in a chartered Cherokee with an ex-Coast Guard search and rescue pilot. They spent all that afternoon and the next day out over the Gulf Stream, coming back to Key West to refuel. They flew a pattern between the Keys and as close to Cuba as they dared. Whenever they spotted a sport fisherman or an object that looked like a life raft, they went in for a closer look. Gordon hadn't realized how difficult it would be to spot an object on the ocean surface, even from a relatively low altitude. Conversely, if you flew too low, you couldn't cover large areas. After the second day, discouraged but unable to give up hope, he headed back to Washington.

★

Santiago and Kate were a good distance east of where Gordon was looking. They were drifting ENE with the Gulf Stream current, and a fifteen-knot breeze out of the southwest gave them an extra push. Their present course would take them to a point off Key Largo where the Gulf Stream runs fast and deep near the shore inside the rocks and whirlpools of Turtle Reef.

They made drinking water with a hand crank that reminded Kate of the ice cream maker her parents used when she was a child. She liked the uncooked Dorado that Santiago caught, cleaned, and hung up in strips to cure in the hot tropical sun. There were no more Cuban search planes, only an occasional airline jet overhead and ships that appeared off in the distance and quickly disappeared hull down over the horizon.

Kate had always tanned easily, and there was the occasional rain-squall that came along to wash things down and cool them off.

"Does it look to you, Santiago, like the rain shower over there is coming this way?"

"Yes, señorita, we'll get it."

The approaching squall gave Kate an idea, but she was uncertain about asking him. He seemed to guess what she was thinking.

"Why don't you take off your clothes and let the rain wash off the salt? When you're finished, I'll do the same."

That was a wonderful idea, Kate thought. "Will you look the other way, Santiago?"

"I will stick my head in the sea," he said. "Don't be too long."

Kate laughed as the first drops of rain from the squall came over the raft. Standing naked in the cool, clean rain, rubbing her fingers through her wet, salty hair, was as close to heaven as she was going to get on that day. Why didn't she think to bring soap from the boat?

Santiago sighed and nodded when she nudged him with her foot, signaling that she was through. "Now you will do the same for me, no?"

"Of course," Kate said, as Santiago was quick to remove the pants he'd cut to shorts length. She couldn't help noticing he was aroused. She wondered if he'd peeked at her little dance in the rain after all.

During the first couple of days at sea, Santiago was too busy organizing their survival to pay much attention to Kate. Since her rain shower, Kate felt she was under his gaze most of their waking hours. He didn't make any advances, but there was no doubt in her mind that he'd considered it. Once or twice their bodies touched in the middle of the night. She didn't think he touched her purpose-fully, but she couldn't be sure. She considered talking to him, heading him off at the pass by telling him how she felt. Maybe she was overreacting. He hadn't tried anything.

She decided if he made a pass she would resist, but not to the point of getting herself thrown overboard. On the other hand, if he forced himself on her, he might need to get rid of her to avoid rape charges when they arrived back in Florida. *Stay friendly*, she advised herself, *but not too friendly*.

Later that day, she offered to help him locate the leak in the soft-er pontoon that was losing air. They worked alongside each other, Kate trying to hold the air valve steady while he pulled a piece of tape tight to make the fitting more secure. He slipped and fell back-ward. As he did, the buttons on his pants pulled free. He saw her looking at him, and it was like a match had dropped on spilled gaso-line. He moved back to her. She tried to pull away, but his hold on her was tight and his arms were strong. He pinned her against the side of the raft.

"No, Santiago. I don't want to do this. Please get a hold of your-self." She squirmed free and rolled to the other side of the raft.

Kate's sudden move left the Cuban on his knees with his shorts around his ankles. It might have been the pants wrapped comically around his feet, or the strength in her voice, but he closed his eyes. "I'm sorry, señorita," he said and rolled backwards off the raft pon-toon and into the sea.

★

Santiago displayed no more overt sexual aggression. He spoke to her as if nothing had happened between them. That was fine with Kate. It was like losing a tennis match. You didn't need the opponent telling you how sorry she was that you lost. What almost happened didn't happen. Better just to put the experience in the bank and move on.

"Tomorrow morning we'll have our swim," Santiago said as Kate awoke to the early light. "The angle into the shore must be just right so we'll have the current mostly with us."

They ate an extra ration of Dorado and drank more water than usual to prepare for what they knew would be an ordeal. There was no *halfway*, no *almost* or *just about*. They'd make it all the way to shore, or they'd die.

Kate listened as the Cuban continued to paint a verbal picture for her. "Señorita, I should explain to you why I must swim for the beach. You do not need to do this. You can stay in the raft. As you drift around the bend to the north, you will pass many boats off Miami and Key Biscayne, all the way to Fort Lauderdale and Palm Beach. You understand that if I get picked up at sea, they send me back to Cuba."

"I understand that, Santiago," Kate said. "But I'm not staying on this raft alone, okay?"

He nodded. Further conversation was unnecessary.

★

Gentle breezes and blue skies are not always the case in the deceptively calm waters of the Florida Gulf Stream. The day before, a long cold front coming off a deep low-pressure system in the high plains, unusually severe for that time of year, brought heavy winds and rain into Dallas and New Orleans. As the raft closed in on Key Largo and the point of the Stream's final bend northward around the Florida landmass, the same front battered Alabama and the Florida Panhandle with hail and isolated tornadoes. The tip of this string of squalls moved in a comma shape southeast into the Gulf of Mexico. Now, late in the afternoon before their morning swim for shore, the first signs of land appeared in the distance, but the approaching storm painted the western horizon black.

Santiago's plans for making a landing at the northeast end of Key Largo needed to be put aside for a serious fight for survival. Another day and they might have been home free.

"The wind direction will swing around to the north. That low line of dark clouds will roll in here with high winds, possibly with gusts reaching hurricane force," he explained. "Waterspouts may form up. Heavy rain and lightning will dance across the water. The wind will blow hard from that general direction for as long as two days. All the while, the strong Gulf Stream currents will move the raft north and east, right into the full force of the wind, making for a very rough ocean. Come on, we've got to tie everything down," he said. "First, we'll take down the canopy."

They faced a long night. Surviving would be a challenge. Sailor's luck, they'd left all the life jackets on the sport fisherman.

★

"I hope you don't mind, Gordon," Charles Black said. "I know you've got a lot on your mind right now, but what you have told me is pure gold. We'll spend an hour or so with her, and then I've told the back-room boys they can have you for the afternoon. Tomorrow, she'd like you to meet with a selected group of Senators and a few from the House."

Cox looked like a caged animal. "Whatever, Charlie, I can't concentrate enough to do any decent work in the office. I might as well amuse your agencies."

The President was first. She grabbed and hugged Gordon as he came across the room to greet her. "God bless you, Gordon. I'm so sorry. I thought she was going to save you from yourself, but we couldn't save her."

"Don't count her out yet, Rebecca. Just keep those planes and ships out there looking for her. She'll turn up. I'm sure of it." Gordon felt the need to get on with the debriefing. Otherwise, he wouldn't be able to do it. "I know your time is tight this morning. Where do you want me to start?"

"We think you were close to being in the middle of something down there, Gordon," the Chief of Staff said. "What's your sense of the situation?"

"My sense is we were being used as a catalyst in a mixture of deadly politics. It's my fault that Kate's gone. I should have seen it coming."

Gordon paused to clear his throat. The President reached to hand him a glass of water, but stopped as Gordon motioned with his hand that he was alright. As he continued, the President could see that his thoughts kept wandering back to Kate. This was not the sharp analytical mind she was used to seeing in Gordon Cox.

"Some were using our presence to bolster their own position. This was certainly the case with Eduardo Santos, Deputy Minister of Defense. Others, like the young woman lawyer who was our guide for the time we were there, saw in us a sign of hope that Cuba would come to be an independent and economically affluent member of the international community. I wish I knew what part our friend Santiago played in all this. Kate and I were sure that he went to Cuba on a mission for a group in Miami. His instructions might have been to do us harm. That's what Santos told us, but I'm not so sure. It seemed he somehow had been trapped into taking some pretty unusual steps. He'd been discovered, but instead of being jailed or shot, he was being used, perhaps by the very people that were telling us he was working for Miami."

"What's Fidel's situation?" Black asked.

"Your information that he's had a mild stroke was probably accurate, but no one is making anything of it. One has the sense that he's not leaking power, so he can't be in all that bad shape. At the same time, it seems there are two major movements being readied by those close to the throne for the day when that power is up for grabs. One is a deal with China, which I'll tell you about later. The other is getting in bed with Venezuela to finance a major modernization of Cuba's infrastructure. Opposed to both of these initiatives is, we think, a small group of middle level, younger, Cubans who would instead look to the international community, including the United States, to invest in Cuba's future. But to accomplish this they'd need to destroy the status quo and all those who are dependent on maintaining it. The trouble is they don't know what this country will do when the shooting starts."

"Do we know who those people are?"

"No, but if we had Santiago deChristo in our clutches, we could probably piece it together."

The President looked at Charles Black. "Tell him, Charles."

"Gordon, you mentioned that Santiago has a brother whose name is Orlando, as I recall."

"That's right," Cox said. "The police were bringing him in for questioning as they were hunting down Santiago. I only know what happened to Santiago."

"General Orlando deChristo flew into Mexico City three nights ago and asked for political asylum."

Cox looked hard at Black, his eyebrows almost at his hairline. "Anyone with him?"

"A young woman, but it wasn't Kate," Black said, watching a glimmer in Gordon's eyes dissipate. "This guy's contacted us through the Embassy in Mexico City. He wants to exchange information for cash so he can live in the style to which he's accustomed."

"He could certainly fill in the card. He might even be part of the group his brother Santiago was hinting at. Our presence may have contributed to his problems. The Cubans were sure that Santiago had come back to Havana to do mischief."

The President made eye contact with her Chief of Staff, and addressed Cox. "Gordon, you must be exhausted. We can pick this up again later."

Cox nodded.

The sessions following with the FBI were the worst. The agents used up all their smarts, first by implication, and then aggressively, trying to make the case that Kate and Gordon created their own crisis. They ridiculed Gordon's knowledge of Cuba and its connections in Miami wherever it conflicted with their own view of the world.

The CIA knew what they were talking about when it came to Cuba. They seemed to have a better grip as well on the state of things in Miami. After a long day, Gordon retreated to his flat, drank two martinis, and woke up the next morning fully clothed in a living room chair with the television still on.

★

Kate was amazed at how quickly the waves increased in size when the first squalls hit. The sea rose in a matter of minutes from gentle one to two-foot wavelets into steep, angry walls of water. In the pre-dawn hours, they heard—rather than saw—the waves. Every tenth wave or so came at them in the night like an express train. The sea pummeled them and pushed the raft into a spinning skid, almost flipping it upside down. All the while the wind screamed at a high pitch. Kate and Santiago shouted to be heard above the chaos that ruled all around them.

"The wind direction is still west," Santiago shouted above the din.

Santiago's mind raced through the sequence he knew was

coming, as he considered their odds of survival. *As the wind clocks around to the north, the seas will get bigger and much steeper; we're being driven toward the reef at the southwest point of Key Largo; in close to land the seas will rise up and break with awesome force over the reef; if we are lucky enough to reach the coral at a break in the reef line, conditions won't be much better; there, the currents swirl around in circles, making the wave action more unpredictable and huge holes appear in the water over the sharp coral heads.*

The already soft side of the raft grew steadily softer. The raft folded almost in half each time a massive wave surged at them, the force throwing the two of them against each other in the center of the raft as the wave rolled beneath them.

When it finally happened, Kate didn't see or feel it coming. Suddenly upside down under the raft in the water, she reached out for anything solid. She took in a mouthful of salt water, and surfaced, spitting and coughing. She could barely see the raft. It was ten or fifteen feet away, still upside down and skidding wildly across the water. She turned her back to the wind and the breaking seas to keep the salt water from filling her lungs. By the time she caught her breath, the raft was almost out of sight. She couldn't see the Cuban anywhere.

Stripping off the heavy shorts, she swam hard for the orange shape moving downwind. She swam as she had along the California coast, surfing down the face of the big waves and breast stroking in between. When she finally caught up to the raft, she could see the canopy was completely torn away. Santiago clung to the other side, trying to right the raft with the help of the wind.

The Cuban's surprise was evident when Kate appeared out of the surf. He motioned for her to help him flip the raft. As they put their combined weight on one pontoon, the wind caught the underside and hurled the raft ten meters downwind, where it landed right side up.

Kate took off again in pursuit of her only hope to survive. The water-soaked sweatshirt held her back, and she pulled it off over her head. Five more minutes of steady swimming and body surfing got her there, exhausted and half drowned. She hung on, quite literally, for her life. She was surprised not to see Santiago.

Kate focused on her own situation. She feared the onset of hypothermia as she struggled to get back into the raft. Weak and shivering, she managed to wedge a knee between the grip line and the composite material of the raft. She drew from deep inside herself and found the strength to heave her upper body onto the pontoon. She tumbled inside.

To stabilize the raft, Kate spread-eagled her body into a four-corner brace, trying to keep it from buckling. She maintained that position until she passed out.

★

Cox's office took on a siege-like atmosphere. "Any word, Gordon?" was the query of the day. Emily Harris received a flood of calls from Kate's parents and her friends from Georgetown. She protected Gordon as much as she could. The story Gordon agreed on with Bob Stevens and Kate's mother, as well as the White House, was that she'd mysteriously disappeared while returning to Miami from Nassau. Some like Brad Howe thought they knew better, but were reluctant to probe.

Having slept all night in his lounge chair, Gordon arrived at the office later than usual. It was Friday and that was the day he met with the full partnership to lay out the following week's major matters and associate assignments. He was invited to a dinner party at the Canadian Embassy, which he declined for no reason other than that most of the starch had gone out of him.

Emily Harris did what she could to comfort him, but Gordon wasn't responding.

"Do you want me to stay around for a while tonight, Gordon?" she asked before locking her desk and heading home.

"No thanks, Emily. We're finished for today. Give my regards to your mother."

"Sure will," she said, the mention of her mother shortening Emily's day by an hour or so.

Cox was leaving the office thirty minutes later, facing his own empty evening, when the phone rang. The Attorney General was on the line.

"Gordon, Conner here," the AG said, rushing into the next sentence in case Cox was tempted to hang up. "I'm sorry if something has happened to your associate."

Cox was not in a fighting mood. "Thank you, Conner, we're not giving up on her."

"Do you mind telling me what happened?"

"No, I don't mind, but does it have to be right now?"

"No, of course not. I thought I'd ask you to meet me for lunch tomorrow. It's Saturday, maybe you'd rather we meet for a drink. Look, I've been off base on a lot of this Cuban business. I'd like to start over. We'll make it informal. How about it?"

The last person in the world Cox wanted to spend any time with was Conner Omega, but a meeting presented an opportunity to get a few answers. He knew the AG wanted to find out what was going on with the Cubans. Maybe he could turn the tables.

"Meet me at the Madison Bar at one. We can have lunch at my club down the street," Gordon said.

The next morning Gordon made note of the points he needed to discuss with Conner Omega. First on the list were the circumstances of John Carver's death. Next, Omega's relationship with Carlos Diego, and third, whether the AG had learned of Cox's undertaking for the President on the now well publicized Cuban plan to litigate over use by the U.S. of the Guantanamo Bay Naval Base as a prison.

★

Kate rolled around in six inches of water. She tried to rise to her knees, but the raft flooring buckled under her weight and the sides folded in over her shoulders.

She slowly became aware that she was still at sea. The wind had lessened and the waves no longer resembled marauding herds of wild elephants. She held onto the pontoons with arms extended and balanced on her knees to shorten the distance to the horizon. She saw a bird before something else caught her eye. She squinted, wondering what to make of the pencil-like shape in the distance. She decided what she was looking at was somehow connected with land, but she couldn't tell if it was getting any closer.

She thought about making a swim for it, but decided she was too weak and the distance greater than it looked. She splashed water out of the raft so she wouldn't drown if she passed out again.

Some inestimable time later, Kate was jarred awake by a lifting sensation and then a hard hit on the bottom of the raft. Stars filled the sky, and the night air sent a chill through her body. Jarred again, she realized the motion was wave action grinding the raft against something solid. Was it coral? Or sand? She put a hand over the side and grabbed a fistful of beautiful soft sand.

The scene was wild and surreal in the darkness. She could make out the dim profile of a clump of trees bending to the wind on the other side of the beach, and off in the distance, what appeared to be the headlight of a car moving along a road.

She swung a bare leg over the pontoon and rolled into a half foot of water with a sandy bottom. She crawled on all fours across the sand to a clump of bushes that afforded some protection from the offshore wind. Then she moved around in tight circles, scratching in the weeds and bush like a dog feeling for the best place to lie down. Shivering and lightheaded, she huddled into a tight ball and lay still until rays of light from the east danced across the Florida Straits and sprinkled through the scrub bushes around her. The sun warmed the white sandy beach and began to raise patches of salt on her skin.

SIXTEEN

"I saw her move," one boy said.

"She looks really hot. I hope she's not dead," said the second, digging his toes into the warm sand and straining to get a better look through the bushes.

Kate uncurled and propped herself up on her elbows. The two boys, nine or ten years old, jumped back. She sat up, instinctively covering her bare breasts with folded arms. "Where are we?" she asked, blinking as she peered through the leaves at the boys.

"The beach," the first boy answered, and then realizing he'd left something out, added, "This is Largo, Key Largo."

She turned her arm to look at her wristwatch, which was no longer there. "What day is it?" she said, looking to the more curious of the two.

"Saturday. It's Saturday morning."

"Are you alright?" the second boy asked.

"Can you get me something to wear?" she said, looking from one boy to the other.

"You can have my shirt," the first said, pulling it over his head as he spoke.

"I've got a bathing suit in my pack," said the other.

The young boy's trunks covered Kate's hips and below her midriff, leaving a gap of four or five inches to the bottom of the t-shirt she struggled to pull on over her head.

"Where are you from?" the second boy asked, handing Kate a half full bottle of water.

She blew a strand of hair from her right eye, and crawled out of the bushes. She sat cross-legged, facing the two youngsters.

"Thank you, young man," she said, taking and drinking the water. She looked around as if missing something more than just her clothes. "Where's the raft? Did you see an orange life raft?"

Both boys shrugged their shoulders.

"I guess the tide took it out," she said, and then belatedly answered the boy's question. "I was in a life raft in a storm. I don't know how I got here. Just washed up on the beach, I guess. It was cold last night," she said, shivering.

"Are you Cuban?" asked the second boy.

Kate laughed. "No, I'm an American. I live in Washington, D.C. You know where that is don't you?"

They both nodded.

"I need to get to a telephone, boys. Do you live nearby?"

"My mother's not home," the first boy said. "She doesn't let me take anyone into the house when she's not there."

Kate turned to the second boy. "I live pretty far from here," he said, "but there's a phone in the General Store up the road."

"Can you take me there?" she said, trying to get to her feet.

The boys watched as she lost her balance and tumbled forward. She lay there unconscious, her nose and right cheek digging into the sand where she'd landed. The two of them stared wide-eyed down at her.

The second boy put his hand on her temple and pronounced Kate alive. "What do we do now?"

"I'll go get help," the first said. "You stay here. I'll find Mr. Harris. He'll know what to do."

"Oh, no," said the second, "I'm coming with you."

"Okay, but leave the fishing poles here. We can run faster without them."

★

The Coast Guard Cutter Resolute radioed its base in Key West.

"Roger, Bravo Hotel Zulu, three miles off the light at the south entrance to Key Largo; no one aboard. It's pretty beat up and one side is almost deflated. No markings, but there's fishing gear and dried up slices of Dorado in the creases. It's an expensive life raft. It could be from that sport fisherman Headquarters is so anxious for us to find. Roger that, Bravo Hotel Zulu, but hear this. We picked up a Cuban male out there last night. He's playing dumb, and won't answer our questions. We guess he's about forty-five to fifty years of age. He was holding onto a water soaked, wooden beach chair. We picked up an EPIRB signal not ten miles from our position and homed in on it. Damn near ran him over when we got near it. Can you confirm he goes to Bahama Charlie's for further processing? Roger that. We'll report when we make contact. . . . This is Coast Guard Hotel India 2734, standing by."

★

Charles Black was talking with the President, whom he thought seemed unusually agitated.

"No, you should absolutely *not* relay that message to Gordon. No news is good news for him. An empty life raft is not going to do anyone any good. We keep it to ourselves. I take it they've found no sign of the boat."

"No, ma'am."

"Tell them to keep looking."

"It's been over five days now."

"I'll tell you when to stop, damn it. The Coast Guard's out there all the time, anyway."

"Yes, ma'am."

★

[218]

The sheriff was on the phone with his County Supervisor in Key West, who happened to be a woman that he usually refused to meet halfway.

"She has no identification, and the boys found her on the beach jackass naked. First Aid is working on her now . . . What? . . . She's pretty dehydrated, and they're trying to raise her body temperature. Probably some hooker who fell or was thrown off one of those big motor boats. I'm holding her until we get prints and numbers back from the Feds."

The Sheriff paused, listening to his supervisor on the other end of the line.

"What? Hell yes, I'll let her make a phone call—just one, mind you. That's right. She says she's a law student and works for a firm up in Washington. She's a Gary Hart style bimbo, I reckon. No, I don't care who she calls, but I don't have to believe a word she's said neither."

Kate couldn't remember Gordon's home number and she knew it was unlisted, so she called the office. No one was on the main switchboard that Saturday morning. The only extension she could remember was her own. In desperation, she left a message for herself.

"Anyone, this is Kate. I'm okay, but they're holding me at a police station in Key Largo. Here's the number. Please tell Gordon I'm alright, and I love him. And will someone please tell these bozos down here who I am?"

★

Conner Omega waited for Gordon in the Madison Hotel Lounge, a drink on the table in front of him. Gordon arrived on time and ordered a tomato juice.

"I hear you're going to Mexico," Omega said as Cox took his seat.

Cox shook his head. He had no idea what the AG was talking about.

Omega sneered. "No?" he said. "Well, suit yourself. No word on your associate?" He was going to say girlfriend, but thought better of it. There was no point in getting Cox agitated before their conversation even started.

"Nothing yet," Cox said, as his drink arrived.

"A lot of Cubans make it across. I reckon she will, too."

Gordon gave him a severe look. "I hope you're right."

"Who's handling the fisherman case for you now?"

"I'm handling it myself. Speaking of which, you owe me an answer.

"Good Lord, Gordon, the man's dead."

"And your department is doing nothing to find his killer."

"The man died in a drunken driving accident. He missed the turn where the old road used to be and drove off into twelve feet of water. His blood tested way over the limit. Besides, his death isn't a federal matter."

"You're aware of the fact the man never touched the stuff."

"That's what they all say, Gordon. You know that."

"We can produce credible witnesses who will attest to his abstinence."

"What are you telling me?"

"I'm saying that we're not going to let this matter go away. We think he was murdered. Your department has jurisdiction, because the act committed was in connection with an arrest made by your people using excessive and unconstitutional measures, and because he was out on bail from a federal warrant." Cox saw the smirk he disliked so much come across Omega's face. "Take it seriously, Conner," he said. "*I* am."

"You're reaching on this one, Gordon."

"We'll see. Tell me, Conner, what's your relationship with Carlos Diego?"

"Who?"

"Diego, otherwise known as The Orphan."

"I know him. That's all."

"Are you aware that he sent a man to Cuba two weeks ago to spy on what I was doing there?"

"No, I was not, but what if he did? We should do more of that sort of thing, if you ask me."

"Do you know a man by the name of Santiago deChristo?"

"I don't know him. Why? Should I?"

"No you shouldn't, but my guess is you've just forgotten."

At that moment, Omega's cell phone rang. He nodded at Gordon, then took the call. Cox excused himself to visit the men's room. He strolled the length of the lounge, acknowledging two people he recognized, but not stopping to talk. As he walked back through the hotel lobby, he happened to glance at a television set with several people gathered around it. Pausing to watch the cable news segment, Gordon welcomed the diversion from the meeting with Conner Omega. He walked closer to see two boys being interviewed about their find that morning of a body on a beach in the Florida Keys.

"It's our fishing spot. We go there Saturdays to fish," one boy was saying.

"He thought she was a mermaid," the other said, laughing. "She didn't have any clothes on."

"I did not think she was a mermaid," protested the first.

"I gave her my bathing suit," said the second boy.

"Did she say what happened?" the reporter asked.

"She said she was in a life raft, but we didn't see one around."

"Did she tell you her name?"

"No, but she said she lived in Washington."

Gordon stopped breathing as he listened.

"What else did she say?" the newsperson asked.

"Nothing. She fainted. We went to get help."

"Thank you, boys." Turning to face the camera, the reporter continued. "There you have it. A mermaid on the beach at Key Largo. Police there are holding the woman pending verification of her story and confirming her identity. She wore no clothes when she was found. I guess that means no pockets and no driver's license. This is Gladys White for Fox News, Key Largo, Florida."

Cox rushed into the Lounge, where Omega was still on the

phone. He took a last sip of his drink. "Gotta go, Conner," he said, and ran out the door.

It was three blocks to Cox's office. He ran the whole distance, and was gasping for air as he showed his security card to the guard on duty and got in the elevator.

The firm's switchboard was closed, and he dialed information for the first time in years. The impatience stored up in him came through in his voice over the phone.

"The police station in Key Largo, Florida . . . yes, operator, and please hurry."

There were two numbers, and he took a guess and dialed. A man answered. "Sheriff's Office, Deputy Hall."

"Hello, my name is Gordon Cox. I'm calling from my office in Washington, D.C. I understand you have a woman in your custody. May I ask if her name is Katherine Stevens?" Gordon waited, his pulse racing as he said a silent prayer.

A voice sounded in the background, not speaking to him but to another person at the station. Then Gordon heard the man on the other end of the line speak.

"Benny, I got a man here that knows her. Least ways, he got her name right." Then, prompted by his superior, he asked Gordon, "What'd you say your name was?"

"Cox, Gordon Cox."

"Hold on," the man said, and there was scuffling as the phone was handed over to another.

"Hello, this is Chief Orbiter. What can I do for you?"

Gordon cleared his throat. "You're holding a woman in your facility who's told you her name is Stevens. The United States Coast Guard, myself, and the President of the United States have been looking for her for five days. Put her on the phone, please."

"Give me your name again."

"My name is Cox, Gordon Cox. Now, put her on the phone."

"Don't get your shorts in a wad there, buddy boy. My deputy is bringing her over here now."

"Hello?"

"Kate, is that you?"

"Gordon! Oh my God, Gordon, where are you?"

"Are you alright?"

"I think so. A bit dehydrated and weak, but I'm okay."

"I'll be down there as soon as I can. I'm going to ask some friends in Biscayne to drive down, pick you up, and take you to their home. I just hope they're home on a Saturday afternoon. Sit tight. We'll have you out of there in no time."

"Thank God. How'd you know I was here?"

"You made CNN, FOX News, and every other newscast in the country today, courtesy of the two boys who found you."

"They were cute, those two, but this place is the pits. What are your friends' names?"

"Carol and Jake Webber. Jake and I went to law school together. He works for a bank in Miami. Carol is a diminutive blonde fireball of energy. She's an architect, and has designed most of the board-rooms in the Southeast. You'll love both of them. I'll call back with the details after I've made the arrangements. Now, better put the Sheriff back on."

Gordon spoke hurriedly, "Thank you, officer. The President will be very pleased you were able to rescue Ms. Stevens. I'm arranging to have her picked up in a couple of hours."

"Mr. Cox, I got that right? C–O–X?"

"Yes, Chief, that's right."

"I'm gonna need some ID from you or from her. At this point, I ain't releasing nobody."

Gordon started to say, "Call the Coast Guard," but changed his mind. "I'll see you get whatever you need, Sheriff, but wait for the faxed documents. It may take a few minutes. What's your fax number?"

★

When the news concerning the life raft recovery was transmit-ted to the White House Staff, no mention was made of the man fished out of the sea hours earlier. Otherwise, Charles Black might have put two and two together and concluded that Santiago had also survived the journey across the Gulf Stream. Having him around to add to the intelligence, or subtract from the misinformation, obtained from his brother would have been priceless.

Santiago was being held incommunicado and was on his way to Guantanamo Bay. He hadn't given the Coast Guard his real name since that would be a red flag to people like Eduardo Santos, who'd be waiting for him at the Cuban end of the exchange.

★

Carol Webber sent regrets to their dinner hosts for Saturday evening. She and her husband Jake drove to Key Largo, collected Kate, fed her a light home cooked meal, and put her to bed in the guest quarters of their town house on Key Biscayne. Gordon arrived in a rented car late that night.

"How is she, Carol?" as he came in the front door.

"She seems okay. They said at the Sheriff's Office in Largo that she was dehydrated. A nurse came in and gave her an intravenous solution, and her energy and cognition picked right up. She's sound asleep. You can go up, but I wouldn't wake her. Take your jacket off and sit down," she said, pointing at the kitchen table. "Jake's on the phone in the den. How about a drink?"

Jake Webber joined them around the table, and Carol made them all a drink.

"You are a man of infinite surprises, Gordon," Carol said, sitting in her kitchen with a three quarters full bottle of gin, half a six-pack of Quinine water, and a store of limes on the table in front of her.

Gordon placed his hand on Carol's arm, and stretched his head around to look in Jake's direction.

"Thank you both for doing this. It was pretty spur of the moment."

"No problem," said Jake. "She had quite an experience out there. That was one hell of a storm that came through here the last couple of days."

"Yes, thank God she's alright," Gordon said, raising his gin and tonic in a toast to his hosts.

Carol moved around the kitchen table and fixed her husband a drink. "So who is she, Gordon, besides the woman who made the evening news?"

"The love of my life," he said, watching Carol's slow smile emerge as she returned to her seat.

Jake gave Gordon a winner's fist pump. "I told you, honey," he said.

"So what was the love of your life doing naked on the beach in Key Largo?" Carol asked.

"I'll tell you what, Carol, let's ask her in the morning," Gordon said.

"Seriously, Gordon," Carol said, laughing, "what's going on? Tell me it's a state secret or something important enough to make me miss the Ryans' dinner party."

"She's important to me. What we were doing, I thought, was important for the country. Will that do it?"

"For now," Carol said. "But, Gordy baby, she's about the age your daughter would be if you had one."

"Come on, Carol," her husband said. "Leave the poor man alone."

"Don't you get any ideas now, Jake Webber," his wife cautioned. She turned to Gordon, "I suppose you'd like to stay in the same room?"

Gordon put his hand back on Carol's arm. "I know what you're saying, but what do you do when it happens?"

"You follow your heart," she said.

"Yes, I would like to sleep in the same room. I'd like to be there when she wakes up. We'll see how she feels about me in the morning."

"Gordon," Carol said, "I just spent five hours with that lovely creature. She is so hooked on you, it scares me. If Jake fished me out of the Gulf after five days and a force ten storm, I'd tell him to come back next Christmas."

Gordon smiled. "Well, thank you again for rescuing her. I owe you."

Sunday morning dawned clear and windy, the storm front having moved through south Florida and out to sea off the Atlantic coast. A shadow passed between Gordon and the sunlight streaming in a short corner of the window looking east, and it woke him. The blink in the light was Kate, passing as she came from the bathroom and slid her arm under the sheets of Gordon's bed. He turned as she climbed in next to him, and they embraced.

"Do you know what time it is?" she whispered into his ear.

He ignored the question and kissed her warmly on the mouth.

"Wow," Kate said. "Who cares what time it is?" and she moved her hands down his back and pulled him closer. "What I mean is, are our hosts still asleep? I think these walls have ears."

Gordon smiled but shook his head. "We better get down there. Carol doesn't need the walls to figure things out."

The Webbers were seated at the breakfast table as Kate and Gordon slowly descended from the second floor wrapped in oversized terrycloth robes.

"Look who's up," Carol said, as her guests reached the bottom of the stairs.

"How are you feeling, Kate?" Carol asked, as Gordon held a chair for Kate at the breakfast table.

"I feel pretty good," she said, "a little weak. I drank all that water in the pitcher you gave me last night. It was like pouring it in the ocean."

"Bad dreams?" Carol asked.

"No, not really," Kate answered.

"Well, you certainly don't look any the worse for wear," Carol said. "How about some scrambled eggs?"

Carol steered the conversation away from Kate to more mundane news of the day, and Jake made Kate laugh relating old stories of his reveling with Gordon in Harvard Square between law school classes.

After breakfast, Kate and Gordon went for a walk along the bay. By themselves and able to speak more freely, they rushed to fill in for the lost time.

"It must have been terrible for you, Gordon."

"For me?" he said. "You're the one they took, and who had to go through that storm."

"If it had been the other way around, I would have hated it. Suddenly, I disappear. You had no way . . . Hey, you know what?" she said, sliding closer to the feelings inside that were surfacing. "Do you remember the last words I said to you before they carted me off?"

"How could I forget?"

"Oh, you're cheating. Do you remember or not?" she challenged, a big smile giving away that she wasn't serious.

"Maybe I just want to hear you say the words again."

"I'll say them again and again, but first you tell me."

"You said, and I quote . . ."

"Yes? Stop stalling. You're acting just like a lawyer."

"I am a lawyer."

"What did I say?"

"You said, 'Hold that thought, I'll be right back.'"

"So, are you still holding it?"

"I am, indeed."

"Good, so stop and come here."

As he did, Kate threw her arms around his neck. They held one another in a tight embrace that lasted through tears and many other emotions.

Kate continued her stream of consciousness. "I thought so many times in that lockup . . . that I hadn't told you how I felt. You'd never know, and they would rob us of that. I prayed to see that dimpled chin and that big Roman nose again, so I could tell you that I love you."

"My life was over."

"No, it wasn't, but that's a very good thought," she said, leaping into his arms again and holding on tight.

"It's alright now," was all that Gordon could manage.

"So you talked to Mother and Father," Kate said, as Gordon nodded and they moved further along the beach. She could feel her drive returning, forging links back to the life that had almost gotten away from her. "How did they cope with the last few days? Mother was the strong one, right?"

"They both were strong. They know you're back, and they desperately want to speak with you."

"I'll call them both when we get back to the Webbers'." Her thoughts racing to make up for lost ground, Kate asked, "Gordon, are you still worried about the age thing?"

"It's not that."

"What is it, then?"

"Kate, I've lived alone for a long time. I'm not sure I'm capable of loving anyone the way you deserve to be loved. You need a young pup, not an old hound."

Kate stopped, hands on hips, "We're perfect for each other. I'll never have to worry about your leaving me for a younger woman. You'll already have her," she said laughing. "And if by love you mean possession and all that insecurity I see in men closer to my own age, you can have it. I need more space than most men would ever tolerate. I'd say we're a great match." She moved closer to his side.

"Okay, Kate," he said softly, holding her hands in his. "Let's see if we can make it work. But you need to call your mother and father before they send the Boy Scouts after us."

"I guess everyone else has been looking for me."

They circled back through the complex of expensive townhouses toward the Webbers' front door.

"So what's next, lovely man?" Kate said. "I have to admit I'm nervous about being back in the office."

"After what you've been through?"

"It's totally different. I could deal with the fear I felt being locked up. I assumed the best or the worst, and prepared myself for both. Going home is a huge change. I left as a summer associate, and I'm going back as the girlfriend, or whatever. I've never been in that position, and we won't have the anonymity we had in Havana. We'll be in the Washington fishbowl."

"We can handle it. If the office becomes difficult, you can find an excuse to go back to law school early, and work in the apartment."

"That's a copout."

"Not really, but I agree the best move is to face up to things. If you're sure we're doing the right thing, then what should we care what others think?"

Kate stopped and wrapped her arms around Gordon's neck as they stood at Carol and Jake's front door.

"What about Emily Harris, the person you depend on? She's in love with you."

"Emily? No."

"Emily, yes, of course. She idolizes you."

"Emily and I get along. We understand each other, but . . ." Gordon stopped talking as Carol's excited voice sounded through the open front door.

"Hey, you guys better get in here. It looks like you might have started something."

Kate and Gordon followed their hostess into the house.

Carol kept talking. "We turned on the Sunday morning news. The big story is about the President sending you guys to Havana to give comfort to Army officers plotting against the Cuban government. They made one of their patented monologues last night. They're accusing the United States of an act of war. What's his face from Caracas has been chiming in."

The television news reporter was finishing the piece on Cuba as Gordon walked across the den where the T.V. displayed pictures of crowds and street scenes of Havana.

"You'd better call her," Kate said.

Gordon nodded, and turned to Carol.

"You can use the phone in my office," she said.

Cox called the private number he had for Charles Black. The White House Chief of Staff picked up on the second ring.

"When will you be back in Washington?" he asked, preempting any discussion of the subject over the phone.

"We're on our way," Gordon said.

"Call me when you're ready. Has the press been onto you yet?"

"No. They don't know where we are. The last person I spoke to was the Attorney General. That was yesterday around noon, when I heard Kate had washed up on the beach."

"Okay, get back here as soon as you can. I'd fly out of West Palm or Fort Lauderdale if I were you. A whole lot of people are watching Miami International for you to show up there."

SEVENTEEN

Ernesto Legra's reward for shining the light on General Orlando deChristo was permission to travel to Mexico to locate and bring back his sister. Second Minister Santos did not expect Ernesto to get the better of Orlando deChristo, but he reveled in the nuisance it would be for the General to deal with the determined young man.

Ernesto flew to Mexico City on a chartered flight. He breezed through customs and immigration with diplomatic papers. No one discovered the .45 caliber pistol in his luggage. The Cuban Ambassador didn't know whether to laugh or cry when Ernesto bragged about getting his sidearm through all of the checkpoints. He chalked it up to his youth and to luck. It was also unnecessary. The Embassy took his weapon and gave Ernesto an unmarked, untraceable revolver made in China. Then, they took his passport and all other identification . . . just in case.

The Cuban Embassy gave him directions to the General's apartment, along with the flat's telephone number. Late that night, Ernesto arrived at the hotel they'd arranged for him, slid into bed, and slept for eighteen hours. He caught sight of his sister for a few moments on his third day in Mexico City. Ana and the General came out of the apartment building together and climbed into a black car waiting at the curb. Ernesto followed by taxi. Their first stop was a clinic, which according to the sign in front, specialized in prenatal care. The second was the United States Embassy. Ernesto concluded that the traitor was taking his sister to the United States, or worse, giving the Americans valuable state secrets.

Ana was, in his eyes, a traitor to their family and to Cuba. She would be better off dead than in this traitor's arms. But Ana had been brainwashed. He would rescue her, and take her back with him to Havana. A few months' rehabilitation and she'd be good as new. He wondered if their stop at the prenatal care facility meant his sister was pregnant. He cursed the General to hell, and came very near making a charge across the street and onto the Embassy grounds, shooting at everything and everyone in sight.

He watched as the two finally appeared and walked hand in hand to the waiting limousine. Hatred for the General welled up within him again, and Ernesto decided then that he'd come to this place, at this time, for a reason.

★

"The White House limo is here, Kate." Cox shouted loud enough through the closed bathroom door to be heard over the noise of the shower.

"Already? Okay, I'll be out in ten. I've got multiple coats of salt and grime still coming off. I want to look my best for our President."

"Move quickly, but don't rush. Didn't Goethe say something like that?" Getting no response from Kate, Cox moved back to his study and turned on the television.

A rebroadcast of the morning's session at the United Nations was on the air. Cox watched long enough to get the gist of what was being bantered around the General Assembly. The Cuban argument that the treaty for the Guantanamo Bay naval base was null and void was getting some play, although the news announcer oversimplified and therefore misstated the Cuban legal position. A lawyer with the State Department was interviewed but refrained from comment, other than to say they were looking into the Cuban position.

Gordon turned off the set and got some juice out of the refrigerator.

"Who will be there?" Kate asked, as the limo pulled out from the hotel entrance to the Watergate complex, avoiding the two or three journalists that were waiting in the shadows at the west entrance to the condominium apartments.

"Just Charles and the President is my guess. That's the way Rebecca plays it."

"They must be pretty angry with the way things turned out."

"I'm sure they're disappointed, but you'll find the President is very quick to get back on her horse. She doesn't stay on defense very long."

"What do you want me to say?"

"Just be yourself, Kate. Tell it exactly as you saw it, no compromise. Charles can be fooled, but not Rebecca. She has a sixth sense when it comes to sorting out the truth."

The President greeted Kate with an outstretched hand and dancing eyes. "We meet again, Katherine. May I call you Kate?"

Kate blushed and smiled. "I would be honored," she said.

"Good. You've had an adventure, haven't you, young lady?" the President said, still holding onto Kate's hand. "Are you okay?"

"Yes, Madam President, I'm fine now."

Small talk prevailed as two stewards from the kitchen staff came into the office. Trays of coffee and light sandwiches were placed on a table by the wall.

"Please help yourselves, everyone," the President said. She turned to Gordon as the staff persons left the room. "How much do you know about the pundit traffic out there?"

"Very little," he said.

"Alright then, Charles, why don't you fill us in?"

Charles Black opened the notebook on his lap as Kate and Gordon, who were famished, joined the President at the side bar.

Black found the place he wanted. The others rejoined him and gave him their attention.

"We got wind of what the Cubans were up to before Kate's rescue made the news. They obviously thought both you and the man on the raft with you were killed when your boat sank. They knew Gordon was back home and very upset. They were worried that your loss would be sufficient excuse for us to do something rash, like invading the Islands, or tightening the noose of the Embargo by persuading the Europeans to join us. So, they went on the offensive, accusing us of committing an act of war by sending two spies to Havana to meet with insurgents. They were clever in using real but partial facts to assemble a credible picture. They even used our meeting in Nassau, Gordon, as part of the conspiracy they manufactured. They had all the names and places right."

"Eduardo Santos," Gordon said, glancing in Kate's direction. She nodded, agreeing it had his signature written all over it.

Black paused to write down Santos' name on his clipboard. "The Deputy Defense Minister?" he asked.

Gordon confirmed it with a nod of his head.

The President showed impatience. "Get on with the story, Charles."

"Yes, their version went something like this. We sent you two to Havana under false pretenses to make contact with General Orlando deChristo, and to provide a link between his efforts and the CIA. The President's initiative to end the Embargo was all a cover for her real intentions, to foster an overthrow of the Cuban regime. Kate's abduction was staged for effect by Santiago deChristo, and as the Cuban government began to take action against those intent on armed rebellion, Kate was whisked off by the General's brother to return to Key West. These two spies were tracked down at sea and dealt with, and the General was forced into exile."

"So there you have it. The Cubans were righteously indignant: 'We will not be bullied. The Americans are not to be trusted,' and in one quick move Cuba once again has put down a U.S. led insurrection and found and dealt with Cuba's most famous traitors, Santiago and Orlando deChristo. That's the picture they painted."

"Clever," Gordon said. "We know now that Santiago had nothing to do with Kate's abduction, and it's at least doubtful that his brother was involved. What about the lawsuit filed in The Hague?"

"Yeah," Black said, "We'll need to talk about that more, but right now it's the spy nonsense we've got to deal with."

The President addressed Kate, "What happened to the Cuban on the boat with you? The General's brother?"

Kate took a deep breath. "Yes, Santiago was his name," she answered, and paused to collect her thoughts. "I really don't know what happened to him." Gordon heard for the first time the sequence of disasters that overtook the raft. Kate ended by saying, "When I reached the raft after the second capsize, he was gone. It was a struggle for me to climb in. The seas were horrible. I couldn't breathe. The wind picked up the salt water in the wave crests and blew it right down my throat. I tried to look around for him, but I never saw him again. There wasn't anything I could have done."

The President nodded thanks to Kate, and seemed engrossed in thought. "It's too bad you didn't have one of those rescue beacons." Turning to Black, she asked, "What're they called, Charles?"

"EPIRBs," he answered.

"Yes, one of those would have been helpful."

"We had two of them," Kate said.

Charles Black coughed. "Two of them?"

"Yes, Santiago took one off the boat, and there was another in the abandon ship bag."

"Were they both in the raft when it capsized?"

"The first time we turned over? Yes, they would have been."

"So they might have deployed. Were they on automatic?"

"I don't know."

The President interrupted. "Charles, how do those things . . . what'd you call them . . . eburbs? How do they work?"

Black suppressed a smile. "They're radio beacons that send a signal to satellites, giving their position. There are several types. Most can be placed on a manual setting, or switched on to become activated when immersed in salt water. Well, I guess any water, but they'll start beeping right away, and last for a day or so on fresh batteries."

Kate raised a hand as if she were in class. "Come to think about it, Santiago had one of those beacons tied around his waist. I think it was the one he took from the boat deck. But it wasn't blinking or anything."

"So he might have had it in the water when you two were separated?" Black said.

"I think it went wherever he went," Kate said. "My impression was he wanted to keep it nearby so it couldn't activate unless he wanted it to. He was always afraid the Coast Guard would find us out there, and send him back to Cuba."

"So," the President said, "if he was in the water with that thing beeping, isn't it possible that one of the Coast Guard facilities picked it up?"

They all exchanged glances, and then Black exited the Oval Office and headed for a secure telephone.

"Well, that raises some interesting possibilities," the President said. "We've been all around the bush here trying to figure the best way to counter this propaganda from of Havana. There's no easy answer. We can't get around the two men being brothers. The world is not going to believe they weren't in cahoots here, and that makes Kate appear an accessory." She glanced at Gordon. "And Charles and I look like damn fools."

Cox responded to the President's eye contact. "If by some miracle Santiago didn't drown out there, and we find him, we might piece together a response, but I don't think you want to fight this matter in the press."

"God, no," she responded. "We've already lost that battle. I want to use diplomacy. I want to make something good come of this. I'm hoping this will make us a positive force in some places, as well as open up the dialogue with Cuba. Who knows, we may even have the Cubans in Miami on our side. We need this man Santiago to tell his story. The part that's hard to explain is his going back into Cuba. Why did he do that?"

"To see his aging mother," Kate said.

The President's eyebrows curled upwards, and she looked at Gordon over the half-glasses balanced on her nose.

"That's what he told us," Gordon said.

The President's expression relaxed. "Good," she said. "That's a story that the press will love, even if they don't believe it."

They all looked up as Charles Black reentered the room. "The Coast Guard is on the case. We should know something within the hour. Do you know how many false alarms they receive each day from things like EPIRBs? Up to thirty," Black said, answering his own question. "So where are we?" he said to no one in particular.

"Let's talk a moment about the other deChristo," the President said, "the one now in Mexico City. I understand he wants to talk to us," she said, looking at her Chief of Staff.

Black nodded and addressed Gordon. "He says he'll only speak with the President."

"Will he come here?"

"I don't think so, but he's apparently willing to give us firsthand intelligence," Black said. "Somebody's going to kill him if he stays in Mexico."

"He'd be protected in Miami," Gordon said with tongue in cheek.

"He could be valuable," Black insisted.

Gordon became more serious. "Maybe there's some way you can talk the Mexicans into providing around-the-clock security?"

"Good point," the President said. "See what you can do, Charles. Have State come into this, or the CIA. It's your call. Now, what's our answer to Havana's claim that you two were sent in there to make contact with insurgents?"

Kate watched as the President and her Chief studied Gordon.

"You need a fall guy," he said.

★

Ernesto waited across the street until the General left his apartment about ten o'clock in the morning, Mexico City time. He gained entrance when Ana, recognizing his voice, buzzed him in. She greeted him with a hug, and marveled at how grown up he looked in his new suit.

"What are you doing here, Ernesto?"

"I've come to take you away."

"Ernesto, the General has promised to marry me. I will have his child."

"That's not possible, Sister. He's already married. You know that."

"But we are in Mexico. He will end that marriage, and when we return to Cuba, that black-hearted family of hers will have to respect us."

Ernesto silently damned the man who'd taken control of his sister, and apparently now had impregnated her.

"He's filled your head with nonsense. Come, and be quick. We have much to do."

Ana had a thousand questions. She looked at her older brother with a mixture of love and apprehension. Ernesto was too headstrong. Their father had been like that, and his life had ended badly.

"Please, sit down, Ernesto. I'll make you some coffee."

Ernesto would not be deterred. "I will not drink his damn coffee," he said. "No, we are going to confront your general. We'll see what he has to say when he's standing in front of a man."

Ernesto looked wildly around the suite of rooms. He went back into the bedroom where his sister and Orlando slept. He spit on the still unmade bed.

"Put on your clothes. We're going to pay a call on the United States Embassy."

As they left the apartment, Ernesto let the pistol in his pocket warm to the temperature of his hand.

★

"Gordon, you've got that look again," Kate said, turning on the light by the side of the bed as Cox returned to the bedroom from answering the phone in his study. "What did Charles Black have to say?"

"How do you know it was Charles?"

"No one else would dare call you at one in the morning."

He laughed and sat on Kate's side of the bed. "They found Santiago. He was on his way to Gittmo, but the President ordered him brought back to Washington. He'll arrive here in a couple of hours. They want you and me to meet with him this afternoon."

"What's the deal?"

"He gets a permanent visa in exchange for helping us debrief his brother."

Kate whistled. "That's good. Don't we also want him as a witness in our case for the captain's widow?"

"Yes, and we want him to do it because he was fond of Carver. It'll be very effective."

"Hmm" Kate said, and reached her arms around Gordon's neck drawing him close enough to plant a wet kiss on his mouth. "Now that we're up and fully awake, my darling . . . "

★

Kate and Gordon spotted the Cuban as they came through the waiting area at the navy yard opposite Haines Point. He was thinner from his ordeal at sea, and clean-shaven, but unmistakably it was Santiago.

Kate walked up to him and put her hand firmly on his shoulder.

"Hello, señorita," he said, starting to stand as she sat down across from him.

Santiago and Gordon shook hands.

"Dr. Cox, thank you for bringing me back from the dead."

Gordon joined them at the small table. "Don't thank me," he

said. "It was the President who figured out what had happened to you based on what Kate reported. It all went over my head."

"What happened?" Kate said. "I lost sight of you after the raft got away from us."

Santiago forced himself to look in her direction. "One of those waves carried a heavy wooden plank in its crest," he said. "It hit my shoulder hard. I still have trouble moving my arm. I had no choice but to hang onto it."

"And that's when they picked you up?" she asked.

"No. The wood kept me afloat okay. I was going to try to swim for shore when it became light. Then I saw the Coast Guard, and they hauled me on board." He paused before changing the subject. "What's going on?" he asked, turning to Gordon. "They said you'd fill me in."

Gordon nodded to Kate, and she handed the Cuban an official looking card with white and green printing under the United States Seal. "Compliments of the White House Chief of Staff, here's your new permanent visa," she said. "In five years you can apply for citizenship."

They watched as Santiago nodded with a mixture of pleasure and disbelief in his eyes.

"We want you to visit Mexico City," Gordon said. "The men you see in the other room," he continued, "one is with our State Department and the other two, I'll let you imagine what they do. They are going to Mexico, at the request of our President, to interview your brother Orlando."

Kate watched as the Cuban's mouth dropped open.

"In Mexico?" he mumbled.

"He flew in there the night you and Kate took off from the Marina Hemingway."

The Cuban's eyes narrowed. He whistled softly before wetting his lips with a swipe of his tongue.

"Your brother's prepared to talk with those men, and answer their questions. They'll return to Washington and report to the President on what, if anything, you are able to learn."

"What do you want me to do?"

"You'll help us evaluate what your brother tells us, attend a press conference, and answer questions from the reporters. The permanent visa is in exchange for telling the truth. Are you with me so far?"

"What about Orlando?"

"We want you to tell us when he's telling us the truth and when he's not."

Santiago shrugged. "Orlando doesn't lie. He does crazy things, but he doesn't lie."

"Does he play games?"

Santiago paused. "Yes, he plays games. He's always playing games."

"So we'll ask you to keep score. Orlando requested this meeting. He claims he wants to tell the White House what's really going on in Havana and what the future holds. We assume he intends to ask for U.S. Government assistance. We want you to help us separate fact from too much imagination."

Santiago smiled, his face lighting up as he looked from Kate to Gordon. "It will be my pleasure. Will he know I'm there? Will I see him?"

"That's up to you. My judgment would be to save that until we think we need it. If, as you say, he doesn't normally shade the truth, then you can remain behind the scenes if you so choose. When the meeting's over, you can do as you wish."

"I'll think about that." The Cuban leaned back for a moment, twirling the visa card in his fingers. "This visa . . . ?"

"Yes?" Cox answered.

"It's Diego proof?"

"Absolutely."

"Do I still do the fishing?" he said, glancing at Kate.

"That would be the payback for getting you a boat," Kate answered.

"I won't need you to get me a boat, but I'd like to help out the widow, for a while anyway."

Kate and Gordon looked at him for an explanation.

"Diego gave me a boat, his bribe for going to Cuba," he said with a smile on his face. He turned to see Cox's reaction. "It's in Key West, unless he's taken it back since he thinks I'm dead."

Cox laughed hard. "What do you think of that, Katie?" he said. "We'd better make sure he hasn't taken it back." He turned to Santiago. "Is it registered in your name?"

"Yes, the papers are under the floor in the garage behind my house."

"I thought you lived in the old wrecked boat?" Gordon said.

Santiago grinned. "He gave me a house, too."

All three of them laughed so hard the government officials in the other room turned and gave Gordon anxious glances.

Kate looked at Gordon. "I think you just found your fall guy," she said.

★

Ana and Ernesto took a taxi to a location near the U.S. Embassy. Ernesto told his sister to be quiet as they sat on the grass behind a bank of shrubs, concealed from the two Marine guards posted in front of the building.

Ana saw Orlando first as he exited the building in the company of two personal bodyguards who'd been posted by the Mexican government to guard the General's life. She stood to wave to him, but Ernesto put his hand on her belt and jerked her down. The General set the pace, as was his style. One of the bodyguards walked in front of him, the other lingered behind.

Ana watched as Ernesto jumped to his feet and tossed what looked like a ball high into the air and across the street. The fragmentation grenade bounced as it landed six or seven feet in front of Orlando, and then skipped past him into a small flower garden near the walkway. There it exploded in a tight ball of red and orange, spewing out pain and death in small pieces of sharp metal.

Orlando was sliced in half across the middle. The cutting edges hit one of the Mexican bodyguards on a diagonal from the left ventricle up through his throat, taking out his right eye for good measure.

Ernesto's mistake was waiting, gun in hand, to see if he'd hit the target. If he'd been trained in places like Mindanao, Ceylon or Kabul, he'd not have lingered. A Marine bullet took him down.

Horrified, his sister watched him crumble and die. She was crying and twisting in grief when the U.S. Marine Sergeant lifted her off the ground and carried her, kicking and screaming in Spanish, across the street and onto the Embassy grounds.

★

The Attorney General and Charles Black were in heated discussion as Gordon Cox was ushered into the meeting.

Black turned to Gordon and smiled. "Conner doesn't think his friend Diego makes a good fall guy."

Cox nodded, and shook Black's hand before doing the same with Omega. He set his briefcase on the floor and joined them at a small round conference table similar to the one in his own office. The AG moved to explain his position.

"Diego's a fighter. He's not going to take a fall for anybody, especially under these circumstances. You're asking him to admit he sent the General's brother to Cuba to subvert your mission. There are a couple of things wrong with that idea. First, he's not going to do it; and second, it will cast Diego in the spotlight, which he'll use to further his own agenda."

Black was shaking his head. "It would make him a hero, wouldn't it? Conniving with Cuban insurgents is exactly what he wants everyone to think he does everyday. What am I missing here?"

"He'd expect to go to jail," Gordon pointed out. "I think that's Conner's point."

"That makes him a martyr," Black said. "He might like that even better."

Cox laughed, but the remark produced a thin smile from Omega.

"Diego is trouble," Omega insisted. "He's not going to go quietly."

"Meaning he'll involve his friends," Black said.

Omega bristled. "What's your point, Charlie?"

"You know damn well what my point is. He'll drag you into it, Conner. Why don't you admit that's your problem?"

Gordon watched the AG's face redden as he rose from the chair. "That's enough of that crap, Charlie. I'm not going to sit around here and help you make me the fall guy for her mistakes."

"Sit down, Conner, and stop acting like a child," Black said. "Gordon's little mission to Havana would have worked out just fine if Diego hadn't sent the General's brother in there to do his mischief. He needs to admit doing it, and make a formal apology to the President. Then you, as Attorney General at the direction of the President, in a coordinated and linked move, are going to send those three Cuban spies back to Havana to make up for Diego's foolishness."

"And that's the end of it?"

"You're also going to get Diego to agree to a favorable settlement of the case Gordon's handling for the widow of that poor fisherman."

"And what happens if Diego won't play ball?"

"Then the Justice Department indicts him on espionage charges, and Gordon brings a wrongful death action against him in Miami. Santiago deChristo is a key witness in each case."

"And if I refuse to indict?"

"You'll be asked for your resignation, and you, too, will be called as a witness in both cases against Diego."

Omega looked venomously at Cox. "And he'll be the next Attorney General," he said, nodding in Gordon's direction.

"No," Black answered. "Gordon will be too busy negotiating with the Cuban government to obtain some relief for what Castro took when his revolution came to power, not to mention defending the century old treaty that gave us the Guantanamo Bay Naval Base."

The Attorney General's gaze went from Charles Black to Gordon and back again. "How's that going to work?"

"Gordon?" Black said. "Why don't you educate our man here?"

The White House Chief's phone rang as Gordon reached for his briefcase. Cox and Omega waited as Charles Black took the call. Both men knew it had to be important, because Black had left strict orders not to be disturbed.

"When?" Black said. "Are you sure? . . . "What's his name? . . . Hernandez?" he said, and looked piercingly at Gordon. "Hold on a minute." Black put a hand on the phone to block any transmission. "Conner, would you mind letting me speak with Gordon alone for a few minutes?"

"What's going on?" Omega asked.

"Later, please, Conner. Just wait outside for a moment."

"It involves Cuba." Omega persisted.

"Conner, I need to speak with Gordon for a few minutes, now."

"Okay, okay," he said, and left, heading for the nearest phone to call his office.

Black took a moment to return to the telephone. "Mr. Cox is right here. I'll ask him. I'm putting you on hold. Don't hang up."

Gordon closed the briefcase he'd opened to arrange some papers, and waited.

"There's fighting in the streets of Havana, Gordon. We're in touch with this man Hernandez, who's reportedly involved on the side of the rebels. He called the State Department through a contact in Toronto. He told the Under Secretary you'd be able to fill in the missing lines of his communiqué. They're afraid over at State that we're being set up again by the Cubans. The CIA seconds that opinion."

Cox leaned back in his chair. His thoughts went back to his very first meeting with José Hernandez, and to the frank political discussion that the two men had had that day, including what the United States must do when the counterrevolution begins in Cuba.

Black continued. "Hernandez also claimed the Cuban government has called in a force from Venezuela to help put down the insurrection. Our reconnaissance flights have confirmed a large convoy about halfway across the Caribbean Sea on a course that would intercept the southeast coast of Cuba by tomorrow afternoon."

"What sparked it?" Cox asked.

"General Orlando deChristo was assassinated this morning. Word has circulated within the Cuban Army that this was the work of an intelligence officer in the Cuban Ministry of Defense who was killed by one of the Marine guards at our Embassy. The General was a very popular soldier. When word leaked out concerning the identity of the assassin, the Army reacted. This quickly escalated to a full-scale rebellion that was probably in the works anyway. In fact, General Orlando was probably going to lead it. Funny thing though, all the fuss they made over our sending you to Havana, getting mobs out into the streets and those long speeches and histrionics, made it much worse for the government. The rebels didn't need to get people all revved up. They'd already been primed."

"And Hernandez is supposed to be one of the keys?"

"Yes," Black said, "and Hernandez wants us to use the Embargo law to stop the Venezuelans from landing in Cuba. How's that for a prime bit of irony?" Black said, winking at Gordon. "Hernandez told the messenger to tell you that your friend Eduardo was the first to go, and his immediate boss—he said you'd know who that was—is in custody. They want no interference from any outside source, and are trusting the United States will stay out, as well as keep everyone else out, until it's over. He said you would be able to explain the importance of those measures, and this makes the State Department think you're being used again by the Cubans to embarrass us."

"Hernandez also warned us that the Cuban United Nations Ambassador is very well connected and popular within the General Assembly, and we can expect a loud cry from the Chinese, the French, and possibly the Russians to send in help to prop up the old regime or at least to support the action being taken by Venezuela. He made no comment on Fidel Castro's whereabouts or health, and refused to answer questions other than to refer to you."

"Excuse me," Black said to Cox, and after listening to the person on the other end of the line for a few moments, he closed off his phone conversation. "Come on Gordon," he hustled, getting up from his chair, "the Secretaries of State and Defense are both on their way to the White House. She wants us over there ASAP."

Charles Black knew the President wouldn't want the AG at the meeting, but Black considered Omega more of a problem being loose somewhere in the gardens of government than close at hand, where they could keep an eye on him. In fact, Black resigned himself to not letting Omega out of his sight until the business in Cuba had run its course.

"Come on, Conner," he said, as they rushed through the reception area outside his office. "We're all going over to Pennsylvania Avenue. I'll brief you on the way."

Omega put down the phone in his hand, and followed.

★

"Using the Trading with the Enemy Act to keep the Venezuelans from reinforcing Castro and ending up in control of Cuba appeals to my sense of historical irony," the President said. "What do you say, Mr. Attorney General," she said, looking at Conner Omega sitting between Black and Gordon Cox at the table. "Will it pass muster?"

Brilliant, thought Charles Black. She'd neutralized the AG, who she hadn't wanted there in the first place, by asking him the central question. One to which Black knew she already had the answer.

Omega drew a deep breath. "The law gives you no authority to use force. The Justice Department looked into that years ago to slow down the companies who were getting special deals and moving into Havana, but their research concluded the law gave us no basis to act in international waters."

"What about the Monroe Doctrine?" she asked, looking around at every person in the Oval Office.

"That's an interesting idea, as notice to the world that we'll tolerate no armed activity at our back door," the Secretary of State answered. "The problem is we haven't enforced it in decades. From a purely technical standpoint I'd have to say any basis it might have provided has lapsed. Besides, it only applied to nations outside the hemisphere, and that would exclude Venezuela."

The President's gaze settled on Gordon Cox. "Any ideas?"

"Madam President, isn't the move by Venezuela an invasion? Haven't we been asked to help Cuba?" Gordon could see the Secretary of Defense, seated on his right, nodding his head. "After the fuss is over, you can fill in any missing pieces if the insurrection succeeds. If it fails, the victorious Cuban status quo will scream, but they also might be pleased that Caracas didn't become their new capital city. The only precedent you'll be establishing is helping a fellow Western Hemisphere nation avoid a hostile takeover. Nothing wrong with that, and it's a doctrine that might come in very handy in the future, if not in Cuba, then elsewhere in the hemisphere."

"That sounds pretty close to the Monroe Doctrine to me," the Defense Secretary said.

The President tilted her head to the side, showing she reserved opinion. She looked back toward Gordon.

"So you'd ignore the embargo ruse suggested by this man, Hernandez?"

"Yes, because that's something you want to get rid of anyway, and it waters down the strength of the doctrine, whatever you call it. All we're talking about here is making a *prima facie* case. The whole world will know we wanted the insurrection to succeed, and that's why we kept Venezuela out. The world will probably believe the CIA started the whole thing anyway, but the nations in this hemisphere will also rejoice that the U.S. and Cuba are friends again, after fifty odd years. On the other hand, if we don't take action now, no one in this hemisphere is going to thank us."

The discussion went on for two more hours, during which time the Navy, Coast Guard, and Air Force were placed on alert to carry out a mission in the Caribbean Sea. One issue kept splitting the assembled group into two factions. "How do we know this guy Hernandez is not a stalking horse for the Cubans to embarrass us again?" the Secretary of Defense demanded to know. The same general doubt was expressed by State, and they both quoted comments coming from the CIA as well as their own intelligence people.

"We've already put our forces on full alert, with orders to stand off until we give the word. I don't think we ought to risk a fight with the Venezuelans before we have some confirmation that this guy Hernandez is what he says he is," concluded the Defense Secretary.

The President started to respond by saying time was short, but paused mid-sentence to glance at Cox. "What is it, Gordon?" she said. "You look like the little boy in the back row with the answer for the teacher."

Cox let his eyes tour the room. "What's happened to the young Cuban woman who was with General deChristo in Mexico?"

The President focused hard on Gordon, her expression demanding an explanation for his sidetracking solutions to the crisis they were trying to manage.

Cox cleared his throat. "With the General dead, this young lady could be a key source of intelligence. I would love to get her and the General's brother in the same room responding to questions concerning the General's activities leading up to his flight to Mexico. She might be able to identify the real players. She'd probably trust Santiago if he were there. The Secretaries are right. Without the General, we're missing too much information. Before we go muscling our way in, let's find out what she knows. And it's very important we don't let the Cubans get hold of her."

The Secretary of State looked skeptically at the President. "She's very young. Only sixteen, I think."

"And," Gordon said, "according to Santiago deChristo, she's very bright and mature for her age. I'm betting her brother was involved in the assassination of the General, as we believe he was in Katherine's abduction. This young woman has a great deal of critical firsthand knowledge to offer us if we can get her to cooperate."

"Do we know where this young woman is?" the President asked, looking at the Secretary of State.

"Yes," the Secretary answered. "She's being held at the Embassy in Mexico City pending a decision whether to send her back to Havana."

"Get her here," the President ordered.

"I can't do that unless she's willing to request it."

Frustrated, the President turned to Cox for help.

"Send Santiago down there tonight," Gordon said. "He'll have her back here tomorrow."

"That's not appropriate, Madam President," the Secretary of State protested. "You'd be accused of kidnapping her."

"I don't care if it's appropriate or not," the President said, and looking to her Chief of Staff, she instructed, "Charles, you and Gordon get that Cuban fisherman over to State ASAP, and go with him yourselves to Mexico if you have to. I want that young woman back here by tomorrow morning. Time's a wasting." Turning to the Secretary of Defense, she said, "Harry, get our naval forces in position off the Cuban south coast. I want no contact until we corroborate Hernandez' story. But be ready."

★

"Are you alright?" Santiago asked Ana Legra as the chartered Boeing 757 taking them to Washington reached cruising altitude.

Ana gave Santiago a half smile, and turned nervously to face Gordon and Kate, alone with them near the rear of the plane.

By prearrangement, Kate spoke first. "Hello, Ana. Thank you for coming back with us today. Are you excited about going to the United States?" and she paused for Santiago to translate.

Ana interrupted. "I think you speak Spanish," she said to Kate.

"Not very well," Kate said, "but I will try if that's what you would like."

Ana smiled, and nodded. Gordon thought to himself that Santiago's description of Ana as being smart might have been an understatement.

Kate struggled at first, but with some help from Santiago, she gained confidence as she went along. Gordon followed up in English as needed.

"Has Santiago explained that you will not be sent back to Cuba unless that is what you wish?"

"Yes."

"Has he also told you why we need the information you can give us?"

"You want to know who were Orlando's friends and enemies."

Kate smiled. That answer was right to the point. "Yes," she said.

The young Cuban woman looked piercingly at Cox. "Why did your Marine guards kill my brother?"

Santiago injected himself into the conversation at this point. "You know dammed well why they shot him, Ana. Don't play games. Dr. Cox does not wish to destroy the name of your brother or mine. Why don't you tell them in your own words what Orlando was doing, and with whom he was doing it? Tell them what you told me."

The more she talked, the more Ana opened up. Orlando was clearly involved in planning an armed rebellion. She was unable at first to name any coconspirators, but Gordon's mentioning of names, starting with José Hernandez, brought instant response.

"Yes, he was one of them. I saw him only one time. That was by peeking through the door into the room where they all met."

Other names brought responses like, "Yes, he was the man who kept my friend Maria. I saw him the time we all went with our men to the Isle of Youth. That was one of several times some of the men took their girlfriends along."

In between Ana's descriptions, Santiago commented to place the activities in perspective. "They usually met in Santiago de Cuba, because that city is quite close to the American naval base at Guantanamo Bay. They thought they might be able to escape to there if their sessions were raided. Orlando always suspected they had a mole within their group."

Gordon stood quietly at one point, and walked forward in the aircraft to where three men were sitting hunched together around a small speaker. He removed the microphone from his lapel, and sat down. He made eye contact with each of the men in turn, and spoke softly.

"It would appear, gentlemen, that our man José is for real. What do you think?"

The man from State was elected to comment by a nod from each of the other two.

"It was all in Spanish. Besides, what does this really prove?" he said. "Even if we believe what the woman says, it's not enough to order the Navy to engage."

Cox paused, and looked to the other two men for comment. Getting none, he spoke to the officer from the State Department.

"What you say may be true, or not," he said. "I encourage you to pass that thought on to the White House when I make the call."

"Are you going to make the call from here?" one of the men said, with a note of apprehension coming through in his voice.

"Those are my instructions," Gordon said. "The Venezuelans are only two hours from landfall in Cuba."

The one hard, dispositive fact of Ana Legra's testimony was confirmation of the association between José Hernandez and Orlando deChristo as coconspirators plotting the overthrow of the Cuban regime. This information was communicated by Gordon from the aircraft's cockpit to Charles Black in his office.

"What say our friends from the State Department and the Agencies?" Black asked.

"Here," Cox said, "I'll put them on," and he gave the handset to the gentleman from State.

Gordon's message, corroborated without enthusiasm by the others on board, became the basis for the President's urgent phone call to the President of Venezuela, and the United States Navy's stubborn confrontation of the Venezuelan convoy as it approached the Cuban coast. No shots were fired.

Word went out from the State Department the following day recognizing the new government in Havana. In a joint communiqué orchestrated by the President and issued under the banner of the

Organization of American States, *sans* Venezuela, Cuba's neighbors offered support to Hernandez' group, now in full control in Havana.

★

Cox paid the two men who'd moved Kate's belongings from her apartment. "You guys made quick work of that," he said. "Thanks," and he left them at the closing elevator door on his floor.

Kate was in the den on the telephone. She and Gordon had decided to hold off the lengthy conversations that Kate needed to have with her parents until she'd moved in with him. She called her mother first, because she thought that would be the more difficult.

Gordon closed and locked the front door to the flat, walked through the large living room, and poked his head into the den. Kate was ending the second of her two calls.

"Gordon, they're both coming," she said in a panic. "They'll be here Saturday afternoon. I think I'm going to die. It'll be bad enough having Mother and Father in the same room, but discussing our relationship . . ."

"It will probably be more difficult for them."

"How do you figure?" she said, calming down.

"Well, for starters I'll be in the room too. Remember me, the guy who took your mother home to meet my family?"

Kate grimaced. "It'll be moments of truth all around, won't it?"

Gordon nodded. "That's why you need to be the strong one. I can't come on too strong without offending at least Elizabeth, and probably your father as well."

"Oh God, I can never be a match for Mother."

"Sure you can. They both want what's best for you. All you have to do is convince them that the best is us."

"You don't even believe that yourself, Gordon. You'll probably agree with them."

"I love you, Katie. That's what I intend to make very clear to both of them. If I'm any judge, that's what they're waiting to hear . . . or will be once they've been convinced you're really in love with me. Our plans for a long engagement while living together may cause more trouble than anything."

"No, I think they view that as a safety net."

"Maybe it is?"

Kate's eyebrows shot up, and she gave him a withering look. "Absolutely not, it's exactly the opposite. Together into eternity," she said, stood up from the desk, and threw her arms around Gordon's neck.

"So, relax," Gordon said, with his arms tugging at Kate's waist, holding her close. "They're not going to say no. The worst they can do at this point is blame each other."

"Mother's already done that," Kate said, extricating herself from his embrace and plopping into a soft chair.

Gordon laughed. "Yes, but if she'd married me, neither of us would be here."

That made Kate laugh. "You really are outrageous. You know that don't you?"

"Yes, but I'm lucky."

"Okay my love," she said, blowing the imagined lock of hair from her right eye. "I'll give it my best shot."

"Atta girl. Now, how about a welcoming glass of champagne? It's not every day we move in together."

Kate rose out of the chair and followed Gordon through the living room. "You should know I told Mother we'd let her hold an engagement party here in D.C. That subject is going to come up when they're here, because she'll want your advice on where to hold it, and she's insisting Father pay for half."

Gordon nodded, popping the cork from 750ml of champagne. "That won't be a tough sell if I know your old man."

"My old man?" Kate said in mock surprise, taking the glass that Gordon handed her. "He's only three years older than you are."

"Yes, but he's still your old man."

★

Kate left her desk at the *Law Journal* for the twenty-block walk home to the Watergate complex. A head poked out from the law school administration office as she passed.

"Ms. Stevens, there's a young woman here to see you."

"Who is it, Jean?" she asked.

"Lara Peron. She says she knew you in Havana."

Kate ran into the reception area. The two women hugged as tears ran down their cheeks. Kate escorted Lara back to her *Law Journal* desk. They laughed, cried, and revisited their time in Havana.

"I was told you were lost," the Cuban woman said.

Kate did not pull her punches. "Your fighter planes tried their best, but in the end it was the storm we had to survive."

Lara lowered her eyes and nodded.

Kate continued, "I was kept in the place where your political prisoners were jailed and tortured. I heard awful things going on while I was there."

Lara changed the subject out of many years of habit, reacting when the truth came too close to penetrating the old Cuban party line. "Thank you for keeping your word and not disclosing my brief on Guantanamo while you were still in Havana. I wouldn't be here today if you had."

"Your new leaders, are they going ahead with the case to get Guantanamo Bay back into Cuban hands?" Kate asked.

"We don't want to trade China for the USA. That was Eduardo Santos' idea. We'd like the deal to be more like what the USA did with the Panama Canal and the Philippines, and not give up our sovereignty. We'd settle the case for some comfort in that area, and maybe some fair market rent. God knows we could use the money to rebuild our economy."

Kate smiled. "When's your first meeting with Gordon's team?"

"We'll wait until the changes in Cuba are complete. I'll return to Washington for those meetings. It will be later this summer. Will you be here then?" she asked.

"I'll be taking the bar exam."

Lara reached out to Kate. "I hope we can stay friends."

"Of course we will," she said.

The Cuban woman let her eyes turn away for a moment. "Kate, I hate asking you this question, but we've lost track of Ana Legra. She's the young girl who was with General Orlando deChristo in Mexico. Do you have any idea what could have happened to her? The Mexican foreign office told us she was shipped back here by your State Department, but they won't tell us anything."

Kate hesitated. "I've no idea where she is," she said, finally.

Lara squinted and looked at her. "She's not being held against her wishes is she? She's not in jail or anything like that?"

"I'm sure she's not, Lara," Kate said, "but I can ask around if you want.

"Is it true she was carrying the General's child?"

"Yes, that's true," Kate answered, resisting the impulse to tell her friend the whole truth. Ana was doing well and living with Santiago and his brother's newly born son in a small house in Key West, Florida, ninety nautical miles NNE across the Gulf Stream from Havana.